AUTUMN BRIDES

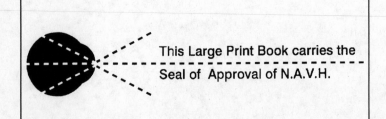

AUTUMN BRIDES

A YEAR OF WEDDINGS NOVELLA COLLECTION

KATHRYN SPRINGER, KATIE GANSHERT, AND BETH VOGT

THORNDIKE PRESS
A part of Gale, Cengage Learning

GALE
CENGAGE Learning·

Farmington Hills, Mich • San Francisco • New York • Waterville, Maine
Meriden, Conn • Mason, Ohio • Chicago

GALE
CENGAGE Learning

LIBRARY OF CONGRESS CATALOGING-IN-PUBLICATION DATA

Autumn brides : a year of weddings novella collection / by Kathryn Springer, Katie Ganshert, and Beth Vogt. — Large print edition.
    pages cm. — (Thorndike Press large print Christian fiction)
    ISBN 978-1-4104-8388-1 (hardcover) — ISBN 1-4104-8388-6 (hardcover)
    1. Christian fiction, American. 2. Love stories, American. 3. Weddings—Fiction. 4. Large type books. I. Springer, Kathryn. II. Ganshert, Katie. III. Vogt, Beth K.
PS648.C43A96 2015b
813'.01083823—dc23   2015028283

Published in 2015 by arrangement with The Zondervan Corporation LLC, a subsidiary of HarperCollins Christian Publishing, Inc.

Printed in Mexico
1 2 3 4 5 6 7 19 18 17 16 15

CONTENTS

■ ■ ■ ■

A September Bride

KATHRYN SPRINGER

■ ■ ■ ■

To Lindsey, Norah, and Ashley:
the real summer brides!

ONE

Annie Price didn't know why Mondays had such a bad reputation.

This one happened to be perfect. Sunshine. A smooth stretch of open road. A scented breeze sifting through the sunroof of her car.

Flashing red-and-blue lights in the rearview mirror.

The police car those lights happened to be attached to triggered a strangely familiar, built-in reflex, and Annie's foot tapped the brake. One of the cardboard boxes lining the backseat tipped forward, and a wave of Styrofoam packing peanuts spilled over the side, flowing underneath the seat and pooling around her feet. Along with the antique spoon collection Annie had spent the last half hour carefully packing *inside* that box.

She steered onto the shoulder of the road and waited for the squad car to drive past. Except . . . it didn't. It pulled up right

11

behind her.

There was no time to contemplate the exact nature of her crime because a county deputy quickly appeared at the window, blotting out the sun like an eclipse in brown polyester.

Annie's gaze glanced off the gold badge centered above his pocket and followed a row of perfectly aligned buttons all the way to a face that looked as if it had been carved from a chunk of granite. Angular jaw. Sculpted cheekbones. Hair a rich sable brown, cropped close to his head to discourage any type of wayward behavior.

And speaking of wayward . . .

Annie squinted at her distorted reflection in the deputy's mirrored sunglasses and noticed one of her curls had gone rogue. Leaning forward for a better look, she tucked it back in place.

The deputy whipped off the sunglasses and a pair of eyes as blue as the cloudless sky locked with hers.

"Do you know why I stopped you?" His crisp tone matched the September morning, leaving Annie to wonder if he always sounded that way or if it was part of the uniform.

"No." Was this a trick question? Annie caught her lower lip between her teeth.

"Don't you?" she ventured.

The blue eyes narrowed. "You have a brake light out. And your tailpipe is hanging by a thread."

Actually, the tailpipe was hanging by a piece of binder twine — a little detail Annie knew because she was the one who'd tied it in place — but she decided it would be best not to correct him.

"I know." Annie flashed what she hoped was a See-I'm-An-Honest-Upstanding-Citizen smile. "I just haven't had time to get them fixed."

"Well, now you have five days." He didn't return the smile.

Annie contemplated offering him one of the leftover donuts from her early morning get-together with the historical society, but he would probably arrest her for trying to bribe an officer of the law.

"Thank you for bringing it to my attention. I'll take care of it right away," she promised.

Instead of leaving, the deputy took a step closer. Annie dragged in a breath and held it while he took a slow but thorough inventory of the interior of her car. She knew the exact moment he zeroed in on the spoons.

"Those don't belong to me," Annie said quickly.

One eyebrow lifted. "Is that so?"

"I mean, I'm just . . . transporting them. For a friend."

There you go, Annie. That sounded so much better.

His expression remained unreadable. "I'll need to see your license and registration, please."

"Of course." Annie twisted toward the glove compartment, but the seat belt chose that particular moment to resist the sudden change in position and held her firmly in place. Acutely aware the officer was watching her every move, she finally managed to free herself from its grip.

Could the situation be any more embarrassing?

Apparently the answer to that question was yes, because the door on the glove compartment gave way — she really needed to get that loose hinge fixed too — and released an avalanche of the miniature candy bars Annie kept on hand for emergencies. On the bright side, the empty compartment made it easier to locate the envelope holding her insurance information.

"Here you go." It took every ounce of Annie's self-control not to grab one of the candy bars and devour it while the officer verified she hadn't stolen the car. Or the chocolate. Or the silver spoons scattered around her feet.

A discreet glance at her wristwatch told Annie she had exactly seven minutes to get to work, unlock the door, and brew a pot of coffee for her first customers.

"Everything is in order, Officer?" Somehow, it came out sounding more like a question than a statement.

The deputy handed her the envelope, and Annie couldn't help but notice the papers looked tidier now than they had the first time she'd stashed them inside. "License, please."

"It's right here, in my —" Annie stared at the empty spot on the passenger seat, where her purse should have been riding shotgun.

"Let me guess," he drawled. "You don't have it with you?"

"No, I . . . no. It's in my purse. Which is . . . somewhere. Else." Panic shorted out the circuits in her brain. "I have one, though. A license." Annie knew she was rambling, but she couldn't find the shutoff valve to staunch the flow of words. "I never go anywhere without it. Except today, of course."

"Of course."

Was that a tiny spark of amusement Annie saw in his eyes?

She couldn't be sure, because the sunglasses slid back into place, shielding his expression.

Heart beating in double-time, Annie silently retraced her early morning route. She'd stopped at the bakery for the donuts and then swung by the gas station to fill up the tank and buy a package of red licorice for Mr. Gunderson, whose arthritis was acting up again. After that, she'd driven to Caroline McCready's house. The older woman had recently made a generous donation to the historical society, and the committee members offered to pack up some of the more fragile antiques. Annie volunteered to be the designated driver, transporting the items to their new home at the museum. She'd deliver them during her lunch hour, when she also planned to give Mr. Gunderson his licorice.

She wasn't getting anywhere, and she didn't want him to think she was just stalling. Maybe if she started at the beginning . . . She'd showered and dressed, and then a few minutes before she'd left her apartment, her friend Lorna had called to ask about a box of old playbills Annie had discovered while cleaning out the storage closet at the bookstore, so . . .

"I know where it is!" Annie clapped her

hands together. "My license . . . I left it at the bookstore!"

The deputy didn't appear nearly as thrilled as Annie that her short-term memory had returned. In fact, he looked downright skeptical. "Are you talking about Second Story Books?"

"Yes." Annie didn't know whether to be relieved he'd actually heard of it or terrified he might be a regular customer. Although she couldn't imagine Deputy Tall, Dark, and Disturbing being comfortable in the bookstore's whimsical setting, with its pastel furniture and cheery yellow walls. "I must have left my purse on the counter."

"The bookstore doesn't open until ten."

Rats. Regular customer.

"That's true, but I can get in." Annie pointed to the cluster of keys hanging from the ignition like a miniature set of wind chimes. "I'm the manager."

"The manager . . ." He paused, the word hanging in the air between them, almost as if he were giving her time to retract the statement.

"I've only been there a few weeks." Annie tried to ignore the prickle of unease that rappelled down her spine, one vertebra at a time. "But I love Red Leaf. Everyone is so friendly."

"Name and date of birth, please."

Well, almost everyone.

"Anne Price. With an *e*. But everyone calls me Annie. And my birthday is October twenty-fourth?" *Don't make it sound like a question!* "Yes. October twenty-fourth."

"I'll be right back."

Before Annie could blink, the deputy turned on his heel and strode away.

"Jesse!" Lorna Kent answered on the first ring. "I didn't expect to hear from you until this evening. Did you take the day off?"

"No, I'm on duty." Jesse kept an eye on the rust-stained vehicle parked on the side of the road. "And I just pulled over a woman named Annie Price who claims she's the manager of Second Story Books. The last I knew, that title belonged to someone else."

Jesse half expected to hear a shriek. At the very least, a gasp of disbelief. Not . . . laughter.

"Well . . . you've been gone for three weeks, sweetheart," Lorna declared. "A lot can happen in that amount of time. I decided to make a few changes."

Changes?

His mother was as predictable as an eastern sunrise. She thrived on routine, whether it was the menu for Sunday dinner — baked chicken, creamed peas, and mashed potatoes — or watering the row of African violets on her kitchen windowsill from left to right every Wednesday while she watched *Jeopardy.*

"Are you telling me that you actually turned the bookstore over to a . . . stranger?" The unexpected announcement might have rattled any preconceived notions Jesse had about his mother, but there was one thing he did know for sure — he'd never seen Annie Price before.

He would have remembered.

"Annie isn't a stranger. She happens to be a member of my book club."

An alarm went off in Jesse's head. He knew of only one book club that his mother faithfully attended. "You met her on the *Internet?*"

"It's an online group, yes," his mother confirmed. "But Annie and I have gotten to know each other quite well over the past six months. There were talks of layoffs where she worked, and as it turned out I happened to have an opening at the bookstore."

"An opening —" Jesse's back molars snapped together. "You gave her *your* job!"

Along with the keys to the front door — and the safe.

"Believe me, Annie was an answer to my prayers." Lorna's voice dropped a notch. "And I think moving to Red Leaf just might have been an answer to one of hers."

Jesse didn't doubt that for a second. Scam artists were always on the lookout for an easy mark. Someone like his mother, who assumed the best in everyone in spite of what she'd gone through in the past. Experience had taught Jesse that trust was something a person had to earn.

"You don't know anything about this woman, Mom."

"I know the things that matter. Annie is a hard worker, and she's already gotten involved in the community. Everyone on the committee loves her."

"What committee?" Jesse's fingers tightened around his personal cell phone.

"She joined the historical society. In fact, we were together a few minutes ago. Cricket McCready asked the committee members to meet at her house this morning to pack up the items she donated to the museum."

"Spoons." The word rolled out with Jesse's sigh. "I saw them."

The explanation for the spoons being in Annie Price's possession didn't exactly put Jesse's mind at ease. Why would a woman in her mid-twenties with no ties to the town join the local historical society?

"You saw them? What did you do, search her vehicle?" Lorna teased.

"Of course not." Unfortunately, Jesse didn't have probable cause. "It was a courtesy stop. Her brake light is out."

"I knew it had to be something like that." Lorna sounded way too confident. "Annie is as sweet as maple syrup. I can't imagine her doing anything wrong."

And therein lay the problem.

Jesse's gaze cut back to the vehicle. The topic of their conversation was leaning out the window, looking not at him but at a flock of geese flying in a perfect V formation over the trees. The breeze toyed with a short platinum curl, and Annie pushed it back into place — without using his sunglasses as a mirror this time.

She caught his eye and pointed at the sky, the smile on her face warm enough to melt right through Jesse's Kevlar vest.

The woman was trouble, no doubt about it.

The radio attached to his belt crackled, and Jesse heard the county dispatcher sending officers to a fender bender at an intersection a few miles away.

A formal written notice would have to

wait. Jesse pointed to the road and waved her on.

If possible, Annie's smile grew even wider. She waved back, ducked inside the car, and put it into gear.

"Are you still planning to come for dinner tonight?" His mother's question yanked Jesse's attention back to the moment as he strode toward the squad car. "I have a surprise for you."

"I think you already filled your quota for the day," Jesse said drily. "But I'll be there."

To find out what was going on.

He wasn't a fan of surprises . . . or change. And no matter what his mother claimed, Jesse could trace both of them to a common source. A curly-haired sprite with a smile so captivating it had the power to make a man forget his own name.

Annie Price.

TWO

"I have the perfect book for you, Lily." Annie smiled at her pint-sized customer, who resembled the heroine of the story with her long blonde braids and gap-toothed grin. "This was one of my favorites when I was your age."

The girl's mother looked at the title and smiled. "*Little House in the Big Woods.* It was one of mine too. Thank you, Annie."

"Don't forget to sign up for the activity night next Friday. We're going to have a lot of fun." Annie winked at Lily as she rang up the purchase. "Let me know when you're finished with this book — there's a whole series about Laura and her family."

Lily bobbed her head. "Okay!"

The little girl and her mother left the bookstore, and Annie flipped the sign in the window to Closed. Lorna was expecting her for dinner, but a steady stream of customers all afternoon meant there were still a few things that needed Annie's attention before she could leave.

Not that she was complaining.

Less than a month ago, Annie had eaten alone in her studio apartment every night, but now she actually had a friend to laugh with over a home-cooked meal several times a week. She was also the manager of a quaint little bookshop located above a bakery on Main Street, where the scent of cinnamon and yeasty bread dough drifted through the metal grates in the floor and scented the air, sweeter than any fragrance a candle company could manufacture.

Thank you, God.

The prayer reverberated in Annie's heart, as clear and sweet as the chimes that sang out a greeting whenever a customer came into Second Story Books. Because she knew it could only have been divine intervention that had led her to Red Leaf.

Annie loved everything about the northern Wisconsin town, from the street made up of red bricks that cut through the center of town to the pots of yellow mums that brightened every corner. It could have been the setting for one of her favorite books, although Lorna had laughed the first time Annie had voiced the thought out loud.

"Oh, the town is real all right," Lorna had

24

said. "Not perfect, but real."

Annie happened to think it was both.

She paused to pet the enormous gray tiger cat curled up on the window seat. Esmeralda spent the majority of her day in the bookstore rather than in Annie's adjoining apartment. A preference as contrary as the feline herself, because Esmeralda didn't particularly care for books — or people.

"I'll be back to get you in a couple of hours." Two lime green eyes cracked open long enough to glare at her.

Annie chuckled. "Sorry for disturbing your nap, Essie. Don't get into trouble while I'm gone."

The cat formally dismissed Annie from the room with a flick of her crooked tail and fell back to sleep.

Reaching underneath the counter, Annie retrieved her purse and experienced a flashback. A flashback that featured a taciturn deputy. Her pulse spiked just remembering the encounter.

Annie found it odd that he had called someone on a cell phone rather than the radio attached to his belt, but when he had waved her on she decided not to stick around and ask why. She planned to replace the brake light, get the loose tailpipe fixed, and never have to deal with the man again.

He had a whole county to protect and serve, right?

Comforted by the thought, Annie locked up the bookstore, stopped by her apartment to pick up the chocolate cake she'd made for dessert, and took the stairs two at a time until she reached the ornate wooden door that opened onto the sidewalk.

"Hey, Miss Annie!" Across the street, Arthur Gunderson paused in his daily ritual of sweeping away any flotsam and jetsam that dared to wash up on the sidewalk in front of his hardware store. He hailed her with the push broom. "Thank you again for the licorice."

"You're welcome!" Annie waved back as she got into her car. They'd met the day she had wandered into the hardware store to buy a set of shelves for her living room wall. Not only had Arthur told her which kind to buy, but he had insisted on helping with the project despite his arthritis.

"Because that's what neighbors do," he'd told her.

Annie had cried when he'd left, because she had never even *met* the people who lived in her last apartment building, let alone her neighborhood. From the day she'd moved to Red Leaf, everyone had treated her like she was family. It meant everything to a girl who'd never had one of her own.

Annie parked in front of Lorna's bungalow and hurried up the sidewalk. Balancing the cake plate in one hand and a folder bulging with craft ideas for the bookstore's upcoming activity night in the other, she climbed the steps and wedged her toe in the screen door before slipping into the foyer.

"Sorry I'm late, Lorna!"

"In the kitchen." Her friend's lilting voice provided a wonderful benediction to a day that had gotten off to a trying start.

"You'll never guess what happened after I left Caroline McCready's house." Annie kicked off her shoes and noticed another — much larger — pair on the rug near the door. She hoped that meant Lorna had taken her advice and invited Michael Garrison for dinner. He was a regular customer at the bookstore and attended their church, and Annie was sure the high school principal who'd recently retired and moved to Red Leaf was totally smitten with Lorna. Annie had a hunch the feeling was mutual. "A police officer noticed my brake light was burned out and he pulled me over. I have five days —"

"Four." The man sitting at Lorna's kitchen table rose to his feet. "And don't forget the loose tailpipe."

27

Annie almost dropped the cake.

It wasn't Mr. Garrison — it was *him.* The deputy who had stopped her that morning. He may have exchanged his uniform for faded jeans and a flannel shirt, but the look of authority hadn't changed. Maybe he was working undercover. Or . . .

"Are you *following* me?" Annie blurted.

One sable brow lifted. "Guilty conscience?"

"Looking at the evidence." Six feet tall. Broad shoulders. Sky-blue eyes. And standing right in front of her.

Lorna's bemused gaze bounced back and forth between them. "Jesse mentioned he pulled you over on a courtesy stop this morning." She chuckled. "It wasn't the way I'd planned for you and my son to meet, but I guess it means we can dispense with formal introductions."

Her son?

Annie's breath tangled in her lungs.

Come to think of it, Lorna *had* mentioned she had a son in his late twenties, but Annie hadn't thought to ask where he lived — or what he did for a living. In the book club's chat room, the moderator had a strict rule that the discussion be focused on the novel the group had chosen, not the personal lives of its members. Even after she and Lorna had become friends and e-mailed each other on a regular basis, there had been too many other things to talk about. Plans to be made.

Aware that Lorna was watching, Annie forced a smile and held out her hand. "It's nice to meet you. Again."

A split-second passed, long enough for her to realize Jesse Kent — *Deputy Jesse Kent* — didn't feel the same way. Then his hand closed around hers, toasty warm as a wool mitten.

It made the shiver that coursed up Annie's arm even more alarming.

"Anne Price." Without the sunglasses, there was no hiding the glint of speculation in his eyes. "With an *e.*"

So this was the surprise his mother had mentioned.

Jesse should have known. He released Annie's hand and took a step back, but the scent of her perfume, something light and sweet, lingered in the air the way her smile had lingered in his thoughts long after she'd driven away.

"When you mentioned the bookstore, Jesse had to call me and find out what was going on." Lorna grinned. "He was attending a three-week training course in Arizona, so I didn't have a chance to tell him that I

29

made a few little changes while he was gone. At least not in person."

Jesse shook his head. "Hiring a manager for the bookstore isn't exactly what I'd call a little change, Mom."

"Oh, Annie is more than qualified." Lorna bustled over to the stove. "Why don't you two get to know each other better while I finish the vegetables? Michael should be here any minute."

Jesse frowned.

Michael?

For the first time, he noticed the table was set for four. So much for his keen powers of observation.

"Michael is coming over for dinner?" Annie's face lit up as she grabbed an apron from the drawer next to the sink.

Jesse narrowed his eyes. Annie had been in Red Leaf for three short weeks and already knew her way around his mother's kitchen?

"Who is Michael?" Jesse kept his tone casual. Because a good cop collected all the facts before he reached a conclusion.

"A friend." The wooden spoon in his mother's hand picked up speed, and a slice of carrot bounced out of the skillet and landed on the counter. "He moved to Red Leaf about six weeks ago."

"Yeah." Jesse pinned Annie with a sideways glance. "There seems to be a lot of that going on."

Color bloomed in Annie's cheeks and she looked away. It occurred to Jesse the man in question could be Annie's date for the evening. For reasons he couldn't explain, the thought didn't sit well.

"I met Michael at the bookstore," Lorna continued. "When he found out the historical society needed help, he volunteered to head up the carpentry crew refurbishing Stone Church. I invited him over for dinner so we could coordinate the details for the workday on Saturday."

"Things must be progressing pretty quickly." Too quickly, in Jesse's opinion, and not only with the historical society's pet project.

Over the past few years, his mother had rallied a small but faithful band of volunteers who'd decided it was important to stay connected with their roots. The committee had restored an old homestead and turned it into a museum before turning their attention to the hundred-year-old church located on the same property.

"They are — thanks to a wonderful group of volunteers." His mother turned from the stove to wink at Annie. "We decided to hold the museum's grand opening at the end of the month. If you aren't working this weekend, you should stop by. We could always use another pair of hands."

The timer on the stove began to chirp and Jesse grabbed a pot holder. "Sounds like the meat loaf is ready."

"It's not meat loaf, sweetheart." Lorna breezed past him and opened the refrigerator.

"But . . . it's Monday."

"I decided to try to duplicate one of Annie's recipes instead. Orange chicken with cashews. She brought it to a potluck at church last weekend, and it disappeared so fast, I didn't even have a chance to try it!"

Church potlucks. Committees.

Annie had certainly made herself comfortable — not just in his mother's home but in the community.

"Where did you live before you moved to Red Leaf, Annie?"

As far as questions went, Jesse didn't think it was a difficult one. But Annie's gaze shifted over his shoulder, as if she'd find the answer written on the wall.

"Madison," she finally said.

"Red Leaf must be quite a change. We roll up the streets when the sun goes down." Jesse slid a glass casserole dish from the oven. Golden pieces of chicken rested on a bed of rice. Bubbles burst, releasing the aroma of orange and ginger into the air. He had to admit, it looked better than meat loaf. "Not much excitement here."

"I prefer the peace and quiet."

To what?

Jesse hadn't become a cop without learning to read people's body language. And everything — from the tension in Annie's slim shoulders to her averted gaze — told him that she wasn't comfortable answering questions about herself.

Because she had something to hide?

Jesse had planned on signing up for a weekend shift, but maybe it wouldn't be a bad idea to help the historical society for a few hours instead.

After all, his mother *had* suggested that he and Annie get to know each other better.

THREE

"Hello! Sorry I'm late!"

Jesse didn't have an opportunity to follow up on Annie's statement. A man strode into the kitchen — *didn't anyone knock anymore?* — carrying an armload of sunflowers.

"Those are beautiful, Michael." Lorna's gaze dropped to the bouquet, and Jesse couldn't help but notice her cheeks had turned a delicate shade of pink.

Or that Michael Garrison was closer to his mother's age than Annie's.

"I bought them at the farmers' market." Smiling, the man transferred them into Lorna's arms. "Didn't you say yellow is your favorite color?"

"You have a good memory." His mother giggled. *Giggled.*

Unbelievable. Jesse slid a glance at Annie. She looked way too pleased by the exchange, as if she were the reason Jesse's mother and Michael Garrison were staring at each other like there was no one else in the room.

And maybe she was.

"Michael, I'd like you to meet my son."

The man's head swiveled in his direction. "Jesse," he boomed, stretching out his hand. "Lorna told me all about you."

Funny, she never mentioned you, Jesse thought as he shook Garrison's hand.

"Everything is ready." Lorna glided over to the sink. "I'll put these flowers in some water, and then we can sit down."

Jesse watched his mother and Annie begin to transfer the food from the counter to the table, a synchronized choreograph so smooth it looked as if they'd done it a hundred times.

As he went to sit down, he and Annie both reached for the same chair — at the same time.

"I'm sorry." A wave of crimson flooded Annie's cheeks. "I didn't realize this was yours."

"Don't be sorry." Lorna chuckled as Michael pulled her chair away from the table and waited for her to sit down. "We don't have assigned seating in this house!"

That might be true, but Jesse couldn't help but notice Michael Garrison claimed the chair at the head of the table.

His father's chair.

Jesse tore his gaze away and tried to focus his thoughts on something else before they got tangled up in the memories.

"Annie, would you like to say grace?"

"Of course!" The platinum curl that seemed to have a mind of its own dipped over Annie's eye as she bowed her head.

Jesse locked his hands together. Not only because they were about to pray but also because he was tempted to push that wayward curl back in place.

"Lord, thank you for all the gifts your hands provide," Annie said. "For friends and for family."

And for wisdom in dealing with them.

Jesse tacked on a silent request of his own after the round of amens.

There was no other opportunity to interrogate — *question* — Annie about her move to Red Leaf. The upcoming workday dominated the conversation not only during dinner but afterward, when his mother ushered them into the living room for dessert.

"I'll call the rest of the crew and tell them to be there by eight o'clock." Michael helped himself to another piece of the chocolate cake Annie had brought. "We still have a few more pews to restore before the wedding —"

"Wedding?" Jesse interrupted. "What wedding?"

Three heads turned in his direction, and Jesse realized he'd spoken louder than was necessary.

"Viola, our committee treasurer, had a wonderful idea to encourage people to attend the open house. We're going to reenact Elizabeth Weston's wedding at Stone Church." His mother patted Annie's arm. "Annie has been reading through Elizabeth's journals and taking notes so the ceremony will be as authentic as possible."

Jesse frowned. "Who is Elizabeth Weston?"

"She was the daughter of Frederick Lowery, one of a group of investors from Chicago who brought the railroad to this part of the state." Judging from the expression on his mother's face, Jesse would have thought he'd asked who Abraham Lincoln was. "Elizabeth's September wedding was the event of the season. She and her husband, Patrick, started a school in town. They built their first home on the land her parents deeded to them as a wedding gift."

"Without them, there wouldn't be a Red Leaf," Michael added.

"That's right." Lorna's smile of approval landed like a spotlight on the man who somehow knew more about the town's history than Jesse, who'd lived there all his life. "We want the open house to celebrate Elizabeth and Patrick's commitment to the town. It's so important to connect with the past."

Jesse didn't say what he was thinking.

It was important to learn from it too.

Annie stared at the pyramid of boxes that had been constructed on the sidewalk while she was getting ready for work. She'd stumbled upon it — literally — when she ran downstairs to get a cinnamon roll from the bakery before she started the day.

But apparently, a deliveryman had started his day even earlier.

With Lorna's blessing, Annie had allocated a portion of the monthly budget to funding some new ideas she hoped would bring more traffic into the bookstore. Every single one of those ideas had been packaged in a box that appeared to weigh more than she did.

The flight of stairs leading to the second floor suddenly seemed a lot steeper.

One step at a time, right, Lord? Unless, of course, you want to send a knight in shining armor to come to my rescue!

She was contemplating which box to move

first when a familiar vehicle turned into the alley.

Annie suppressed a groan.

I said a knight in shining armor, Lord! Not a bulletproof vest!

Honestly, wasn't there a cat stuck in a tree somewhere? Someone who needed help crossing the street?

It had been obvious at Lorna's house that Jesse didn't approve of her, although Annie had no idea why. It couldn't be just because of her brake light and tailpipe. She'd hoped that Red Leaf would be a new page to write on, but once again, it seemed she would have to prove herself. At least when it came to a certain deputy.

The squad car rolled to a stop beside the curb and Jesse's tall, athletic frame unfolded from the driver's seat. It wasn't fair the guy was even better looking than she remembered, either. Not that she'd been remembering him. Much.

Annie parked her hands on her hips as he strode toward her. "I still have two days."

The sunglasses came off and those bright blue eyes got a bead on her. "Two days?"

"Brake light. Tailpipe."

"I'm glad you remembered, but that's not why I'm here." Jesse nodded at the boxes. "I stopped over at Mom's last night, and

39

she mentioned you were expecting a delivery today."

"Thanks, but I can handle this." To prove it, she grabbed one of the boxes — and tried not to wince when the muscles in her lower back protested. "I don't want to keep you."

"Technically, I'm on a break." He lifted one of the containers as if it didn't weigh any more than a shoe box filled with tissue paper.

Annie chose one of the smaller ones and followed him up the flight of steps. By the time she reached the top, Jesse had already set the box down in the office and was walking over to the window seat, where Esmeralda had settled in for the first of her daily naps.

"Is this your cat?"

"Yes, but don't —" *Touch her.*

The words died in Annie's throat when Esmeralda, former alley cat turned professional diva, went for Jesse's hand. And rubbed her furry little face against it like he was her favorite person in the world.

"What's her name?" Jesse scratched Esmeralda's ragged ear, which jump-started an equally ragged purr.

"Traitor," Annie muttered.

"What?"

"Esmeralda — but I call her Essie. She

40

doesn't usually" — *like?* — "take to new people very well." *Or anyone else for that matter.* "She has a better view of the birds from the bookstore window than she does from my apartment. And a more comfortable place to watch them."

Jesse straightened, and she could see a muscle work in his jaw. "You're living in the apartment? What happened to Mrs. Daily?"

"She decided to move in with her daughter." Annie realized Lorna hadn't told her son that, either. "Tracie's divorce is final, and she needed someone to watch the children while she's at work."

"Tracie's divorce . . . you know more than I do about what's going on in town," Jesse said with a shake of his head.

"Well —" Annie shrugged. "Red Leaf isn't very big."

"But peaceful and quiet."

He'd just repeated a comment she had made at Lorna's house, leaving Annie to wonder what other tidbits of information he'd filed away.

"I better get the rest of the boxes up here." She dodged his searching gaze and made a beeline for the stairs.

Jesse followed, the heavy tread of his footsteps matching the beat of her heart.

Once again, he chose the largest box.

41

"What do you have in here?" Jesse grunted.

Dreams.

If she said the word out loud, would he laugh at her?

Annie decided it wasn't worth the risk.

"Books, of course . . . and some special things for the children's area."

"There isn't a children's area."

Annie couldn't hold back a smile.

"There is now."

More changes.

For years Jesse had tried — unsuccessfully — to convince his mother to hire some help so she could take a weekend off. She'd juggled everything, from ordering the books to dusting the shelves and everything in between.

He couldn't believe she'd given Annie Price carte blanche over the entire store.

"You must have a lot of experience." Jesse veered into the office and set the box down on the floor. "How long did you manage the last bookstore where you worked?"

"I wasn't the manager," Annie murmured. "I worked in . . . another part of the store."

Something in her tone tripped a silent alarm inside Jesse's head. "Which part?"

"The coffee shop."

"You managed the coffee shop?"

"No . . . I was a barista."

"A barista."

Jesse felt the ground tilt beneath his feet, not an uncommon feeling since Annie Price had barged into his life.

He had asked his mother a few questions about Annie last night, but Lorna hadn't provided much in the way of information. Just the opposite, in fact. His mother had been curiously vague, which either meant she didn't *know* the answers or she was keeping something from him.

"Did my mother know that when she hired you?" he asked.

"Of course she did." Annie's expression clouded. "Lorna said it meant I knew how to smile, multitask, and make great coffee — and that's all she was doing here."

"Uh-huh." Jesse knew that wasn't true — and judging by the expression on Annie's face, so did she.

"I was surprised when Lorna offered me the position too." Annie wouldn't look at him now, and Jesse felt a hard tug on his conscience. Maybe Annie was as sweet and sincere as his mother claimed.

Or maybe not.

Brad Rawlings had put on a good show, too, and look how that turned out. Maybe his mother was willing to walk down that road again, but Jesse was no longer the naive young kid he'd been when Rawlings waltzed into their lives. He hadn't been able to protect his mother then, but he wasn't going to let anyone take advantage of her now.

What was Annie really looking for? And why did she think she was going to find it in Red Leaf?

FOUR

"There you are!"

Caroline McCready, affectionately known as "Cricket" to her friends because of her diminutive size, rushed up and looped her arm through Annie's. "We've been waiting *forever* for you to get here!"

"I had to work at the bookstore until one." Annie turned to wave at Michael Garrison as Cricket towed her up the steps of the church the historical society had spent the summer restoring. "What's going on?"

"I'll tell you when you get inside."

A cheer erupted from the group of women gathered around the organ at the front of the church.

"Annie!" Viola Holmes surfed down the center aisle of the sanctuary's recently waxed hardwood floor on her white Keds. "You're our last hope."

Annie struggled to hide a smile as she looked to Lorna for an explanation of the women's strange behavior.

"We have a surprise," Lorna said.

"We have an emergency," Cricket corrected.

"And we need *you* to fix it." Yvonne Baker pointed to a large white box on the floor next to the organ. "Take a look."

"Okay." Slightly reassured by Lorna's wink, Annie knelt down and lifted the lid. "It looks like a . . . wedding dress."

"Not *just* a wedding dress." Lorna grinned down at her. "Elizabeth Lowery-Weston's wedding dress."

"How —" Annie sucked in a breath, unable to believe she'd heard her friend correctly. "Where did it come from?"

"Viola did a little research and found the names of some of Elizabeth's distant relatives who used to live in the area," Lorna explained. "She contacted the people on the list and invited them to attend the open house."

Viola bobbed her head. "I also mentioned that we planned to have a reenactment of Elizabeth and Patrick's wedding. A few weeks ago, I received an e-mail from a woman who said she was sending something we could use for the event. I assumed it would be a pair of lace gloves or a piece of antique jewelry, but then a delivery truck showed up yesterday — with this."

"The woman inherited the gown from a great-aunt who claimed it was the one Elizabeth had worn on her wedding day," Lorna said. "We compared it to a photograph hanging in the museum, and it's a perfect match."

"It's so beautiful." Annie traced her finger over a swirl of tiny seed pearls that trimmed the bodice. "I'd be afraid to take it out of the box."

"We already did," Yvonne declared. "And that's where the emergency comes in."

Annie rocked back on her heels and scanned the circle of faces above her. "The gown isn't in good condition?"

"It's in perfect condition," Viola said. "But did Elizabeth happen to mention in her journals that she was . . . shall we say . . . vertically challenged?"

"Short," Yvonne said with her usual bluntness. "She was short."

Annie held down a smile. "I can't recall reading a reference to her height, no."

"We can't have the gown altered, either." Lorna tipped her head and studied the gown. "It's on loan, and Viola promised we would return it in the same condition it arrived."

"What about Mrs. McCready?" Annie

47

ventured. "She's petite."

Cricket chuckled and patted her hips. "I might be the right height, but I'm afraid the rest of the measurements are a bit off."

"She's right." Viola sighed. "Everyone on this committee is over fifty years old and too . . . round to fit in this dress."

"Well, almost everyone." Lorna's eyes sparkled as the committee members turned their attention back to Annie. Their eyes were sparkling too.

"Oh no!" Annie stumbled to her feet. "I can't play the part of Elizabeth. It should be someone who grew up in Red Leaf. Someone with strong ties to the community."

And that someone wasn't her. A detail she remembered every time Jesse's gaze settled on her.

"Who made up that rule?" Yvonne lifted the gown from the box. "I say try the dress on and see if it fits."

"I don't —" Annie's protests fell on deaf ears as she and the wedding gown were hustled into a small room at the back of the church.

"Come out when you're done," Yvonne commanded as Annie shut the door. "We want to see what it looks like!"

With everyone smiling and nodding, Annie didn't have the heart to refuse.

The room, once used for storage, wasn't much larger than a closet, and there was no mirror on the wall. Bracing one hand against the wall, Annie wriggled out of her blue jeans and stepped into the dress.

She could hardly believe this wedding gown was the one Elizabeth had written about. Annie had volunteered to read through Elizabeth's personal letters and journals and been caught up in the romance between two people who came from different worlds.

An only child, Elizabeth was expected to make a match that would be advantageous for her family — until she visited the area with her father one summer and fell in love with Patrick Weston, a young circuit preacher.

Elizabeth's deep faith and her strength of character shone through every entry in her journal. Instead of a grand society wedding, the young heiress insisted on exchanging vows with Patrick in a small church made from fieldstone. Agnes Lowery had wanted her daughter to wear a gown from Paris, a stunning creation that would have everyone talking, but Elizabeth wanted something simple.

The result of their compromise was the

gown Annie now wore.

And it was a perfect fit.

A sudden commotion outside made Annie curious. She stood on her tiptoes to peek out the window and saw a pack of preadolescent boys wrestling with one of the adult volunteers in the grass.

It had been Michael's idea to ask the pastor of their church if the youth group would like to partner with the historical society on the project. So far the response had been wonderful, and some of the teens' parents had even stayed to help out.

Annie smiled. Whoever they'd tackled was being a good sport about it.

The man rose to his feet, tipped his head toward the sky, and released a loud victory whoop.

Jesse.

She pressed her nose against the glass, certain the glare from the sun was playing tricks on her.

But no, it was Jesse. And he was . . . laughing.

It was like seeing another person. A man perfectly at ease in his surroundings.

And why wouldn't he be? Annie asked herself. Born and raised in Red Leaf, Jesse didn't have to earn his place in the community.

Unlike her.

The boys swarmed around Jesse again, and Annie couldn't help but smile as he let them wrestle him to the ground, this time pretending they had the upper hand.

"What's taking you so long, Annie?" Yvonne bellowed. "My wrinkles are getting wrinkles."

Annie tore her gaze away from Jesse. "I'll be right there."

Without the benefit of a mirror, she couldn't do much with her hair except wrangle a few stray curls back in place. She grabbed a fistful of satin and stepped out of the makeshift dressing room.

Annie expected the women to applaud — or at least *smile* — when she walked out, but absolute silence greeted her instead.

She glanced down at the dress, wondering if she'd left a trail of seed pearls behind. "What's wrong?"

"Wrong? Nothing!" Viola clapped her hands together. "It looks like we found our bride!"

Cricket bent down to adjust the gown's flowing train. "There's only one thing missing."

"What's that?"

"A groom!"

"You don't have one yet?"

"There've been so many other things to do, we hadn't gotten that far," Lorna admitted.

"Don't worry. We'll find one for you." Yvonne said the words as matter-of-factly as if they were discussing a new winter coat.

"Or maybe someone will find her." Viola's voice sounded dreamy, and Annie remembered the last book the woman had purchased was a romance novel.

"She'll take the bachelor behind door number one!" Getting into the spirit of things, Cricket threw open the church door like the hostess of a game show and everyone burst out laughing.

Because Jesse stood on the other side.

Jesse hadn't seen Annie arrive, but there she was. Vivid green eyes, flushed cheeks, and platinum curls askew — as usual — but it was the dress she wore that stripped the air from his lungs.

A wedding gown that looked as if it had been custommade to fit her slender frame. Jesse didn't know what kind of fabric it was, but there was a lot of it. It pooled around her feet and sparkled like sunlight on freshly fallen snow.

"Annie is going to be our bride for the reenactment," his mother explained.

"The dress is a perfect fit." Viola Holmes sighed. "Just like Cinderella's slipper."

Jesse heard Annie make a noise that sounded suspiciously like a groan. "I didn't mean to intrude." He took a step backward. "Mr. Garrison wanted me to check the purchase order for a load of lumber that came in yesterday."

"You aren't intruding at all." Cricket Mc-Cready fluttered over and took hold of his arm. "In fact, I would say your timing couldn't be better."

"We were just discussing the need for a groom." Yvonne Baker, Jesse's sixth-grade science teacher, was smiling the same way she'd smiled just before announcing a pop quiz. And even though Jesse was almost thirty years old, it still had the power to make him squirm.

"I'm sure Jesse is busy." Annie spoke for the first time.

Yvonne shrugged. "I don't know why he can't fit it into his schedule. All he has to do is put on a nice suit and stand in front of the church."

"That's all any groom has to do." Viola reached up and brushed a blade of grass off Jesse's shoulder, the remnants of his impromptu wrestling match with the boys he taught on Sunday morning. "I'm sure it won't be difficult for Jesse. He was a natural when he played the part of Joseph in the Christmas program."

He had also been ten years old, but that thought took second place to the one that broke through the fog that had clouded Jesse's brain the moment his gaze had locked on Annie.

"You want me to be the groom?"

"What a wonderful idea!" Cricket gave his arm a squeeze. "Thank you for volunteering."

"I'm sure Mr. Gunderson wouldn't mind playing the part of Patrick," Annie interjected. "He said he would help with the open house that day."

"Arthur is almost seventy years old!" With a slash of her hand, Yvonne crossed the hardware store owner off an invisible list. "If we want the reenactment to be as authentic as possible, we need a younger groom. Patrick was twenty-five." She speared Jesse with a look. "How old are you?"

"Twenty-nine."

Yvonne nodded her approval. "Close enough."

"So, you'll be our — Annie's — groom?" Viola said.

Jesse glanced at Annie. He knew he

54

shouldn't. He could tell she didn't *want* him to. But for some reason, that didn't stop him from saying two simple words that contained the power to change a man's life.

"I will."

FIVE

Annie wasn't quite sure how the situation had gotten so out of hand. The thought of Jesse acting as her groom made her knees feel all weak and wobbly.

She raised her hand. "I think —"

"It's settled then," Yvonne interrupted. "Now we can get back to sewing curtains for the museum."

"And leave the rest of the details to the bride and groom!" Viola adjusted the rhinestone bifocals perched on her nose and flitted toward the door.

Along with everyone else. Leaving her alone with . . .

"Wait!" Annie tried in vain to round them up. "What details? I don't know what you have planned for the rest of the wedding!"

"Oh, we hadn't gotten that far yet," Cricket said cheerfully.

"You're the one who's been reading Elizabeth's journals." Yvonne marched past her.

"But she didn't describe everything." Annie dove in front of Viola and blocked her path, no easy feat in a dress with a long train. "I have no idea what to do."

"All young women dream about their wedding day." Viola smiled and squeezed her arm. "If some of the details are missing, fill in with some of yours."

Annie shot a panicked look at Lorna, but she'd pulled Jesse aside and was talking to him in a low voice.

No help there. She wasn't sure how to convince the committee to find another bride, and it wasn't only because Jesse had volunteered to be the groom. In spite of what Viola claimed, Annie hadn't dreamed about her wedding day. Until a few months ago, she hadn't dared to dream at all.

If only she hadn't told the committee she would fill in wherever necessary. If only she were *taller*.

Holding back a howl of frustration, Annie retreated into the little room to change back into her work clothes. By the time she emerged a few minutes later, everyone — including Jesse — was gone. And Annie was able to breathe again.

Something she'd forgotten how to do when Jesse had smiled at her. Groom or not, she did her best to avoid him for the rest of the day.

"I'm going to give Viola a ride home now."

Lorna breezed into the sanctuary as Annie was climbing down from a stepladder. She'd volunteered to wash the windows in the church while the other women sewed curtains.

"I'm almost finished too." Annie tucked a rag in the back pocket of her jeans.

"The windows look amazing." Lorna shook her head. "I know that was a lot of work."

Annie stepped back to inspect the glistening stained glass panels. Every one of them told part of an amazing story. Jesus standing next to a woman drawing water from a well. Jesus praying in a garden. Jesus holding a basket filled with fish and loaves of bread.

"It didn't feel like work," she admitted. "It felt like reading a book."

Lorna's smile told Annie she understood. "Which one is your favorite?"

"That one." Annie pointed to the one where Jesus was reaching down to rescue a lamb.

Their eyes met, and Annie knew Lorna understood that too. It was the reason they'd become close friends over the past six months.

"I still have to put the cleaning supplies away, but you don't have to wait for me," Annie told her. "I can lock up the church when I leave."

"There's one more thing." Lorna held out a small cedar box. "Yvonne discovered these combs while we were sorting through some old jewelry the mayor's daughter donated to the society a few days ago. They might not be the ones Elizabeth wore on her wedding day, but the committee took a vote this afternoon and everyone agreed they would look beautiful in your hair."

Annie opened the tiny gold clasp on the box and peeked inside. "Those aren't real diamonds, are they?"

"The size of peas?" Lorna chuckled. "I doubt it!"

Annie nibbled on her lower lip. "They're gorgeous, but shouldn't they be on display at the museum?"

"They will be on display." Lorna gently folded Annie's hands around the box. "They'll just be displayed on *you*. Yvonne's niece, Julie, owns the beauty salon a block off Main Street, and Yvonne said she would love to help you pick out a hairstyle for the wedding."

"But —"

"No buts." Lorna wagged one finger in front of Annie's nose. "You're the bride. It's okay to have some fun."

Annie's eyes began to sting. "Thank you."

Lorna's expression turned solemn, an indication she knew Annie wasn't referring to the combs. "I should be thanking you. If you hadn't taken over the bookstore, I would still be selling books instead of writing one."

"Promise that I get the first autographed copy."

"Done." Lorna gave her a quick hug. "I'll see you at church tomorrow."

Annie was still smiling when she turned the key in the lock a few minutes later.

Most of the volunteers had gone home for the day, and there was no sign of Jesse anywhere. Mission accomplished. She wasn't ready to face him yet.

Or maybe you aren't ready to face the way he makes you feel.

"Frustrated," Annie muttered as she walked around the church. "That's how he makes me feel."

Along with light-headed, dizzy, and wobbly-kneed.

Jesse Kent was the human equivalent of heatstroke, that's what he was.

A horn honked as a van pulled out of the

parking lot, and Annie waved to the passel of sixth-grade boys who'd spent their Saturday helping Michael's crew refinish the oak pews that had been stacked like cordwood in the basement of the church.

The image of Jesse playing with them on the lawn flashed through Annie's mind. He'd looked younger. More carefree. Apparently there were moments he let his guard down and laughed.

Just not with her.

"Not that you want him to," Annie reminded herself.

The cell phone in her purse chirped a reminder that she hadn't checked the messages all afternoon. She tapped the button to retrieve her voice mail and pressed the phone against her ear.

"This is Steve from Number One Auto Service. Thank you for scheduling an appointment with our service department. We close at 3:00 p.m. on Saturdays, but if you drop your car off by two, we should be able to get to it today."

Oh. No.

She'd totally forgotten about the appointment. Annie cast a panicked look at her tailpipe. Was it her imagination or had it dropped a few more inches since she'd driven the car earlier that day? If there was

61

a downside to living in Red Leaf, it was the fact there were very few businesses, and the ones it had closed up on the weekends as tight as the clasp on Viola's beaded purse. She'd been lucky to get a Saturday appointment at the auto shop.

Annie gnawed on her lower lip. Had Jesse noticed she had neglected to get her car fixed? And what would happen now that she had to put off the repairs until Monday? Would she be issued a ticket she didn't have the money to pay?

"You look deep in thought."

The rumble of a masculine voice — a *familiar* masculine voice — made Annie jump.

"You were waiting for me, weren't you?" she complained. "Isn't that considered entrapment?"

Jesse gave her a look. "When people get defensive, it's usually because they feel guilty about something."

"I do feel guilty!" Annie wailed. "I was in such a hurry to get here today, I forgot about the appointment I made at the auto shop. And now it's closed until Monday. And the five days you gave me is up *today,* and I suppose you're going to give me a ticket?" She paused to catch her breath and Jesse held out his hand.

"Keys."

Annie curled her fingers around them. "You're taking my keys?"

"Of course not. I'm taking your car." Jesse unleashed a slow smile that caused Annie's heart to stall midbeat.

Talk about a concealed weapon!

"My . . . car?" she stammered. "Where?"

The smile moved to Jesse's eyes and spilled into the tiny creases that fanned out from the corners. "To my place. I took an auto shop class my junior year of high school. I'm pretty sure I can replace a bulb and find something a little sturdier than twine to hold the tailpipe in place."

Annie finally got her lips to move, but only one word slipped out. "Why?"

Jesse found that question more difficult to answer than the first one.

A few days ago, his motivation would have been to gather all the information about Annie Price he could. But Jesse had tossed out a few questions about Annie that afternoon in casual conversation, and everyone he'd spoken with had nothing but good things to say about Red Leaf's newest resident.

In spite of Annie's assumption that he'd been lurking nearby, waiting to write up a citation, Jesse had just been worried there

63

was something wrong when he spotted her pacing back and forth in front of her car as he was leaving.

"I'm a public servant, remember?" he reminded her. "You're the public."

Just keep telling yourself that, Dudley Do-Right.

"Really? You're going to fix it?" The sparkle returned to Annie's eyes, and Jesse realized that's what he had been waiting for all along.

"I live a little off the beaten path," he told her. "I can drive your car and pick up my truck later when we come back, or you can follow me."

"You can drive." Annie dropped the keys into his hand and dashed around to the passenger side of the vehicle.

Suddenly he questioned the wisdom of spending time alone with her. Jesse was starting to forget his reasons for wanting to get to know Annie better. He just . . . wanted to get to know her better.

Late afternoon sunlight filtered through the trees as Jesse turned off the main highway.

"You weren't kidding when you said your house is off the beaten path," Annie said when he slowed down to let a doe and two half-grown fawns cross the road.

"It's on Jewel Lake, although the lake is more like an oversized pond. I moved there after I got hired by the sheriff's department. I'm close enough to Mom that I can help out if she needs something and far enough away that she can't steal the remote control when I'm trying to watch a football game."

"Lorna is amazing."

"Agreed." Jesse didn't miss the wistful note in Annie's voice. "Do your parents live in Madison?"

"No." Her expression clouded a split second before she turned to look out the window. "Oh, look at that log cabin! Isn't it adorable?"

"It's mine . . . and I prefer the word *rustic.*" Jesse turned down the gravel driveway.

"Adorably rustic, then." Annie ended the debate with a smile. "Did you build it yourself?"

"Dad bought it to use as a hunting cabin, but I insulated the walls so it could be used year-round and added the deck." Jesse regretted the words as soon as they slipped out. He didn't talk about his father.

He still felt the sting of his dad's absence, like a wound that had never completely healed. They'd spent hours at the cabin, catching fish off the rickety dock and exploring the woods together.

His mom had been forced to sell it to pay for Jesse's college tuition, but the moment he'd been hired by the sheriff's department, Jesse had contacted the couple who'd purchased the land as an investment property and bought it back.

"How long has he been gone?"

Jesse's throat tightened under Annie's searching gaze. He'd been trained not to show emotion, and yet he had the uncomfortable feeling that she could see right through him.

"He died when I was eight."

"I'm sorry." Her voice was whisper soft and so was the hand that stole out and touched his arm.

"So am I."

Jesse turned off the ignition and they both got out of the car. Annie wrapped her arms around her middle as a cool breeze danced across the water and ruffled the leaves of the poplar trees.

"You can wait inside if you want to," he offered. "The evenings are getting chilly." And he wouldn't mind putting a little distance between them even if it meant deviating from his original plan to get Annie alone so he could question her more about her reasons for moving to Red Leaf.

66

"Or I can help you."

Right now, with her winsome smile wreaking havoc with his pulse, Jesse couldn't help but think that Annie Price posed more of a threat to his heart than to the town.

SIX

The prelude had already started when Annie slipped into the church. Ordinarily, she was on time for the Sunday morning service, but not today. She had hit the snooze button twice in what had proved to be a futile attempt to wring out a few more precious minutes of sleep. Sleep she'd lost because of Jesse.

After he'd fixed her car, Jesse had barely spoken when they'd driven back to Stone Church so he could pick up his truck. Annie couldn't shake the feeling that Jesse thought he'd already said too much. Did Lorna know how much Jesse still missed his father?

Annie's gaze scanned the congregation, searching for her friend, and there was Jesse, sitting next to her in the second row. Annie shouldn't have been surprised to see him.

Maybe it was her imagination, but Jesse happened to be *everywhere*. The bookstore.

Stone Church.

Her head.

And worse yet, her dreams.

"Excuse me." Annie squeezed into the back row, next to a couple with twin boys and a sweet-faced toddler who promptly held out her stuffed rabbit for Annie to admire. She dutifully patted the bunny's head and was rewarded with a wide grin.

"Just to warn you," their father whispered, "you might feel like you've been stuck in a blender by the time the service is over."

Annie smiled. "I don't mind."

In fact, the children sitting in the row weren't nearly as distracting as Jesse.

Annie's gaze kept drifting to the back of his dark head and broad shoulders. At one point, Jesse turned to listen to something Lorna was saying, and the smile that kicked up the corner of his lips triggered a corresponding kick to Annie's heart.

"But she's not singing, either, Daddy."

The loud whisper and a chubby finger pointed in Annie's direction brought her attention back to the worship team as they took their places at the front of the sanctuary.

Unable to stop the blush that swept through her cheeks, Annie grabbed the hymnal and paged through it until she came to "Amazing Grace." Her heart picked up the melody as she sang the words, amazed by grace all over again.

When the service ended, Annie saw Lorna winding between the clusters of people who'd stopped in the aisle to chat.

"Where were you?" Annie was wrapped in a vanilla-scented hug. "We saved a seat for you up front."

"I came in a few minutes late."

"Michael offered to grill hamburgers for lunch, and there's plenty if you'd like to join us."

Out of the corner of her eye, Annie saw Jesse approaching. Honestly, over the past few days she had developed a strange, inner radar that turned toward him like the needle on a compass.

"I'd love to, but I'm driving over to Vivienne Wallace's house right after church. She left another message last night, asking if I could pick up something for the museum."

Lorna snagged Jesse's arm and drew him into the conversation. "Then I think Jesse should go with you. The 'something' might be heavy."

"That's not necessary," Annie said quickly. "It's Jesse's day off. I'm sure he has better things to do."

"Jesse doesn't mind, do you, sweetheart?" Lorna cast a bright smile at her son. "He turned down my invitation to lunch, too, so I'm sure he has a few minutes to spare."

Jesse opened his mouth and closed it again.

"That settles it." Lorna waved to Michael. "I have apple pie for dessert if you want to stop over later. And that invitation is for both of you."

Annie watched Lorna glide away and then glanced at Jesse.

"I'm not sure what just happened."

Jesse knew exactly what had just happened.

His mother was no longer managing the bookstore, but she hadn't stopped managing other things. Like his life. It wasn't the first time Lorna had set an extra place at the table and tried to play matchmaker. Jesse had become adept at dodging her attempts. His schedule — working many weekends and holidays and dropping everything whenever the pager buzzed — wasn't exactly conducive to forming deep relationships. At least that's what Jesse had always told himself.

"You don't have to come with me." Annie was already moving up the aisle when the words registered, but Jesse caught up to her

71

at the door.

"Mom's right. I should go with you."

Annie hesitated, a response quite different from the one Jesse had seen when he'd offered to fix her car. "I don't want you to go to any trouble," she said after a moment. "You already gave up enough of your free time to help me last night."

Jesse watched a shadow skim across Annie's face and felt a stab of regret. He hadn't meant to make her feel like an imposition, but memories had crowded in like the evening shadows. He hadn't only been remembering the good times with his dad; other memories weighted the air as well. He'd wanted to apologize for his silence, but that would have meant explaining what he was apologizing *for.*

"I don't have plans," Jesse said. "And trust me, you might need an interpreter."

Annie tipped her head. "An interpreter?"

Jesse steered her toward the parking lot. "Have you met Vivienne Wallace?"

"We've only talked on the phone. Do you know her?"

"Everyone knows Ms. Viv." Jesse's lips tilted in a smile as he opened the door on the passenger side of his truck. "She is a little . . . eccentric. Even for Red Leaf."

"Are you implying the people in your

72

hometown are eccentric?" Annie asked when he'd opened the driver's side door.

"Don't tell me you haven't noticed." Jesse shot her a sideways glance as he slid behind the wheel. "The Fourth of July decorations in the diner that stay up all year —"

"Very patriotic."

Jesse ignored the interruption. "And the way Arthur Gunderson sweeps the sidewalk outside the hardware store every day at six o'clock, even though there's not a gum wrapper to be seen."

"He doesn't sweep the sidewalk to get rid of litter." Annie's laughter washed over him like a warm summer rain. "For a police officer, you aren't very observant."

"Not very —" He strangled on the last word, which only gave Annie an opportunity to state her case.

"At six o'clock every day, Miss Greer rearranges her window display across the street."

"The florist?"

"That's right." She lowered her voice even though they were alone in the vehicle. "I think Mr. Gunderson has a bit of a crush on her."

"A *crush*? Mr. Gunderson has to be eighty years old!"

"He's seventy. And what does that have to

do with anything?" Annie countered.

"Nothing . . . I guess." Jesse frowned. "But if your theory is right — and I'm not saying it is — why doesn't he ask her out on a date?"

"I haven't figured that out yet." Annie nibbled on her thumbnail. "Can you think of a reason?"

"I . . . no." Jesse didn't really want to think about it at all.

He drove to the older part of Red Leaf, where the rows of Victorian homes with their turrets, fancy trim, and slanting rooflines resembled the gingerbread creations the Sweet family displayed in the window of the bakery every Christmas.

Before he and Annie reached the front door, it swung open and Vivienne Wallace swept onto the porch. In the folds of her long, multi-colored skirt were three tiny white dogs, each one no larger than the sponge Jesse used to wash his pickup.

"Little Jesse Kent!" Vivienne went up on her tiptoes and reached up to tweak his cheeks. "I wasn't expecting to see you too!"

Little Jesse Kent?

Annie bit her lip to keep from laughing as she glanced at Jesse to see how he felt about Vivienne Wallace's description.

His hands came up and covered hers, and the warm smile on his face stole Annie's breath from her lungs. "It's good to see you, Ms. Viv. This is Annie Price."

"It's nice to meet you, Mrs. Wallace." Annie held out her hand, but Vivienne Wallace ignored it and pulled her in for a hug instead, enveloping her in a sweet cloud of fabric softener and Chanel No. 5.

"Call me Ms. Viv, sweetheart." Vivienne released her and cast a smile at Jesse before motioning them inside. "That's what my students called me."

"You're a schoolteacher?" Annie followed her into the tiled foyer.

"Oh, no. What gave you that idea?"

Out of the corner of her eye, she saw Jesse's lips twitch.

"Ms. Viv was my piano teacher," he explained.

"You play the piano?" Annie knew she shouldn't have sounded so surprised.

"Mercy, no!" the woman interjected cheerfully. "The boy can't play a note. Lorna insisted that he stick it out for six months, though." She winked at Jesse. "Every Tuesday at four o'clock, we played checkers. He certainly had a talent for that."

Jesse grinned. "Only when you let me win."

"Always the charmer, this one." Ms. Viv pursed her lips in mock disapproval.

Jesse flashed a smile that had Annie silently agreeing, although a week ago she would have laughed at the description.

"Follow me." Vivienne snapped her fingers, and the dogs fell into a line as she led the procession down the hall to a room overlooking a garden. A massive stone fireplace took up one wall, a baby grand piano the other.

Vivienne settled in the comfortable lap of a chair covered in bright yellow chintz. "Now, what can I do for you?"

Considering she was the one who'd contacted Annie, the question was disconcerting.

"You mentioned that you had some things to donate for the open house at the museum," Annie said cautiously.

"That's right." Vivienne sighed. "I forget things sometimes. Don't I, girls?" She directed the question at the trio of dogs who'd flopped at her feet and maintained a polite silence. "I'm not sure if this is common knowledge, but a relative of Patrick and Elizabeth Weston's built this house about ten years before the Great Depression."

Annie leaned forward. "I don't remember

76

anyone on the committee mentioning that."

"It's true. My grandparents bought the house shortly after they were married, and the previous owners left the whole caboodle here for them to deal with. I overheard my grandmother complaining to my parents there were things in the attic that dated back to Patrick Weston himself." Vivienne chuckled. "Cricket mentioned you'd been out to her place last week to pick up a donation, and that's what made me remember I had a few things that might be of interest to the committee too."

"That would be great." Annie couldn't hide her excitement. "We're putting together a nice display with the donations that have been coming in."

Vivienne picked up a basket of knitting and began to hum along with the click of the needles.

"Where are the things you'd like to donate, Ms. Viv?" Jesse finally asked. "I'll carry them out to my truck."

Vivienne stopped humming and looked up. "They're in the attic, remember?"

"Is there something specific Jesse and I should look for?" Annie ventured.

"A box of some sort," Vivienne said vaguely. "Believe me, you'll know it when you see it." She patted her knee. "I would have gone up there myself, but I can't climb that flight of stairs anymore. Old opera injury."

Annie didn't dare look at Jesse as she nodded. "Of course."

"Second floor, door in the closet at the end of the hall." The woman wagged one finger under Jesse's nose. "Don't get lost this time."

A pained look crossed Jesse's face. "I won't."

"Jesse would pretend he was a famous explorer and search the house from top to bottom, looking for hidden treasures," Vivienne said. "I'd have to ring a bell to get his attention when it was time to leave."

"I was nine years old, Ms. Viv," he muttered.

Annie rose to her feet and swept her arm toward the door. "After you, Dr. Livingstone."

A hint of red washed over Jesse's angular jaw, and Annie found it as charming and unexpected as his smile.

SEVEN

"Tell me what we're looking for again."

Annie wrinkled her nose in an attempt to hold back a sneeze. "You heard, Ms. Viv. We'll know it —"

"When we see it," Jesse interrupted. "Right."

Annie ducked to avoid the swags of spiderwebs hanging from the wooden beams of the open ceiling. "She said something about a box, remember?"

"Well, that narrows it down," Jesse muttered. "To about a hundred."

Annie clamped down on a smile as she picked her way through the maze of boxes and discarded furniture. "She could open her own antique store up here."

"Look at this." Jesse picked up an enormous ceramic lamp shaped like a mermaid, its entire base encrusted with real seashells. "I can't believe the junk people hold on to."

"It's not —" Annie let out a gasp as her foot sank into a loose floorboard and she pitched headfirst into the bony wooden arms of a Queen Anne chair. A cloud of dust erupted from the velvet seat cushion, filling the air and her lungs.

"Are you all right?" Jesse was suddenly there, his large hands reaching out to steady her.

No. "Yes." Annie's throat tightened around the word.

"Are you sure?" His face was only inches from hers, close enough for Annie to see the exact spot in his eyes where the clear blue deepened to indigo.

"Positive," Annie croaked as she took a step back. "It might be easier if we split up."

A lot easier.

Jesse didn't seem to hear her. He picked up a dusty violin case and shook his head. "Why do you think people keep this kind of stuff anyway?"

"Maybe it's attached to a memory." Annie rescued the case and set it down on a scarred coffee table with a missing leg, held upright by yet another box.

"A memory?" Jesse looked skeptical. "I doubt there's even a violin inside."

"Let's find out." Accepting the challenge, Annie flipped the tarnished metal clasps and opened the lid.

Jesse was right. Instead of a musical instrument, the case was stuffed with old sepia photographs.

Annie picked one off the top. "Look! Here's a picture of Stone Church." In her excitement, the top of her head bumped against the underside of his jaw.

Jesse winced. "Assaulting a police officer is a federal offense, Miss Price."

The sparkle in his eyes rendered her speechless. Jesse was actually *teasing* her.

While Annie tried to piece together a coherent thought, Jesse swept a handful of photos from the pile and began to thumb through them.

"I can't believe these were taken a million years ago and the town still looks the same."

"Aren't you exaggerating a little?"

"Okay, a thousand years ago." Jesse brushed away a layer of dust and tapped a finger against an image of one of the buildings on Main Street. "And I'm almost sure that ugly vase is still in the window of the bank."

Annie peered down at the photograph. "I think you're right."

"Nothing changes around here."

"I love that about Red Leaf," she murmured.

"Wait until you've lived here a few years." Jesse put the photographs back and closed the case lid with a snap. "The waitress at the Korner Kettle will have your coffee on the table five minutes before you walk in the door. It makes you wonder if there are surveillance cameras hidden in the awning. The postmaster calls you at home and scolds you if you don't shovel around the mailbox after a snowstorm. If you go into the bakery on your birthday, Mrs. Sweet gives you a cupcake, and then she lights a candle and makes you blow it out in front of all her customers."

"That's amazing."

"That's one word for it." Jesse brushed his hands against his thighs and left a streak of dust on the faded denim.

"You're blessed," Annie insisted. "To have roots. People who care about you."

"Where are your roots? Madison?"

"Not really. I moved around a lot."

"Military brat?"

"Foster child," Annie said lightly.

Jesse's forehead creased in spite of her attempt to smile away thirteen years of never feeling as if she belonged. Like a player always forced to sit on the bench — part of a team but always viewing everything from the sidelines.

The year Annie turned sixteen, life had taken an unexpected turn when the Martin family took her in. For the first time in years, Annie had been hopeful about the future. The couple had one child, a daughter named Paige, and Annie was looking forward to sharing secrets and dreams with someone her age.

Things had started out well. Paige introduced Annie to some of her friends, and they had some classes together. But Paige wanted to spend her weekends at the mall, shopping and gossiping with her friends, while Annie preferred to stay home and read a book. Paige's mother, Janet, a junior high English teacher, noticed how much she enjoyed reading and asked Annie if she would be interested in tutoring some of her students. Annie had jumped at the chance to help. She started helping Janet grade papers, too, and enjoyed talking about some of the essays the students had turned in.

Paige hadn't seemed to care at first. She had her own interests, and English literature wasn't one of them. Annie sensed a subtle change in Paige's mood over the next few months but hadn't realized she was the cause.

Until it was too late.

Watching the myriad of emotions skim across the surface of her expressive features, Jesse could see he'd struck a nerve. If he was interviewing someone, this was the moment he would push for more information. Instead, he was struck by an overwhelming urge to wrap his arms around Annie. To protect her from whatever memory had extinguished the light from her eyes.

He'd dealt with kids in the foster care system on occasion, and it was difficult to imagine Annie growing up in that world.

Is that what his mom had meant when she'd told him Annie needed a fresh start?

Halfway through his rant about life in a small town, Jesse had realized she was staring at him with a look of wonder on her face, as if what he was describing came straight from a fairy tale. Or a dream.

Jesse's throat began to itch, and he couldn't blame it on the bucket of dust he'd swallowed since climbing the attic stairs.

"We better keep looking. We don't want to be here forever. We haven't had any lunch and my stomach is starting to growl." Jesse didn't miss the flicker of relief in Annie's eyes as he stepped over a crate filled with

84

fake evergreen boughs.

They continued to work their way through the attic as the temperature rose with the afternoon sun. Jesse was no expert, but none of the items they found dated back to the turn of the twentieth century. A split-second before Jesse was going to suggest they call it a day, Annie popped up from behind a steamer trunk.

"I have an idea." Her eyes were shining, her platinum hair curled wildly around her face, and she still managed to look as perky as one of the flowers in Vivienne's garden. "Let's have a contest."

Jesse used the cuff of his sleeve to blot the moisture from his forehead. "What kind of contest?"

"Whoever finds the most unusual item at the end of thirty minutes wins."

"We have to stay up here another half hour? I'm hungry!"

Annie ignored the question. "Me too. But are you in?"

"It depends. What's the prize?"

"A dozen cinnamon rolls from The Sweet Bakery. Front door delivery. And they have to be warm."

"They're only warm at six in the morning."

"I know."

85

Jesse wasn't sure if the spots dancing in front of his eyes meant he was succumbing to the heat or to Annie's smile. "You've got a deal."

"It has to be something new, not something you've found before."

"So no mermaid lamp?"

"No mermaid lamp."

"Fine."

Jesse chose a methodical approach, working in a straight line from the front of the attic to the back, while Annie flitted from box to box, finding strings of old Christmas lights, a wooden rocking horse, an ancient record player. Every find, no matter how dusty and decrepit, was a treasure to her. Jesse knew, because he found himself paying more attention to Annie than the competition.

A bead of sweat trickled down his spine as he discarded yet another box, this one filled with ice skates. He suddenly realized he hadn't heard a sound from Annie, not even a giggle, for several minutes.

"Annie?"

"Up here." Her muffled voice led Jesse to a wooden ladder nailed to the wall. "But don't follow me. It's kind of dangerous."

Dangerous?

"Are you *trying* to insult me?" Jesse

stepped onto one of the rungs and heard a snap.

"Be careful!" Annie called.

Jesse grasped the ladder and felt a splinter pierce his finger. A few seconds later, he reached the top and poked his head through an opening in the ceiling, where he could see a trapdoor had been pushed open.

Dressmaker forms — and more boxes — filled a tiny loft Jesse hadn't known existed.

"Look at this!"

Annie stood in front of an oval stained glass window that wasn't visible from the road. She wore a full-length cape made of purple velvet and a black top hat embellished with a peacock feather that curled around her face like an upside-down question mark.

She turned a slow circle as Jesse climbed the rest of the way up the ladder and cautiously made his way across the creaking floorboards until he reached her side.

"There are boxes and boxes of costumes. Where do you think Ms. Viv got them?"

"Costumes?" Jesse's brows shot up. "My guess is that they're part of her winter wardrobe."

Annie's hand emerged from the folds of the cape to swat his arm. "Be nice."

"I am nice. I'm also serious."

"Someone stitched this cape by hand." Annie lifted a corner and inspected the fabric. The tattered feather drifted over one eye. "Do you think Vivienne really was an opera singer?"

Jesse didn't answer.

Annie glanced up and a frown pleated her forehead. "What's the matter? Why are you looking at me like that?"

"Because I won."

"What?" The top hat listed to one side. "Where is it? What did you find?"

She looked so disgruntled that a smile slipped out before Jesse could stop it. "You."

"Me?" Her lips shaped the word but no sound came out.

Jesse grasped her shoulders and turned her toward a full-length mirror standing in the corner. "Tell me you don't fit the criteria for the most unusual thing in the attic."

"It's the clothes. And the feather." Annie blew at the feather but only succeeded in setting free one of the curls poking out from the top hat.

Jesse couldn't resist. He only meant to brush it away from her face, but the curl wound around his finger like a silver ribbon. His knuckles grazed her cheek, and Annie made a soft sound that drew his attention to her lips.

He cupped her jaw and tipped her face up. In Annie's vivid green eyes, Jesse saw his reflection . . . and something else. Something that looked like . . .

Yes.

Over the thumping of his heart, Jesse was dimly aware of a bell ringing. It took a moment to place the sound, but when he did, he stifled a groan.

"Jesse?" Vivienne's voice floated up the stairs, all the way to the loft.

"Be down in a minute, Ms. Viv."

Annie lurched away, peeling off the cape and hat on her way to the trapdoor.

Jesse exhaled the breath that had collected in his lungs as she clambered down the ladder.

Remember what it is you're looking for.

EIGHT

Annie spotted Vivienne at the bottom of the stairs, wearing a white chef's apron and a smudge of flour on her cheek.

"You look flushed." Vivienne clucked her tongue. "I suppose it's warm up in the attic."

Annie couldn't look at Jesse.

You have no idea, Ms. Viv.

Had Jesse really been about to kiss her?

The thought made Annie's toes curl all over again. She had assumed she was the only one who felt the tiny sparks that danced in the air between them. Until she'd seen them in his eyes.

"Did you find what you were looking for?" Vivienne turned a smile on Jesse, whose expression remained as unreadable as if he were wearing his sunglasses again.

"Sorry, Ms. Viv. There was a lot of —" Annie's foot shot out and pressed down on Jesse's shoe. "A lot of *stuff* up there, but we couldn't find anything that looked like it might have belonged to Patrick Weston."

"I was so sure . . . Oh well." Vivienne didn't look the least bit upset by the news. "You have time to stay for tea? I set up a table in the garden." The woman didn't wait for a response as she forged ahead, the three dogs pattering along behind her. "We won't be blessed with too many beautiful afternoons like this. Have to take advantage of the moment while we can."

"I'm sorry about this," Jesse said in a tight whisper. "I forgot about her standing appointment with Earl Grey."

Annie almost smiled. Almost.

They trooped through a three-seasons room stuffed with wicker furniture and followed Vivienne through a door that opened into the backyard.

"Help yourself." Their hostess motioned to a tray on the wrought iron table. Tiny china cups circled a hand-painted teapot, and peanut butter cookies dusted with sugar were piled high on a matching plate.

Annie perched on the edge of a white wicker chair. "Everything looks delicious."

"These are Jesse's favorite." Vivienne pushed the plate of cookies closer to Annie. "He used to eat half a dozen every time he came over for piano lessons."

She passed Jesse a filled teacup and it all but disappeared when he wrapped his large hand around it.

"You shouldn't have gone to so much trouble," Annie told her as Vivienne poured her a cup of tea.

"It's no trouble," the woman sputtered. "It's a celebration!"

"What are we celebrating, Ms. Viv?" Jesse reached for a cookie.

"Your wedding, of course. I heard you two are getting married."

Annie didn't dare look at Jesse as she hurried to correct the mistake. "It's not a real wedding, Ms. Viv. It's a special event for the museum's grand opening. Jesse and I are just pretending. Playing a part."

Vivienne laughed. "I'm seventy-eight years old. I know the real thing when I see it! David and I were married for fifty years and we looked at each other the same way you two look at each other."

Annie couldn't look at Jesse now.

"We did everything together . . . My husband had this way of making everything an adventure," Vivienne went on. "After David retired, he refused to sit in a recliner and watch the world pass by. One morning I looked outside and he'd dug up the entire backyard. I opened the window and asked him what on earth he planned to do with that enormous pile of dirt. You know what he said?" Vivienne paused.

Jesse picked up on the cue. "What did he say?"

"He said, 'Vivie, I don't see a pile of dirt anywhere. I see a garden!' "

"He planted all these flowers?" Annie reached out and touched the petal of a yellow dahlia the size of her dessert plate. "They're stunning."

"We planted them together." Vivienne's gaze rested on the flowers, but Annie had a feeling the woman was seeing something else. "David designed the garden so flowers bloomed during every season, right up until the first snow. We used to have people over for dinner, and I finally stopped setting the table in the dining room because everyone ended up out here."

The sparkle faded from Vivienne's eyes, and Annie felt a divine nudge.

"Would you like to help me decorate the church for the open house?" she asked. "Fresh flowers would be beautiful, and it would mean more if they came right from the garden and not off a truck."

"Me?" Vivienne pressed a hand against her heart. "I don't know. I don't get out much these days."

"I need you, Ms. Viv." Annie folded her fingers around the woman's other hand. "I'm terrified I'm going to make a mistake."

"You don't have to be afraid. When God gives us a task, he always gives us just what we need to accomplish it, you know."

"I know . . ." Lorna had told her the same thing, but Annie still felt as if she were traveling on new ground. "But, sometimes, isn't what we need . . . people?"

"I suppose that's true." Vivienne's speckled hand gently cupped the upturned face of a brown-eyed Susan. "All right, I'll help. And I'll also make your bridal bouquet for the ceremony that day." She glanced at Jesse and lowered her voice in a pseudo whisper. "You'll be the blushing bride he always dreamed about."

When it came to Jesse, Annie certainly had the blushing part down.

While they finished their tea and cookies, Vivienne talked through what flowers she thought would make good arrangements for Stone Church, a subject probably boring to Jesse. He was quiet, and Annie wasn't surprised when he was ready to go. He still hadn't had any lunch.

"We should be getting back, Ms. Viv." Jesse stood up, leaned down, and wrapped the elderly woman in a hug. "It was good to see you."

"Promise you'll visit again." Vivienne rested her cheek against Jesse's chest. "Next time I'll break out the checkerboard."

"It's a date." Jesse's smile — and the kiss he pressed against Ms. Viv's nest of iron gray curls — melted Annie's heart.

"You come back too." Vivienne nodded at Annie. "We can pick out the flowers for your bouquet."

"I will," Annie promised. "And thank you for the tea."

"It was my pleasure, dear. I'm glad Jesse found someone as sweet as you. You're going to be so happy together."

"Um . . . thank you." This time Annie didn't remind her it wasn't a real wedding.

She followed Jesse outside, her stomach in knots at the thought of being alone with him again. Because the last time they were alone . . .

"I'm sorry," Jesse said a few minutes after they pulled away in his truck.

Jesse's matter-of-fact statement sent Annie's heart into a skid. She was afraid to ask what he was sorry for. Letting his guard down when they were in the attic? For almost kissing her?

"You'll have to tell my mom we came back from Ms. Viv's empty-handed," he continued.

"Not empty-handed." Relief coursed through Annie, and she was afraid to analyze why. "We're going to have fresh flowers for decorations."

"But that isn't what you needed."

Annie tipped her head, remembering that inner nudge she'd felt in the garden. "Vivienne mentioned she had talked to Cricket McCready a few days ago. I think she saw an opportunity to open her home again. To entertain visitors like she and her husband used to do."

"Are you saying she never intended to make a donation to the historical society?"

"She's lonely," Annie said simply. "She needs to feel needed."

"That's why you talked her into donating flowers for the open house."

The flash of guilt on Annie's face confirmed it. "Her garden is beautiful. And I *do* need her. I don't know the first thing about arranging flowers."

Jesse pulled into the church parking lot, where they'd left Annie's car after the service. "You missed your calling, Dr. Price." A smile teased his lips.

"You don't need a degree to know when people are lonely." *Sometimes you just have to look in the mirror.* "People need a little nudge now and then. Like the one Michael gave your mom."

"What do you mean?"

The abrupt change in Jesse's tone made Annie flinch. "Michael was the one who encouraged her to step down as manager."

"Why would he do that?" Jesse's eyes narrowed, and with a sinking heart, Annie realized that Lorna hadn't confided in her son.

"I think you should ask her."

Michael and Lorna were sitting at the kitchen table when Jesse arrived, so deep in conversation they hadn't even heard the back door open.

His mother glanced up and spotted him in the doorway.

"Jesse! Are you back from Vivienne's already?"

"I've been gone most of the afternoon."

His mother smiled at Michael. "I guess I lost track of time."

The man reached out and squeezed her hand. "I'll see you tomorrow morning. Eight o'clock sharp." Then he turned to Jesse. "I heard the fish are biting in Jewel Lake. Interested in going out for a few hours tonight and trying our luck?"

"That's a great idea!" Lorna interjected.

"I can't remember the last time Jesse went fishing."

Unfortunately, Jesse could.

"I better not." He tried to temper his refusal with a smile. "I got behind on some things at home when I was in Arizona."

"Another time, then." Disappointment flashed across Michael's face, but his smile didn't waver as he got up, walked to the back door, and left.

"Can you stay for a few minutes?" Lorna stood before veering toward the living room. Jesse didn't miss the bounce in her step. She sat down on the sofa and patted the empty cushion next to her. "I hoped Annie would be with you. There was no way Michael and I could eat an entire apple pie for dessert, so I have a lot left over."

Michael and I.

Jesse sat down in a chair across from her. "What's going on, Mom?"

"I don't know what you mean." Lorna's blush said otherwise.

"Well, first of all, you quit your job —"

"I didn't quit," his mother said quickly. "I'm still the owner of Second Story Books; I just don't manage the day-to-day operations anymore."

"Annie told me that she never managed a bookstore before." Jesse raked his hand through his hair. "If she needed a job, why didn't you just hire her to help out a few days a week?"

"Annie has all the skills necessary to be the manager. What she needed was someone to believe in her. And I . . . I wanted to be free to pursue some other interests."

"Michael Garrison?" Jesse said before he could stop himself.

Lorna's shoulders straightened and her chin came up. "Like writing a book."

"A *book*?"

"Michael thinks I have a gift." A smile shimmered in his mother's eyes. "For years I've sold books, but I never scraped up the courage to write one."

"I didn't know you wanted to."

"It's one of those things you convince yourself is beyond your reach," she said softly. "I was busy running the bookstore and raising you, and there weren't enough hours in the day to devote to what some might consider a silly dream. Michael convinced me that it wasn't silly. He said if I didn't try, I would always regret it."

"So what's in it for him?"

"Nothing." His mom looked confused by the question.

"You're too trusting, Mom."

"I don't like what you're implying." Lorna

99

frowned. "Michael is a wonderful man. Sweet and smart and kind."

"Like Brad Rawlings?" Jesse hated to say the man's name out loud.

His mother rose from the sofa. "That was a long time ago, Jesse! Did I make a mistake when I let him into our lives after your father died? Yes. But not everyone is out to take advantage and hurt the people who trust them. And if you think otherwise, it means I failed you twice."

The words landed like a blow.

"You didn't fail me at all, Mom." Jesse closed his eyes. "I was the man of the house. I was supposed to be looking out for you. My instincts told me something was off, but . . ." The rest of the sentence stuck in his throat.

"But you were twelve years old and you missed your dad." Tears misted Lorna's eyes. "I was lonely, too, and Brad swept in like a knight on a white horse. He fooled a lot of people. Took advantage of their trust."

In Jesse's mind, Brad Rawlings had done more than that. The guy had shown up in Red Leaf one summer, claiming he was a developer looking for investment property for a vacation resort. Rawlings would show up at the bookstore near closing time and browse through books on local history.

Long conversations with Lorna had eventually led to a dinner invitation.

Looking back, Jesse knew it hadn't been an accident. The widow of the former mayor, his mother had grown up in Red Leaf and was well respected in town. Over the course of the summer, Brad had wormed his way into their lives. He and Jesse hiked miles of trails on the weekends and fished until dark. And all that time, Rawlings was working his charm, convincing people to invest in his so-called business venture.

"Because of him, you lost everything," Jesse said tightly.

"Not the important things." Lorna took hold of his hand. "Do you know why I named the bookstore Second Story Books? Most of the people in town assume it's because of its location, but there's another reason. After your father died, I knew God would provide the strength to go on, even when the easiest thing would have been to pull the covers over my head and stay in bed."

Jesse had no idea she'd felt that way. His mother always had a smile on her face and was the first person to reach out to someone in need.

"Brad Rawlings stole my savings but not

my hope." Lorna smiled. "I trusted God for the next chapter."

"I don't want you to get hurt again, that's all."

"There are no guarantees that won't happen, but love is worth the risk," Lorna said softly. "I know you want to protect me. In fact, I wouldn't be surprised if you became a police officer because you wanted to protect the whole town."

It hit so close to the mark that Jesse looked away. "I love my job."

"I know that. But you can watch over someone from a distance, Jesse, and it seems to me that's what you've been doing for years. You've distanced yourself from the people in this community who care about you." His mother squeezed his hand. "Sometimes I can't help but wonder if the person you're really protecting is *you*."

NINE

Arthur Gunderson was sweeping the sidewalk when Jesse walked out of the bank right before closing time on Friday afternoon. A fire that destroyed a home, two car accidents, and a missing hunter had added hours of overtime to his regular workweek. After digging his way out from under the mound of paperwork, Jesse was looking forward to another weekend off.

"Hey, Deputy." Arthur lifted his broom and Jesse waved back. On a whim, he glanced across the street at The Shy Violet, Miranda Greer's flower shop. Sure enough, just like Annie had claimed, the woman stood in the window, arranging cornstalks for an autumn display.

When Arthur shuffled back inside the hardware store, Miss Greer stopped working. There was no mistaking the wistful look on the woman's face as she stared at his retreating back.

Jesse couldn't believe it. Annie was right.

"Jesse!" Mrs. Sweet, the owner of the bakery, stood on the curb in front of her shop, waving a white towel. "Do you have a minute?"

It didn't matter if Jesse was officially off duty. In a town the size of Red Leaf, everyone knew who he was. That meant people approached him about everything from lost dogs to plugged drain gutters.

"What can I do for you today, Mrs. Sweet?" he said as he crossed the street.

"We need your opinion." Mrs. Sweet's fingers closed around his arm and pulled him into the bakery. The door sealed shut behind them.

"My opinion on . . . ?" Jesse nodded at Mr. Sweet, a softspoken man whose white apron was always askew and hair always standing straight on end. Jesse had a hunch it was because he lived in the whirlwind that was Mrs. Sweet. As long as Jesse could remember, the man had taken refuge at a corner table, shielded by a rumpled copy of the weekly newspaper.

"Your wedding cake." Mrs. Sweet nudged him into the kitchen. "Annie picked out her two favorites this morning, but you should have a say too."

Wedding cake? Apparently the historical

society was determined to make the wedding reenactment the highlight of the open house. And judging from the number of "congratulations" Jesse had been receiving from random people on the street, you'd think he was really going to be a groom and not simply playing a part!

"It doesn't matter what flavor," Jesse said.

"It doesn't matter." Mrs. Sweet's mouth dropped open. "Did you *hear* that, Mr. Sweet?"

The newspaper rattled in agreement.

"We decided to go with cupcakes instead of a traditional layer cake, though," Mrs. Sweet continued. "Annie thought it would be easier for people to deal with while they were touring the museum. I made several different kinds, but she couldn't decide whether to go with chocolate raspberry or vanilla with buttercream. I've got some samples right here for you to try."

Jesse didn't know how it happened, but he found himself holding a fork in one hand and a china plate with two cupcakes in the other. They didn't look anything like the cupcakes the gas station sold. In fact, with all the bling embedded in the frosting, the cupcakes looked more like the pins in his mother's jewelry box.

"Are those . . . pearls?"

"Edible pearls," Mrs. Sweet corrected. "Perfectly safe for human consumption. And so is the glitter."

Jesse cut into the chocolate cupcake first and took a tentative bite.

"Well?" It wasn't Mrs. Sweet's voice.

Jesse glanced over his shoulder and saw a group of customers who seemed more interested in his opinion than the case filled with fresh pastries.

"I like the chocolate one." He lowered his voice. "With the glitter."

Mrs. Sweet nodded her approval. "Annie wouldn't say so, but I have a feeling that was her favorite too. That young woman loves sparkles."

"She does?"

Mrs. Sweet peered at him over her bifocals. "If you're going to be a good husband, you have to become a student of your wife. You have to know what makes her sad. What makes her smile. Isn't that right, Mr. Sweet?"

"Yep," came the muffled response.

"You realize that Annie and I are only pretending to get married?" Jesse said slowly.

Mrs. Sweet didn't seem to hear him. "Annie is such a sweetheart. She loves to sneak down here and watch me decorate the cakes. I asked her what she found so fascinating, and she said she's never had a birthday cake. Not one." Mrs. Sweet clucked her tongue. "Can you imagine that?"

"No." Jesse's mom still made a big deal out of birthdays. Balloons and presents and candles on the cake. The idea that Annie had missed out on something as simple as a birthday cake made Jesse's stomach curl. What kind of families had she been placed with? And for how long at each place? She hadn't gone into details, and Jesse had resisted his natural inclination to press for more information.

It was ironic, considering he hadn't had any qualms about digging deeper into her background the previous week. Nothing had turned up during his initial background check, but he'd left a message with a friend he'd met at a conference. The officer had lived in Madison all his life, working his way from patrol to investigations. If there was anything in Annie's past, anything to do with the police, Lance would probably know about it. Or could find out. Too bad he was still out on vacation when Jesse had called.

Guilt left a bitter aftertaste in Jesse's mouth. He'd made that call the day he'd pulled Annie over. Before he'd spent an afternoon in a musty attic with her.

Before he'd wanted to kiss her.

Oh, who was he kidding? He still wanted to kiss her.

"Thank you for coming in and being our second taste tester," Mrs. Sweet was saying.

She made it sound as if Jesse had had a choice.

"No problem," he said dryly. "I'm off duty anyway."

"Then you won't mind running this upstairs." Mrs. Sweet picked up a large white box and placed it in Jesse's hands before he could protest. "Annie is hosting a special event at the bookstore tonight, and she ordered three dozen of my famous sugar cookies."

"Sure." Strange how the thought of seeing Annie could burn away the fatigue from a twelve-hour day.

"Wait! There's one more thing!" The woman beat him to the door and topped the box in his hands with a white paper sack.

"What's this?"

"A custard-filled Bismarck." Mrs. Sweet looked shocked by the question. "It's your favorite. I gave you one every Saturday morning when your mom opened the bookstore. You would sit in the window seat and watch the cars go by until every speck of it was gone."

The newspaper lowered an inch and Jesse saw a pair of twinkling blue eyes. "Usually got more on your face than in your belly, though."

Jesse glanced at the window seat, its red-and-white checked cushion inviting people to linger for a moment.

After his mother had opened the bookstore, Jesse had spent as much time in the bakery as he had upstairs. The owners had been patient, even when Jesse left fingerprints on the display case and got underfoot. Mr. Sweet had read interesting headlines out loud and shared from the stash of peppermints he kept in his apron pocket.

Mrs. Sweet planted her hands on her hips. "You didn't think I'd forgotten, did you?"

Mrs. Sweet hadn't forgotten. Jesse had.

Why had she thought this was a good idea?

Annie stared at her reflection in the office mirror and adjusted her tiara.

More than a dozen children, boys and girls ranging in age from six to ten, had signed up to attend her first activity night at the bookstore. She hadn't anticipated such an overwhelming response. Lorna, of course, was thrilled. Annie was terrified.

On the flyers she'd posted, Annie had encouraged the children to dress as their favorite storybook character. She had even filled an old trunk with an assortment of hats and other articles of clothing in case someone had forgotten.

Annie decided to be Cinderella only because she'd found a wrinkled ball gown that Lorna had once used as part of a window display in the back of the storage closet.

Not because she was hoping to meet a prince.

Annie touched her fingers to her lips, and in the mirror she watched a slow blush creep into her cheeks. She had to stop thinking about the look in Jesse's eyes when his hand curved around her cheek.

She had to stop thinking about him, period.

Annie hadn't seen Jesse all week, and even though Lorna had mentioned he'd been working a lot of overtime, she couldn't help but think their last conversation had something to do with it. From the look on Jesse's face, Annie could only assume Lorna hadn't told him the reason Michael had encouraged her to hire someone else to manage the bookstore. But it wasn't Annie's place to tell him that Lorna wanted to write a book.

Was it his mother's dream that Jesse didn't approve of? Or Michael? The last thing Annie wanted to do was cause conflict in a family.

Again.

Annie pushed the troubling thought aside and grabbed the list off the counter.

The apple juice was in a pitcher on the table. The craft supplies separated into boxes. The rocking chair in the corner polished for story time.

Essie had even grudgingly allowed Annie to put a jeweled collar on her for the event. All she had to do was run down to the bakery and pick up the cookies Mrs. Sweet had baked.

Annie hadn't sat down once all day, but at least the business kept her mind focused on the task instead of Jesse.

The bells jingled over the door and she grabbed a fistful of blue satin as she dashed out of the office to greet the customer. A woman close to Annie's age grinned when Annie skidded to a halt in front of her.

Behind the boxy frames of the woman's glasses, a pair of chocolate brown eyes sparkled. "Hey, Cinderella. I'm looking for Annie Price. If she hasn't already left for

111

the ball, that is."

Annie grinned back. "She's still here, sweeping floors and dusting shelves."

"It's so hard to find good help these days." The woman flipped a long red braid over one slim shoulder and extended her hand. "Mackenzie Davis. Mac for short. I'm a reporter for the local newspaper and my boss sent me over. He heard about the big event and wants me to write an article for next week's edition."

"That's great!" Annie motioned toward the children's area. "You'll probably want to take some photographs over here before the kids arrive. The tables are already decorated and I have the craft area set up."

Annie suddenly realized Mackenzie — Mac — hadn't moved. "I'm sorry, I'm afraid we have a bit of a miscommunication going on," Mackenzie said. "I'm writing an article about the wedding."

"The wedding?"

"That's right. Everyone is talking about it."

"They are?" Annie squeaked.

"You're going to be front-page news!" Mackenzie promised. "Now, when would be a good time to set up an interview and take a few pictures of you and your handsome groom? I heard Jesse Kent volunteered."

"He didn't volunteer. He surrendered," Annie muttered.

"Somehow I doubt that." Laughter danced in the reporter's eyes. "Jesse and I went to school together, and I know that word isn't in his vocabulary. If Jesse is willing to walk down the aisle, he has a good reason."

Annie had no doubt what Mackenzie thought that reason was.

"His mom is the head of the historical society," Annie said. "I'm sure Jesse just knows they need the extra help."

"Uh-huh." Mackenzie didn't look convinced.

"Jesse is probably really busy, but I'd be more than happy to answer your questions. And I'm sure some of the other committee members would be willing to sit down for an interview too."

Because Annie had a hunch it was the last thing a certain deputy wanted to do.

"My editor really wants the wedding couple to be the main focus of the piece." Mackenzie, it appeared, wasn't going to budge. "I'll call Jesse."

TEN

"Call me what?"

Jesse walked into the bookstore and did a double take when he spotted Annie. The color and sparkles and the shape of her dress reminded him of one of Mrs. Sweet's cupcakes. A plastic crown circled her head, poking from the riot of curls like the tops of a picket fence.

"Busy," Mackenzie Davis drawled. "Are you CinderAnnie's date for the ball too?"

"I'm just the delivery boy." Jesse set the bakery box on the counter. "If you want more information about the fire, Mac, you'll have to talk to the chief investigator. I told you that this morning."

"She wants to interview us for the newspaper," Annie said. "They're doing a feature about our . . . *the* . . . wedding."

"No comment."

"I hear those two words every time I call the sheriff's department," Mac complained.

"This is free publicity for the museum. All you have to do is answer a few questions and smile pretty for the camera."

"Annie doesn't have time for an interview now, but if you stick around and cover the activity night, we might be able to squeeze you in later."

"Fine." Mac lifted the corner of the box and filched a cookie. "I'll be back in half an hour."

"How did you do that?" Annie breathed as the reporter sauntered out the door.

Jesse's lips twisted in a smile. "I've known Mac since kindergarten. The only way to get rid of her is to make her think she got her way."

"She did get her way."

"True. But the bookstore gets its fifteen minutes of fame too."

The phone rang and Annie reached across the counter to answer it. "Hey, Lorna! Everything is ready . . . Oh no. Do you need anything?"

Jesse's stomach bottomed out. His mom had called late yesterday, but he'd been in the middle of taking an accident report so he hadn't been able to answer the phone.

"Don't you dare apologize," Annie scolded. "It's not like you planned to get sick. I'll be fine. Really. And I'll tell you all

115

about the event tomorrow."

Their eyes met when she hung up.

"A migraine." Worry shadowed Annie's expression. "It came on a few hours ago."

"I'll drive over and check on her after I leave," Jesse said. "Unfortunately, Mom gets hit with one once in a while, but she resists the idea of having to take it easy for a day or two."

"I hope I convinced her to stay home tonight."

"She was planning to help out?"

"She was going to read a book during story time."

Jesse shrugged. "I can read a book."

Annie's eyes went wide. "Are you stating a fact . . . or offering to help?"

"Both." Jesse picked up a pair of antennae made from blue pom-poms. "Just don't ask me to wear this."

A smile teased Annie's lips. "But it matches your eyes."

"Sorry. A man has to draw a line somewhere."

And every time Annie sent a smile his way, Jesse forgot where that line was.

"Fair enough." She ducked behind the counter. "I'm not going to turn down volunteer help. In fifteen minutes we're going to be knee-deep in kids."

116

Annie wasn't exaggerating.

At six o'clock, the bookstore began to fill up with parents and children dressed up like pirates and barnyard animals and fairies. Annie glided through the chaos with a smile on her face and greeted most of the children by name. Every time Jesse looked her way, she was in demand, whether it was painting a heart on a little girl's cheek or refilling a glass of juice for a parent.

Jesse smiled when a miniature princess scampered up to Annie.

"You have a pretty crown!"

Annie curtseyed. "Why thank you, Your Highness. And you have a beautiful dress."

"My grammy made it. She made my purse too." The little girl showed off a gold purse decorated with oversized jewels. "But I don't have a crown."

"You don't need a crown, sweetheart," her mother said.

The girl's forehead puckered. "Yes, I do."

"Maybe you can make one," Annie suggested. "I have some pretty beads and pearls on that table right over there."

"Will you help me?" The girl tugged on Annie's skirt.

She glanced at him and Jesse nodded, responding to the question in her eyes. "Go ahead. I'll keep an eye on the rest of the crew."

Jesse herded a group of boys over to the rug and supervised them while they each chose a hat or a costume to wear. When Jesse felt a tug on his sleeve, he expected another request for a cookie or glass of apple juice. It was Annie, her eyes wide with panic.

"What's wrong?"

"No one is leaving," she hissed.

Jesse was confused. "Isn't that a good thing?"

"I expected the parents to drop their kids off, but everyone is staying! I've never talked to a group this size before. What if they get bored? What if they think it's silly?" Annie closed her eyes. "Why did I think I could do this?"

The last sentence came out in a whisper, almost as if Annie were talking to herself.

"You'll be fine."

"How do you know?"

"Because if you can handle a line of cranky Christmas shoppers demanding their double caramel lattes with whip and sprinkles, you can handle this."

Jesse meant every word. And he knew he'd said the right thing when Annie's smile blazed a trail right through his heart.

■ ■ ■ ■

"That wasn't so bad."

Jesse closed the door as the last family left, their arms laden with books and the crafts they'd made.

"How can you say that?" Annie dropped into a pink beanbag chair and groaned. "I . . . I *blinched.*"

"Only on the inside." Jesse winked at her.

Winked. At. Her.

But that wasn't nearly as astonishing as a man who could quote Winnie the Pooh.

"Don't look so shocked." Jesse wandered over to the refreshment table, scouting for leftovers. Maybe he was sorry he'd stayed instead of getting some dinner. "I spent more time here than I did at home while I was growing up. I think I read every book on the shelves. Twice."

Annie tried to picture Jesse engrossed in a picture book and smiled. He'd been great with the kids, patiently gluing felt pieces to cardboard and refilling glasses of juice, reading a Dr. Seuss book with the flair and enthusiasm of an actor auditioning for a Broadway play.

"I heard some people asking when the next activity night was going to be." Jesse scooped up some empty cups and dropped them into the wastebasket.

"I'm going to try to have one once a month." Annie kicked off the satin shoes she'd found at the secondhand store and felt the blood return to her toes.

"This is all that's left, but I noticed you didn't eat anything." Jesse sat down on the floor and handed her a napkin topped with broken shards of the last sugar cookie, pieced together to make a whole one.

Annie's breath collected in her lungs as Jesse's arm brushed against hers. "I was nervous." She was *still* nervous, but for a completely different reason now. "And Mac kept taking pictures. I was paranoid I'd end up on the front page of the newspaper with cookie crumbs on my face."

Jesse tipped his head. "You do have something on your face."

"I do?" Annie squeaked. "What?"

"Glitter."

Annie almost dumped the contents of the napkin onto the rug as she swiped at her cheeks. "Where?"

"Everywhere." Jesse effortlessly captured her fingers in one hand. With the other, he tapped her cheekbone. "Here." Her chin. "Here." Her temple. "And here . . ."

Annie dragged in a breath, unable to look

away as every featherlight touch claimed a piece of her heart.

Jesse's hand stilled, and his eyes searched her face. Annie saw the smile that suddenly lit his eyes. *Felt* it when he closed the distance between them and captured her lips.

Everything else disappeared as Annie wound her arms around Jesse's neck and wove her hands through his hair. He tasted like cinnamon and sugar, and Annie felt the rapid thump of Jesse's heart as he drew her deeper into the circle of his arms.

Annie wanted to stay there forever.

"It was nice of you to check up on me, sweetheart, but I'm feeling a lot better." Lorna managed a wan smile from her place on the sofa. "Annie dropped off a container of homemade chicken noodle soup after work yesterday. She's so thoughtful."

"And sweet. And kind. And beautiful." All adjectives Jesse had heard in the past two weeks. And every one of them fit Annie to a T.

She was also a phenomenal kisser, but Jesse kept that to himself.

"You think Annie is beautiful?"

Jesse shot his mother a wry glance. Even when she was feeling under the weather, nothing got past her. "I thought we agreed a long time ago, no matchmaking."

"Oh, it doesn't look like you need any help from me." Lorna nodded at the newspaper on the coffee table.

Jesse had already seen it. One of his fellow officers had pinned the entire front page to the bulletin board in the break room at the PD. The article, right below a photograph of him and Annie smiling at each other, wasn't nearly as provocative as the headline.

Wedding Bells Are Ringing.

He planned to have a little chat with Mac about that.

"Do you need anything?" Jesse refilled her water glass, a not-so-subtle attempt to change the subject.

"Grandchildren would be nice."

"Mom."

"It's the power of the media." She shrugged. "I keep looking at that headline and my mind starts to wander."

Jesse's mind kept wandering too. Back to the way Annie had felt in his arms. The way she'd responded to his kiss.

He hadn't had an opportunity to see her over the weekend; he'd been called into work after all and had to work Monday too. But Jesse planned to stop by the bookstore and invite her out for dinner after leaving his mother's house. That, he thought wryly, would probably make the front page of the newspaper too.

The phone rang and Jesse rose to his feet. "Stay there, Mom. I'll get it."

Lorna didn't protest as she sank against a pillow, a sign her energy level wasn't quite back to normal.

He picked up the phone. "Kent residence."

"Jesse! I'm so glad you're there. Something *terrible* has happened."

He matched the high-pitched voice to Gwynn Talbot, the mayor's wife, and frowned. "Mrs. Talbot? What's the matter?"

"My daughter accidentally gave some very expensive jewelry to the museum while I was out of town." The words came out in a rush. "Somehow they got mixed in with a box of costume jewelry I'd planned to donate, and I want them back. Immediately."

"It's all right, Mrs. Talbot. I'll let you talk to my mother. She'll find out what happened to the jewelry and make sure it is returned to you as soon as possible."

"I *know* what happened to it!" Gwynn sputtered. "According to Yvonne Baker, Lorna gave the hair combs to that young woman who moved to town a few weeks ago. Annie Price."

Eleven

"Annie?" Jesse's hand tightened around the phone. "I'm sure she'll give them back once you explain the situation."

"I went over to the bookstore a few minutes ago and *explained the situation.*" Gwynn pressed down hard on the words. "Oddly enough, Miss Price claims she can't find them. Those combs are real silver and have diamonds in them. They are worth a lot of money, but more than that, my grandmother left them to me. They have sentimental value and can't be replaced."

"I'll talk to Annie myself. We'll get this straightened out, Mrs. Talbot."

"Thank you, Officer Kent." Gwynn sniffed. "I'll tell my husband you're handling the case."

Jesse didn't care for her choice of words. Or the fact she was acting as if a crime had been committed. "I'll call you when I have more information."

"What's going on?" His mother stood up and clutched the afghan draped around her shoulders. "Why did Gwynn call?"

"Mrs. Talbot claims her daughter accidentally gave the historical society some jewelry while she was out of town. Two hair combs. Do you remember them?"

"Of course I do. Yvonne found them when we were sorting through the donations. We gave them to Annie to wear for the wedding ceremony." Lorna rolled her eyes. "Don't tell me Gwynn wants them back. Honestly, that's so like her to kick up a fuss over a little misunderstanding. From the way she was carrying on, you'd think the diamonds were real."

"They are."

The color drained from his mother's face. "What?"

"She went to see Annie at the bookstore and asked her to return the combs, but when Annie looked for them, she said she couldn't find them."

"Annie wouldn't lie about that." Lorna pushed to her feet. "She must be so upset."

"It sounded that way. Apparently the combs are a family heirloom."

"I was talking about Annie." His mother's bedroom slippers scuffed against the carpet as she paced the length of the sofa. "I'm sure Gwynn's accusation will only stir up bad memories."

Jesse felt a cold finger slide down his spine. "Memories about what?"

Lorna didn't answer.

"Mom? If you know something, it would be helpful if I knew it too."

"It was a long time ago," she murmured. "A person shouldn't be defined by something that happened in their past."

"What kind of something, Mom?"

"Annie got into some . . . trouble when she was sixteen. That's all I know."

Jesse sucked in a breath. Juvenile records were sealed. No wonder nothing had shown up when he had run Annie's name through the computer the day they'd met.

Jesse scrubbed a hand over his eyes. "And you didn't bother to mention it until now?"

Lorna met his gaze straight on. "I didn't think it mattered."

Annie stood on Lorna's front step as the sound of raised voices pelted her like sleet from an early winter storm.

Jesse and Lorna were arguing. About her.

Annie had been so upset after the mayor's wife left the bookstore that she'd closed the shop and spent almost an hour searching for the combs.

She was sure she had left them on the desk in the office, but she looked in her apartment and in her car, too, before going through every desk drawer and cabinet in the shop, her hands shaking from the aftermath of Gwynn Talbot's visit. The woman had barely allowed her to get a word in edgewise, and the conversation had spiraled into a storm of accusations. It was like reliving her confrontation with the Martins all over again.

Annie decided to drive over to Lorna's and tell her about the situation, never dreaming Mrs. Talbot had gotten to her — and Jesse — first.

Tears scorched the back of Annie's eyes as she stumbled down the steps.

"Annie?" Jesse was suddenly beside her. He caught hold of her arm and turned her around.

Her gaze fell on his badge and she swallowed hard. He was on duty.

"I can't find them," she blurted.

Jesse tucked his sunglasses into his pocket, but his expression remained unreadable. "Tell me what happened."

"I know I put the cedar box with the combs on the desk in the bookstore office, and it's gone. I've looked everywhere."

"Who else has had access to the office?"

"No one. I should have put the combs somewhere safer, but I had no idea they were valuable."

"When was the last time you remember seeing them?"

Annie had asked herself the same question a dozen times over the past hour. "Maybe sometime before the activity night? I was so focused on the preparations and the kids . . . I don't really remember. Mackenzie Davis was the only person who was in the office then. Her cell phone had died and she asked if she could use the phone."

"It wasn't Mackenzie." Jesse didn't hesitate. "I've known her for years."

"And you haven't known me more than a few weeks."

Jesse stiffened. "I didn't say that."

"You didn't have to." Annie tried to swallow the knot in her throat. "I'm the outsider."

Maybe she would *always* be the outsider.

"I'm just trying to find out what happened, Annie," Jesse said quietly.

The words echoed in her memory.

Just tell us what happened, Annie.

She did, but no one had believed her. And looking at Jesse's grim expression, Annie doubted that he would, either.

■ ■ ■ ■

"Sorry it's taken me so long to get back to you. I need a vacation from my two-week vacation." Jesse's friend from the Madison police department stifled a yawn. "What was the name again?"

"Annie . . . Anne . . . Price." Jesse stared at a plaque on the wall near his desk at the sheriff's office as he listened to Lance tapping on a keyboard, but all he could see was Annie's face when she'd told him she couldn't find the combs.

He'd driven over to the bookstore and helped her search again. As the minutes ticked by, Jesse's frustration had grown in direct proportion to Annie's silence. It hadn't helped that the mayor had marched into the bookstore, demanding an update.

That was three days ago, and the wedding was tomorrow. He'd been racking his brain, trying to figure out what could have happened to those combs. But Jesse had hit a wall, and now he was praying for a miracle, especially for Annie's sake. The combs couldn't have just disappeared.

Meanwhile, Lance had finally called back. Even though juvenile court records were sealed, as a professional courtesy, officers could share information from the police report with other departments. Jesse hoped his friend could shed some light on what had happened in Annie's past. He didn't know how that would help, but he was desperate for anything that could help Annie.

"Here it is. Price . . . stolen vehicle. Uh, it looks like the officer interviewed the family . . . and the teenage daughter claimed Anne Price said she was tired of living there and took off in the car . . . and then the vehicle was eventually found in a mall parking lot. They picked up the girl a few hours later."

"Did Annie tell her side of the story?"

"Let me see . . . Ah, according to her statement, the Martin girl called after an argument with her boyfriend . . . begged Anne to come and pick her up . . . it came down to one girl's word against the other's. The foster parents decided not to file charges, but DHS sent Annie to a group home the next day. I remember this case now that I read the report."

Jesse's eyes began to burn. "I appreciate you calling back and letting me know what happened."

"No problem. I can fax a copy of the report over if you want to take a look at it,"

Lance offered.

"That isn't necessary." Jesse didn't need it. He knew Annie.

"The Price kid got a tough break, especially if the other girl was lying," his friend mused. "I didn't work the case, but the officer described Paige Martin as the spoiled princess type."

A smile spread across Jesse's face. "Thanks, Lance."

And thank you, God.

Jesse hung up the phone and grabbed his keys.

"Smile! Tomorrow is your wedding day!"

Annie pressed her face into a bouquet of orange tiger lilies. "These are beautiful, Ms. Viv."

Vivienne tucked a sprig of Queen Anne's lace in a bud vase next to the guest book. "I think we're done for now. I'll bring your bouquet tomorrow morning before the ceremony."

Annie scraped up a smile. "I can't wait to see it."

"I made another batch of peanut butter cookies this morning." Vivienne hooked the strap of a red leather purse over her shoulder. "You and that handsome groom of yours are welcome to come over

132

anytime."

"I'm sure Jesse would like that." Annie didn't add that she and Jesse wouldn't be doing anything together. Not now.

Vivienne left, and Annie melted into a pew. Every day after work, she'd been at either Stone Church or the museum, getting ready for the grand opening. It kept her hands busy and her mind off Jesse.

"You look like you just lost your best friend." The tools on Michael's leather belt clanked together as he sat down beside her.

"Just tired."

Michael's eyes filled with sympathy. "It'll be okay, Annie. You'll see."

Annie wasn't so sure about that.

"Lorna hasn't been herself this week." And Annie hadn't seen Jesse since he'd escorted the mayor out of the bookstore.

Michael's eyes sparkled with mischief. "Lorna hasn't been herself because I asked her to go steady."

Annie momentarily forgot her own problems and clasped his hand. "That's wonderful!"

"She hasn't said yes, but I'm determined to wear her down."

"Lorna is crazy about you."

"Lorna, maybe. Jesse, not so much." Michael sighed. "Lorna is afraid he's still hung up on what happened with Brad Rawlings, but she's confident that God will help him straighten it out."

"Who is Brad Rawlings?" Annie couldn't remember Lorna ever mentioning the name.

"Lorna met him a few years after Jesse's dad died. He seemed like a great guy when he came to Red Leaf, until he drained people's savings accounts with a development scheme and took off." Michael's face clouded. "From what I understand, Jesse took the whole thing pretty hard. I'm not surprised he's wary of me, but fortunately, there are no deep, dark secrets in my past."

Annie wished she could say the same thing.

"I have to talk to her."

Yvonne Baker blocked Jesse's path. "You can't see the bride on her wedding day."

Jesse decided that now wasn't the time to point out the obvious.

"Come on, Mrs. Baker." He turned on the charm instead. "I have something for her. A gift."

"Oh, for heaven's sake. Let the man through." Cricket drew herself up to her full height of four feet eleven.

Jesse didn't wait to see who won the argument as he slipped past the women.

Annie was staring out the window, a slim figure in jeans and a faded T-shirt. The wedding gown was hanging on a hook on the wall, shrouded in plastic. Considering they were getting married in fifteen minutes, Jesse didn't take that as a very good sign.

He sent up a silent prayer, asking God for help. People said that actions spoke louder than words, but Jesse had the feeling Annie needed both. She *deserved* both.

"I'm feeling a little overdressed."

Her whole body jerked and she swung around. "What are you doing here?"

"I'm the groom, remember?" Jesse tugged on his lapel and the pungent scent of mothballs stung his nose as he walked toward her. "I'm supposed to be here."

Annie's gaze bounced around the room, lighting on everything but him. "I should get ready," she murmured.

"You're going to need these."

Annie stared down at the combs cradled in the palm of his hand. "How . . . where did you find them?"

"Do you remember Hannah Murphy?"

"Hannah." Annie repeated the name. "Of course. The little blonde girl who came to the activity night. She was dressed up like a princess."

"A princess who complained she wasn't

sparkly like you."

Annie pressed her fingers against her lips. "Hannah took the combs?"

"I talked to her mother. They were out until late last night, and she didn't listen to my voice mail message until this morning. She checked Hannah's purse and there they were. At some point during the chaos of the activity night, Hannah must have ended up in your office instead of the powder room. Kids are curious. The box looked like a miniature treasure chest, and she must have peeked inside. All that sparkle proved to be a temptation."

"How did you figure out it was her?"

"Process of elimination." And Annie's name was the first one he'd eliminated — the moment he'd heard the combs were missing.

Annie frowned, but Jesse didn't have a chance to elaborate because the door swung open. His mother and the rest of the committee members swooped in like a flock of colorful birds. Good thing this room was bigger than the broom closet where she had first tried on the wedding dress.

"You, out." Yvonne pointed to Jesse and then to the door. "And you, into that wedding gown! And, Annie, Gwynn Talbot says she wants you to wear those combs! I think

136

she feels bad for making you feel like you weren't telling the truth about them."

Jesse found himself out in the hall, where Vivienne Wallace stood waiting with a boutonniere. "Hold still." She pinned it to his lapel while Viola fussed with the antique cuff links on his shirt.

Yvonne Baker was the last one in line, and she tried to press a thin gold band into his hand. "Here's a ring you can use for the ceremony."

"That's not necessary." Jesse winked at her. "I brought my own."

TWELVE

"You look absolutely gorgeous, Annie." Yvonne's niece, Julie, one of the many women who'd invaded the room, tucked one of the combs into Annie's hair.

"So does your groom." Mackenzie Davis grinned behind the lens of her camera as she snapped another photograph for the newspaper.

Annie managed a tremulous smile. Her hands were shaking. Her heart was pounding. And Jesse was waiting for her in the sanctuary.

Viola fluttered over. "Pastor Blake says it's time to start."

Arthur Gunderson was waiting in the hallway, every inch the gentleman in a dark suit with a brocade vest and string tie. Someone, most likely Ms. Viv, had planted a white rosebud in the buttonhole of his lapel.

"You look very dashing," Annie told the man.

Arthur's ears turned bright pink as he offered her his arm. "Are you ready?"

Annie took a deep breath. "No."

Vivienne handed her a stunning bouquet just before she and Mr. Gunderson reached the door of the sanctuary. "Not half as pretty as you, Annie, but they'll have to do."

Annie touched one of the delicate blossoms and tears filled her eyes. "They're perfect, Ms. Viv. Thank you."

"None of that now." Yvonne clucked as she pressed an embroidered hankie into Annie's hand. "Time to go inside."

Annie froze when she saw how many people had packed into the small church. Some of the faces she recognized and some she'd never seen before. She clung to Arthur and tried to smile as they walked down the aisle. And suddenly, she was standing in front of Jesse. He looked amazing in the vintage suit that accentuated his long legs and broad shoulders, but . . .

Annie couldn't bring herself to meet his eyes.

Pastor Blake waited until the music stopped, and then he opened a worn leather Bible and began to read.

"Love is patient, love is kind. It does not envy, it does not boast, it is not proud." Annie silently recited the verses along with the pastor. "Love does not delight in evil but rejoices with the truth. It always protects, always trusts, always hopes, always perseveres."

Jesse's hand folded around hers, and it took every ounce of Annie's self-control not to press it to her lips.

This isn't real, she told herself. No matter how much she wanted it to be.

Jesse still didn't know about the police record that stained her past. A dozen times over the past few days, she'd wanted to tell him the truth, but she couldn't stand the thought of seeing the doubt and disappointment in his eyes. It would cast a shadow over their relationship, and Annie didn't know if she could live with that. She'd thought Janet Martin would believe her, but in the end, she'd taken her daughter's side — and sent Annie away.

The organist stopped playing, and Pastor Blake smiled at the congregation. "We're gathered together today to ask God's blessing on this couple —"

"Could I say something, Pastor?" Jesse interrupted.

"Now?" Pastor Blake glanced at his notes and frowned as if he'd somehow misplaced some of the script.

"I have a feeling I might not get another

opportunity."

A hush fell over the sanctuary as Jesse turned toward her, taking both her hands in his. The blue eyes swept over Annie's face, as warm and bright as the base of a flame. It was a good thing he was holding on to her, because Annie felt her knees begin to melt.

"Annie, you came to Red Leaf looking for a new beginning, but I'm the one who needs to start over," Jesse said. "Something happened a long time ago that made me afraid to trust. Afraid to take a risk."

Jesse afraid? Annie would have laughed if he hadn't sounded so serious.

"A very wise person said we shouldn't be defined by something that happened in the past, but that's exactly what happened." Jesse's eyes glistened. "I let the past define *me.* And I'm sorry I hurt you in the process. I didn't even appreciate everything I've been given until I saw it through your eyes. I love you, Annie."

He released her hand and dipped into his jacket pocket. Annie's breath backed up in her lungs when she saw the diamond ring cradled in Jesse's palm.

"You're my dream," he whispered. "Will you meet me right here — in this church —

next September? We'll start our own story
—"

"*Yes.*" Annie couldn't wait a second longer. She wound her arms around Jesse's neck and drew his head down until their lips met. His arms came around her and drew her closer, his strong hands fanning out against the small of her back.

Pastor Blake cleared his throat. "Yes . . . well . . . I guess you may kiss your bride!"

Annie was aware of laughter and people clapping and a joy that welled up inside her heart, filling the cracks with warmth and light she'd never experienced before.

Now she had a name for it.

Annie smiled against Jesse's lips.

Home

ACKNOWLEDGMENTS

Thank you to the amazing, talented team at HarperCollins Christian Publishing for inviting me to participate in the Year of Weddings novella collection — and to Becky Philpott, whose warmth and enthusiasm made this "new kid on the block" feel at home.

I'd also like to thank our three children — Lindsey, Norah, and Reid — who all got married the summer I started writing *A September Bride* and made the research easy!

And always, to Pete. The reason I can write about "happily ever after" is because I'm living one.

DISCUSSION QUESTIONS

1. What was Annie looking for when she moved to Red Leaf? How did she see the town differently than Jesse did? It's easy to take the things we have for granted. What are some ways we can prevent that from happening?
2. Jesse is suspicious of Annie's reasons for moving to Red Leaf. How did an experience from his past color his perspective? What role does forgiveness play when a person needs to move forward?
3. Lorna Kent's secret dream was to write a book, but it took a long time for her to act on it. What was holding her back? If someone asked if you have a secret dream, what would you say? What would you need to do to make it come true?
4. What did Annie see in Ms. Viv that prompted her to ask for help with the flowers? What are the benefits of multi-generational friendships?

5. Annie was falsely accused of something she didn't do. Has that ever happened to you or someone you know? What were the circumstances? The outcome?
6. What was your favorite scene in the book? Why?
7. Pretend you're a wedding planner. What would Annie and Jesse's "real" wedding day be like?

ABOUT THE AUTHOR

Kathryn Springer is a full-time writer and the award-winning author of *Front Porch Princess.* She won the ACFW 2009 Book of the Year award for *Family Treasures.* Her most recent book, *The Soldier's Newfound Family,* hit the *New York Times* bestseller list in November 2012. Kathryn grew up in northern Wisconsin, where her parents published a weekly newspaper. As a child she spent many hours sitting at her mother's typewriter, plunking out stories, and credits her parents for instilling in her a love of books — which eventually turned into a desire to tell stories of her own. Kathryn has written 19 books with close to two million copies sold. Kathryn lives and writes in her country home in northern Wisconsin. Facebook: Kathrynspringerauthor

■ ■ ■ ■

AN OCTOBER BRIDE

KATIE GANSHERT

■ ■ ■ ■

*For my dad — the best father
and Papa Bear around.
I love you more.*

ONE

The suddenness with which life can upend itself is alarming. One second you're two months away from matrimony — unable to find that perfect dress but confident it's out there in the wide abyss of bridal boutiques — and then *wham*. An MRI reveals a tumor in the brain of the man you love more than life.

Only that man isn't your fiancé.

This singular diagnosis turns your entire world on its head. Instead of the bride-to-be, you are the woman who has canceled the cake order and returned the ring, all while apologizing profusely to your wounded ex-fiancé who was nothing but kind and patient.

It's a hard thing to recover from — these sharp, unexpected upheavals.

And just when my life started to normalize, everything went flip all over again. Three weeks fresh and I'm trying to acclimate.

After all, if Dad can do it — if he can go from the picture of health, to the trenches of cancer-battle, to the cruel tease that was four months of remission, to the shockingly cold waters of a two-month time clock, then what's my excuse? In my weakness, I have forced my father to be the strong one, to comfort *me,* yet *he's* the dying man.

This has to stop.

I take a deep breath, inhaling the aroma that is Mayfair, Wisconsin, in the beginning of autumn — a paradoxical combination of fresh air, burning leaves, and the scent of Eloise's famous pumpkin bars wafting from the front windows of her bakery. A flock of geese honk overhead. I look up at the clear blue sky — the dark bodies in V-formation — wondering if I couldn't join them somehow. Grow a pair of wings and take flight to someplace where time and death do not exist.

Instead, I let out my breath, remove the two-day accumulation of mail from the mailbox, and head up the walkway, taking in the modest home of my childhood — buttercream siding with country-blue shutters, flower boxes outside the windows, and a pair of burning bushes that bookend the front, their leaves a vibrant bloodred. It's a house that carried my brother and me from infancy to adulthood and has since treated a pair of empty nesters with kindness these past nine years. At least until the diagnosis.

Will Mom put it on the market after he's gone?

Shaking away the question, I unlock the door, step inside, and blink at the mess before me. Saying yes to cat-sitting while my parents drove up to Door County for the weekend was my first attempt at climbing aboard the be-strong-for-Dad train. If Mom and my brother can hop on so quickly, going about life with smiles and unshakable faith, then surely I can at least feed the cats and empty the litter box. Animals are, after all, my forte. What I failed to remember, as I eagerly agreed to the favor, was that my parents' cats are not normal cats.

Case in point?

The mess of kitty litter and down feathers scattered across the hardwood floor. A groan escapes from my mouth like a slow leak. Off to the side, Oscar lounges beside the emptied-out carcass of a throw pillow.

"Seriously?"

His furry tail twitches lazily.

I head down the hall toward the room with the closet where Mom keeps the cleaning supplies. Floorboards creak beneath my cross trainers as I smooch the air and whistle for the other beastly feline to come out from hiding. The tabby is a no-show, which can only mean she's responsible for the mangled pillow.

I cross the small office that was once my brother's bedroom to set the stack of mail on Dad's desk. Something catches my eye. A familiar leather-bound journal sits precariously close to the desk's edge — a birthday present I gave Dad three years ago, before cancer cast its ugly shadow over our lives. My father isn't much of a writer, but I knew the collection of quirky quotes on the top of each page would make him chuckle.

Trailing my finger down the spine, I find myself wishing I could go back to the time when tragedy was something that happened to other people, or better yet, wishing I could fix what is wrong now. My inability to do anything but cat-sit leaves me with a helplessness I'm unaccustomed to feeling. As I turn away from the desk, the journal falls to the floor with a *whap,* and a piece of paper slips out from its pages.

I bend over, but the words — written in neat, straight script at the top — stop me mid-reach.

Bucket List.

I pick up the paper carefully, delicately —
like it is a find as rare as the Dead Sea
Scrolls. These are my father's dreams. His
dying wishes. The things he wants to accomplish before the end. Carefully written
on the sheet of paper I now hold in my
hand. I sit on the edge of Dad's swivel chair,
knowing this is private but unable to resist
the temptation. If there is something on this
page I can give him or help him accomplish,
how can I look away?

Take Marie to Ireland.

He did. Two years ago, after his surgery.
Before his first round of chemo. Dad got
himself a passport and booked the tickets,
and they flew across the Atlantic. They
spent a whole week visiting pubs, riding
bikes through ancient ruins, looking into
Mom's genealogy.

Let Liam teach me to ride a motorcycle.

He did that too. I'll never forget watching
the pair of them in matching Harley
Davidson bandannas, driving around
Mayfair's town square while Mom clutched
my arm, convinced her two boys would
become one with the cement.

Run a half marathon with Emma.

I smile at the extrabold line crossing this one off, as if showcasing my father's triumph. Dad is not a runner. I was a bit perplexed when he asked if he could train with me, but I welcomed the extra time together.

Fix the boat with Liam.

Just how much time did those two spend in the garage, resurrecting that hunk of junk? All four of us took it out on the lake for the first time this past Fourth of July. I'd strapped on a life preserver and brought rations, sure we'd either sink or be stranded. Turned out, I didn't need either. The day had been a success.

Go on a hot air balloon ride.

Swim with dolphins.

Emotions well in my throat — a hot, sticky mixture of joy and sadness. As much as I don't want my father to go, I'm so proud of the way he's going. Moisture builds in my eyes as I reach the items that are not yet crossed off. *Yet* being the key word, because I know my dad.

Spend a weekend in Door County.

(He'll get to cross that off as soon as he comes home and relieves me of crazy cat duty.)

Take dancing lessons with Marie.

(Mom will love that.)

Walk Emma down the aisle.

The words are like a sucker punch to the gut. I deflate in the chair. Unable to swallow. Unable to breathe. Unable to do anything but press a palm against the pit forming in my stomach.

Two

My brain has switched to autopilot. I'm not sure how I arrived at my small bungalow on the edge of town. At some point, I must have put the page back in Dad's journal, cleaned the mess in the living room, fed the cats, and driven home. But it's all a fog. I keep picturing myself as a little girl, donning my mother's veil and her oversized white high heels, walking down a pretend aisle on my daddy's arm toward Scooby, our very first family dog. A great stand-in groom, may he rest in peace. The memories wrap around my heart and squeeze tight while my mind worries those five words raw.

Walk Emma down the aisle.

The pit in my stomach grows — deepening and widening while I walk haphazardly through the yard. As sick as the discovery has made me, at least I saw it now instead of after, when it would have been too late. At least I have a chance to do something. My thoughts scramble this way and that, grappling for a solution, until one comes — wild and half-baked. What if I called up Chase and told him I changed my mind? Never mind the fact that I ripped his heart out two years ago; we should get married after all. Would he hear me out, or would he hang up the second I announced myself on the other end of the line?

I step onto my porch, over two loose floorboards, and stop. The front door is ajar. My brow furrows at the thin strip of space that leads into my home. Forgetting to lock up is one thing — a common side effect of growing up in a tiny northern Wisconsin town. But forgetting to shut the door all the way?

No, I wouldn't do that.

Which means the latch must be broken — one of many broken things in my well-loved home. It's a perfectly logical explanation, and yet I find myself clutching my purse tighter as I quietly open the screen door. This is the moment in scary movies when viewers scream, "You fool, don't go inside!" I step over the threshold anyway. This is Mayfair. There are no serial killers. There probably aren't even any burglars. Even so, the lack of greeting from Samson has me on edge. A vision of my beloved pooch drugged and dragged into the bathroom while some drug dealer strips my home for cash flashes through my mind. It is the epitome of far-fetched. Knowing this, however, does not stop me from exchanging my purse for the vase on the sofa table.

Muffled sounds come from the kitchen.

I raise the vase over my shoulder, prepared to hurl it at the perpetrator's head. I am creeping toward the noise when, out of nowhere, Jake Sawyer steps into view. I yelp. He jumps. And the vase falls to the floor with a heavy clunk.

"You scared me half to death!" I say, clutching my chest.

"Who did you think I was — Ted Bundy?"

"I had no idea. You didn't announce yourself."

"My truck's in your driveway."

"It is?" I look over my shoulder, as if I might see through the walls of my house. How did I not notice Jake's truck on my way in? Then I remember those five words on my dad's bucket list, the ones that had me on autopilot. "Where's Samson?"

"Out back chasing squirrels." He cocks his head in that way he does whenever he's concerned. "You okay?"

I wave my hand, then bend over and retrieve the vase. Not even a chip. The thing is made of thick, sturdy glass — the kind of material that probably wouldn't have knocked out a burglar so much as killed him. I'm very thankful I didn't chuck it at Jake's head. "What are you doing here?"

He holds up a wrench. "You said your kitchen sink faucet was leaking."

"Oh, right." I return the vase to the sofa table and cup my forehead, trying to gain my bearings. "You didn't have to come over on your day off."

Jake runs his father's hardware store. Arthritis makes it hard for Mr. Sawyer to do much besides chat with the customers, so Jake does all the real work. And whenever he's not working there, he spends time in his gigantic man-shed, making and restoring furniture. He calls it a hobby, but I know better. Jake is a craftsman. If it wasn't for loyalty to his dad, I have every bit of confidence he could turn his "hobby" into a lucrative, full-time profession.

"I figured I needed to fix the leak before Mayor Altman issued you a citation."

I smile, but only just. Our mayor has recently gone on a crusade to make Mayfair a "green" town. His enthusiasm over the cause has failed to spread to the rest of us.

Jake scratches the dark stubble on his chin, studying me like I studied the vase a moment ago. I wonder if he sees any cracks. "I was on my way out to get my toolbox."

"Oh, okay." My conversational skills are riveting today.

He heads outside, the screen door whapping shut behind him. The shock of finding that list, followed by the onslaught of adrenaline, has me out of sorts. I need to go upstairs and get cleaned up for the Fall Harvest Festival committee meeting. My best friend is the committee coordinator and has finagled me into joining in the planning, which means I should march up the stairs, wash up, change into something nice, and forget I ever saw Dad's bucket list. But chirping birds and late morning sunlight woo me outside. I sit on sun-warmed floorboards and rest my elbows on my knees.

Walk Emma down the aisle.

He never would have written those words if he would have known I'd see them, but I did see them and it can't be undone. Those five words are seared into my conscious, worse than the most stubborn of stains.

Jake pulls his toolbox from the bed of his

rusted-out Chevy.

I squint at him as he walks toward me — broad shoulders clad in a flannel shirt, unbuttoned over a simple gray tee, backward Milwaukee Brewers ball cap, with his perpetual five o'clock shadow and eyes the color of the sky overhead. I wait for him to walk past. Instead, he sets his toolbox on the porch and sits beside me, bringing with him the unmistakable scents of cedar and pine. It's a fragrance that will forever and always be Jake. "Something on your mind, Emma?"

Should I tell him what I saw? Should I tell him about my crazy, half-cocked idea? This is Jake, after all. Buddies with my ex-fiancé, sure, but also my brother's best and oldest friend — which would make him like a brother to me, if not for the giant crush I hid over the course of my growing-up years. He's a guy who has the whole *quick to listen, slow to speak* thing perfected. I rub my eyes with the heels of my palms, thankful I'm not one for mascara. "I found my dad's bucket list."

"Bucket list?"

"Everything he wants to accomplish before he . . . you know."

Jake gives a slow, comprehending nod.

"Almost everything is crossed off."

165

"I'm sorry."

"Three are left. One he'll be able to cross off as soon as he returns from Door County. Another I'm sure is in the works. And then the last one is completely outside of his control." I grip my elbows. "But not mine."

Jake raises his eyebrows. "What is it?"

"Walk Emma down the aisle." And there it is, gathering quicker than I can blink — moisture in my eyes. I swipe at a lone tear and look away. "On my way home, I was contemplating calling Chase."

"Chase?" Jake says the name with disgust, like he can't believe my nerve.

"I know, but it's my dad. And this is finally something I can give him. You know how much I've been looking for a way to help. Well, here it is." Selfishly, I want it for myself too. What girl wants the sole memory of her father walking her down an aisle to be of her six-year-old self saying *I do* to an overweight, crooked-eyed Boston terrier?

Jake scratches his jaw. "Do you still love Chase?"

I shake my head, hating the answer even as I give it. I'm not sure if I ever really loved Chase, at least not in the way brides are supposed to love their grooms. He was a safe bet. I knew exactly what our life would be together. Until Dad got cancer and all

166

bets were off, even the safe ones. "But he's a great guy. We get along. People get married for a lot less."

Jake takes off his cap and runs his hand over his dark hair as he looks out at my overgrown lawn and the leaves rustling on the branches of my maple tree. I can guess what he's thinking. Chase and Jake were friends, and I broke Chase's heart. Surely there's some sort of guy code that requires Jake to watch his buddy's back. Keep the ex far, far away. He slides his baseball hat back onto his head. "If you're looking for a groom, I can do it."

"What?"

"I'll be your groom."

I laugh. "Be serious . . ."

"I *am* being serious."

"You can't be my groom."

"Why not?"

"Because you're not . . . I'm not . . ." I fumble my words, trying to grasp one of a thousand different reasons. "You have a girlfriend."

He pulls his chin back. "A girlfriend?"

"That mystery woman the bunco ladies are always gabbing about."

He cocks his head, like he's disappointed I would believe anything that comes from the mouth of a sixty-year-old woman wearing a pink T-shirt with the words *Bunco Babe* on it.

"What — there's no mystery woman?"

He shakes his head, a hint of amusement in his eyes.

"But why?"

"The bunco ladies kept trying to set me up. I kept saying no. So they made an assumption I didn't bother to correct."

"No, I don't mean why isn't there a mystery woman. I mean why would you offer to be my groom? That's . . . that's . . . a little different than fixing my faucet."

Jake's cheeks turn pink, and Jake *never* blushes. He scuffs his work boot against the cement. Drags his broad palm down his face. My ravenous curiosity eats up more and more of my shock the longer he makes me wait. What could possibly motivate him to make such an offer?

"Ben." The name escapes on an exhale — shockingly unexpected.

"You're offering to be my groom because of your brother?"

"Remember when Ben made it to the Lumberjack World Championships in Hayward?"

"He was the town celebrity." I smile a sad smile. Despite graduating in the same class, Ben and I were never close. Our link was always Jake. Whenever we ran into each other, like people do in small towns, that's who we'd talk about — Jake, and how he was liking life in Milwaukee. But now Jake is back in Mayfair, and Ben . . .

"He begged me to come watch him compete. It was a big deal."

"You didn't know what would happen." Nobody did. Not a single person on this earth could have predicted that two days into the tournament, Ben would die in a freak accident. Everyone had high hopes that Hayward would be the first of many world championships for the youngest Sawyer boy.

"Doesn't change the fact that I didn't go."

I pull at the sleeves of my sweatshirt, wishing I could change the subject, wishing I could take away the sadness clouding Jake's eyes. Seems that's all I do these days — wish, wish, wish. Only there isn't a genie in sight and the stars aren't out yet.

"It was the only time Ben ever asked me for anything. And I didn't give it to him."

"Jake . . ."

"Trust me, Emma, you don't want to live with regret." He lets out his breath, then sets his hands on the floorboards behind us, leans back into his arms, and nudges me with his shoulder. "Besides, it'd get the

Bunco Babes off my back. You can be my mystery woman."

The words unleash a flutter in my chest. I tell myself it's a silly, leftover reaction from days long gone. "Okay, but what happens after? I mean, you'd be . . . we'd be . . ." The rising heat in my cheeks makes me want to pull my hood over my head.

He clears his throat. "It wouldn't be a real wedding. I mean, we wouldn't sign the marriage certificate."

"Oh, right."

The crease between his eyebrows deepens. "Unless . . ."

I wave my hand, shooing away whatever his *unless* might be. I mistook his friendship once before. I promised myself a long time ago I would never make that assumption again. "No, of course that's what we'd do. But Jake, you don't have to do this. I mean, it would be . . ."

"Crazy?"

I laugh. "Beyond."

"Crazy's not all bad. I've actually heard that crazy can be fun." He smiles at me then — the kind of smile that is bracketed between a pair of parenthetical dimples. "So what do you say, Emma? You want to be crazy with me?"

It's nothing like my first proposal. There

is no ring or flower bouquet or man on one knee professing his undying devotion. There is no hesitation either. Without letting myself think about the consequences or implications, I say yes to Jake Sawyer. For my dad.

THREE

A cotton candy sunset frames my parents' house as Jake turns the key to his truck. The grumbling engine goes quiet. "You ready?"

I wipe my clammy palms against my jeans. "My stomach's been doing nonstop pirouettes since you picked me up." Up until this point, our less-than-twenty-four-hour-old engagement has been nothing but an enticing idea — one Jake and I talked through at length over an entire pot of pumpkin spice coffee yesterday, after he finished fixing my faucet and I had returned from the Fall Harvest Festival committee meeting. We sat at my too-tiny, can-never-have-more-than-one-guest-over-for-dinner kitchen table and hashed out a plan.

"Are you afraid they'll be upset?" Jake asks.

"Are you kidding? My mom will be thrilled."

"She will?"

"Come on. She's dreamed about us getting married since we were teenagers."

His eyes crinkle in the corners. "No she hasn't."

"Trust me, she has."

He leans back in his seat, the evening's shadows darkening his features. "Huh."

I take a deep breath, annoyed with my pesky conscience. According to doctors, my dad has one month, maybe two, and as far as I'm concerned, there will be no items left uncrossed on his bucket list. Not if I can help it. Whatever confessions I need to make can be made after he's gone. Surely God will understand. Surely, after twenty-seven years of playing by his rules, he will allow me this one indiscretion, if something so gray can even be considered an indiscretion.

"Emma?"

I blink.

Jake's staring at me. No baseball hat. No five o'clock shadow. Not even one of his flannels. His transformation from rugged to dashing does little to improve my focus.

"Sorry, what did you say?"

"I have something for you." This time, he's the one who wipes his hands on his jeans. The show of nerves is comforting somehow, a reminder that we're in this together. He shifts his hips forward, reaches into his back pocket, and brings out his fist. "I thought, since we're engaged . . ."

"Please tell me you didn't buy a ring."

He opens his hand.

My fingers move to my lips.

"It was my maternal grandmother's. I inherited it from my mother. I know it's not a diamond, but it seemed like something you would wear."

"Jake, I can't wear this."

"Sure you can."

I shake my head. Jake should save this for the woman he loves. For the woman he's going to spend the rest of his life with. That woman isn't me. I can't wear his grandmother's ring. But before I'm able to voice any of this, he slips the piece of jewelry onto my finger — a gold band set with an oval-cut pearl surrounded by tiny red gemstones. "Now they'll believe us."

I look at him, this man I've known since I was three. I grew up tagging along with him and my brother, at first wanting to be one of the guys, then wanting to date one of those guys, and here that guy is, putting his grandmother's ring on my finger. I stare down at my hand, reminding myself this isn't real. Jake is only doing me a favor.

Besides, I laid my schoolgirl crush to rest a long time ago. Chase had been proof. "It's beautiful."

He winks, climbs out of his truck, and opens my door, letting in the chill. I swing my legs around and take his offered arm. Together, we crunch through the leaves in the same lawn we used to play in as kids — ghost in the graveyard, kick the can, capture the flag, and every other neighborhood game — when two things happen simultaneously: I notice my brother's motorcycle behind Dad's Lincoln Navigator, and the front door flies open.

Mom stands inside the door frame, beaming from ear to ear, her gray-blonde curls tucked behind her ears, a novel's worth of questions sparkling in her hazel eyes. Nix the gray and the wrinkles and twenty extra pounds, and I am basically her doppelgänger. "If it isn't Jake Sawyer!" She steps forward and gives Jake a tight squeeze, making eyes at me over his shoulder, mouthing his name as if I don't already know it. "What a wonderful surprise!"

"Good evening, Mrs. Tate."

"If I've told you once, I've told you a hundred times." Mom gives his chest a friendly prod with her finger. "It's Marie to you."

The pirouettes in my stomach pick up speed. We might be able to fool my parents, but my brother is a whole different ball game. To say his presence complicates our plans is the understatement of the year. "Liam's here?"

"He got back from his trip this afternoon. I invited him to join us."

Jake and I exchange a nervous glance.

"How was Door County?" he asks Mom.

"Oh, just wonderful. Gorgeous in the fall. Have you ever been?"

"A couple times as a kid."

"It's breathtaking, isn't it?"

He nods earnestly.

Mom looks from him, to me, to him, to me, her eyes dancing. "Should we go inside?"

I want to shake my head. Nope, no thank you. I would much rather stand out here, away from Liam and his prying, astute eyes. Judging by the way Jake's feet do not move, I think he's in agreement with my plan.

"Come in, you two. Come in. Martin, Liam, look who's here!" Mom motions for Jake to go ahead, then takes my arm before I can follow, a question written all over her delighted face. *What does this mean?* As much as I'd like to stand out here where it's safe and attempt to explain my unexpected guest to her, I cannot leave Jake on his own. He's already doing enough.

"Mom."

She lets it go for now, and we join the men, who are busy shaking hands in the middle of the living room. Jake stands with a stiffness in his shoulders while a slightly sunburned, mostly tan Liam looks on with an unmistakable gleam in his eye, as if he's tucked a smirk into one corner of his mouth. We haven't even explained ourselves yet and already he doesn't believe us. I can tell. Trying to ignore him, I smile at Dad. Except for the scar on his bald head and the sharp edges of his shoulders, there is no trace of the cancer spreading throughout his brain. He's even gained back some weight since finishing his last round of chemo several months ago. His warm brown eyes sparkle as he steps forward and wraps me in a tight hug. I don't want him to let go. I want to stay right here, in this moment forever.

"Fun trip?" I manage to squeak out.

"The best." His voice rumbles against my ear, an ocean of calm. It makes the tightness in my throat tighter. My father has always been my hero, but these past two years, especially these past several days, has him superseding hero status. "How were the cats?" he asks.

"Don't get me started."

He chuckles, then lets me go and addresses Jake. "It's a nice surprise to see you here."

"Definitely unexpected," Liam adds.

Jake sticks his hands in his back pockets. "I thought you were sailing around the San Juan Islands or something like that."

"Finished a day early." My brother has an insane job. He actually gets paid — and good money too — to take rich people on outdoor adventures, all in the name of leadership training. He's climbed Kilimanjaro, hiked the Na Pali Coast in Kauai, and almost everything else in between. Technically, he lives in Mayfair. But he's gone more often than he's around. "So what's this?" He flicks his finger between Jake and me. "Are you two together?"

I look at my partner in crime, then back at my brother. "I guess you could say that."

Liam's eyes widen.

I give him my best pleading look.

It only makes the smirk in the corner of his mouth bigger. He gives Jake a friendly slap on the shoulder. "It's about time, man! Emma only had a crush on you all through high school."

Jake cocks his head.

178

My entire face catches on fire. "No I didn't."

"Then what was up with all those little hearts you drew everywhere?" He traces an invisible heart with his finger. "JS plus ET equals true love."

I am going to murder him.

"I think it's wonderful," Mom says.

"Me too. I've always thought you two would make a great couple." Dad claps his hands, then rubs them together. "Now Jake, I hope you're hungry. When Emma said she was bringing a guest to dinner, I think Marie thought the Packers' entire defensive line would be coming."

Jake pats his flat abs. "Starved."

"Anything else happen while we were away?" Mom asks.

I swallow, my throat suddenly parched. This is the perfect opportunity to make the announcement, only I find myself waffling. Liam was not part of tonight's plan. We were going to tell him after we eased into the charade by first telling my parents. I had come prepared for something akin to a warm-up speech, given in front of the safety of a mirror, only to find out there would be no practicing. "Well . . ."

Jake runs his finger under his collar. "Emma and I . . ."

"We're engaged!" I blurt.

"What?" Mom and Dad say the word in unison.

I hold up my left hand, grateful for Jake's forethought. It would have looked extra suspicious if I didn't have a ring.

"Engaged?" Dad asks.

"To be married?" Mom adds, as if there is another kind of engaged Jake and I might be.

Liam coughs, or maybe it's a laugh. I can't tell.

I stare at my parents, trying to gauge their reaction, wondering if we shouldn't have somehow led up to the announcement. Told them we were serious over salads, in love over the main course, engaged by dessert. "We know it's fast."

"More like warp speed," Liam says.

The fire in my cheeks spreads into my ears. My brother is many things — a charmer, an adrenaline junkie, the life of the party — but he's also shrewd and skeptical. And right now his shrewd, skeptical stare bores into the side of my face. I cannot look at him.

"Mystery woman," Mom mumbles.

"What's that?" Dad says.

Her face brightens, a tangible lightbulb moment. "*You* are Jake's mystery woman?"

She laughs — fairy dust sprinkling the air, dissolving some of the tension.

Dad furrows his brow. "What mystery woman?"

"Jake's been dating someone for the past several months. All the ladies of Mayfair have been trying to guess who. Turns out, that woman is our daughter." Mom takes my hand and examines the ring. "This is gorgeous."

"It was Jake's grandmother's."

"Wait a minute," Dad says, apparently trying to keep up with Mom. "If you and Jake have been dating, why did you keep it a secret?"

"They probably didn't want to put pressure on the relationship, Martin. You know how nosy this town can be. I understand wanting to keep things private." Mom looks up from the ring. "What I don't understand is keeping it private from us."

"We're sorry. We, um, didn't want anything to be awkward. In case things didn't work out."

Mom shoos away my apology and examines the ring more closely. "Jake, are those rubies?"

"Garnets," he says.

I take my hand back and peek at Dad, watching the wrinkles gather on his forehead. Time is a funny thing when the end of a person's life draws near. Days that once flew by like discarded seconds turn into twenty-four-hour lifetimes. The definition of fast changes. This engagement came out of nowhere, but my dad's face softens. I wonder if he's picturing me in a white dress, my arm wrapped around his as he walks me down the aisle. I wonder if he's thinking about his bucket list.

This is for you, I want to say.

"This is really what you want?" he asks me.

"Yes."

That's all it takes — one simple *yes.* His face splits into a smile that transforms him into a happy, healthier, younger man. Then he grabs Jake's hand and pulls him in for a hearty thump on the back. "Congratulations!"

Jake thumps him in return. "Thanks."

"Now you'll officially be a part of the family," Mom says.

"Does that mean we get the family discount at the hardware store?" Dad gives Jake a wink. "I want to replace the floor in Emma's old room."

My fake fiancé jumps into this new conversation wholeheartedly and, much to my relief, avoids Liam as diligently as I do.

182

He and Dad chat about the benefits and drawbacks of real hardwood versus laminate as they walk down the hall, toward the room in question. I want to go after them, pretend to contribute to their conversation. Instead, I'm left alone with Liam and my mother — the wolf and the overexcited puppy.

"Emma!" Mom swats my arm.

"What?"

"*What?* You are engaged to Jake Sawyer."

"Will you stop using his last name?"

"I'm sorry, it's all just happening so quickly. My head is spinning."

"Mom, you and Dad only knew each other for five months before you got married. I've known Jake my entire life." I peek sideways at my brother as I say it.

He stands with his hands folded behind his back, eyes slightly narrowed, as if measuring every single one of my words. I want to cup my hand over his eyes and tell him to stop staring.

"Oh honey, don't get me wrong. You know I'm thrilled, it's just . . ." I wonder if she's going to bring up Chase and the fiasco that was my first engagement. We dated on and off for six years before I said yes, and look how well that turned out. "Do you love him?"

"Mom."

Her expression turns serious. "It's an important question, Emma."

"It's Jake. Of course I love him."

"All right then." She smiles. "Have you picked a date?"

"October twenty-fifth."

Her eyes go buggy. "Of this year?"

"I know all of this must be overwhelming, but October's my favorite month. And if we wait until next year . . ." I don't have to finish the thought. The smirk tucked into the corner of Liam's mouth dissolves. All three of us are thinking the same thing.

If we wait until next year, Dad will be gone.

FOUR

Tossing a wave over my shoulder at a couple of men in yellow hard hats conferring in the middle of town square, I hurry across the street. The early morning sun is at my back, and caffeine is the last thing I need with this much adrenaline coursing through my veins. But Monday morning coffee at Patty's House of Pancakes is a ritual, something Lily Emerick and I have been doing since we were old enough to drive. According to Lily, rituals aren't meant to be broken. Besides, I have to tell her the news before she hears it from somebody else.

The upcoming announcement pulls my chest muscles tight.

My parents had no problem believing Jake and I were getting married in a little over a month. Sure, they were shocked, but that quickly gave way to delight, because we are quick to believe what our hearts want to be true. My dad wants to walk me down the aisle. My mom has always wanted me to be with Jake. And they'd much rather focus on a wedding than an impending funeral. Liam, I'm sure, didn't buy it, but at least my parents' presence kept him from verbalizing his doubts. He remained suspiciously quiet throughout last night's dinner, and neither Jake nor I attempted to rouse him.

My best friend, however — straight shooter, no-nonsense, can't-get-anything-past-her Lily — will not be so accepting. Her senses are unclouded by grief, and not only do I need to tell her the news, I also need to convince her to help me. With Dad officially retired as of three weeks ago, I am now the only veterinarian in Mayfair, which means I'm too swamped at the clinic to pull off an entire wedding in such a short amount of time. This is what Lily does for a living — she plans parties and events. So surely she will help me.

I open the door and step inside Patty's, inhaling the salty-sweet aroma of fried sausage and syrup. The place is all wainscoting and wallpaper and wood-framed pictures, with a counter spanning the length of one wall and booths lining the other, a space in between too narrow to fit any tables. I give the place a quick scan, but Lily is MIA.

Patty, on the other hand, lights up like the sky on the Fourth of July the second she notices me in the doorway. Almost as wide as she is tall, she waddles out from behind the counter wearing her pale pink Bunco Babes T-shirt, puts her umber hands on my cheeks in a gesture befitting grandmothers everywhere, and pulls my head down so it's level with hers.

"Um, hi, Patty." This is not her typical greeting.

"Child, how on God's green earth did you keep it a secret?"

Oh no.

"You and Jake Sawyer getting married?" She lets go of my face and shakes her head. "You, the mystery woman?"

A wave of panic rolls through my limbs. Patty is not a soft-spoken woman, and Lily will be here any second. "Where did you hear that?"

"Please. *Where did I hear that?* Your mother stopped in for a to-go coffee after that 5:00 a.m. Zumba class she's always going on about." Patty turns toward two men who sit across from each other in one of the booths, a game of gin rummy between them. The one on the left is Jake's great-uncle, Al, and across from him is Al's best buddy, Rupert — Mayfair's oldest residents.

"Did you hear the news?"

Al looks up from the cards splayed in his hand. Somehow, his sagging jowls, stretched earlobes, and bulbous nose mesh together in just the right way, giving meaning to the phrase "He's so ugly he's cute." This morning he wears his cowboy hat tipped back as opposed to pulled low — a sign to the world that he woke up in a good mood. "What news?"

Rupert — not so decidedly cute in his old age — looks up too, squinting at Patty as though keener eyesight might make up for his pitiful hearing.

"Our very own Emma Tate and Jake Sawyer are engaged."

"What's that?" Rupert asks.

I shake my head. Wave my hands. Consider cupping one over Patty's mouth, but I am not quick enough.

"Emma and Jake are engaged!"

The diner goes quiet.

"Jake Sawyer, my great-nephew?" Al says.

"What other Jake Sawyer do we have in this town, Al? Of course your great-nephew!" Patty turns back to me. "Now let me see that ring. Your mama said it was something."

Eager to dispel her excitement as quickly as possible, I stick out my hand.

"Oh!" Patty brings her hands to her ample chest and leans closer. "But it's an unusual engagement ring, isn't it? Not a single diamond anywhere."

"An engagement ring?"

I shut my eyes. The disbelieving question belongs to Lily. Sure enough, when I look, she stands just inside the doorway, her expression every bit as disbelieving as her voice.

"You mean *you* didn't even know?" Patty's dark eyes widen. "Emma, you kept the news from your best friend?"

"What news?" Lily asks.

"Emma and Jake are getting married."

For a couple of seconds, Lily does not react. She stares, almost bored, back at Patty, until the corner of her mouth curls up, as if trying to meet the downward turn of her scrunched eye. It's a classic Lily face, code for *yeah, right.*

"Speak of the devil!" Patty points toward the window, where my fake fiancé is walking past — his baseball hat in place, carrying what appears to be a heavy load of lumber. "Nobody move. Coffee's on the house!"

If Patty hears my groan, it doesn't stop her. She bustles outside. I watch through the window in horror as she grabs Jake's arm and pulls him inside, lumber and all. When his attention lands on me, he raises his eyebrows.

I shrug apologetically.

Patty grabs a full coffeepot and hurries around the diner like a whirling dervish, topping everyone's mugs. She forces a mug into Lily's hand, fills it up, then scoots me over so I'm standing next to a bewildered Jake. His shock is this palpable thing beside me. We both stand there like a pair of open-mouthed idiots, and I cannot — will not — look at Lily.

"To Emma and Jake." Patty raises her own mug high into the air and waits for everyone else to follow suit. "I've known you both since you were in diapers, and now look at you — the town sweethearts. May your life together be filled with health and happiness!"

"And a passel of Sawyer babies!" Al adds.

My body flushes as mugs clink together and customers take delicate sips.

"What are you waiting for?" Rupert calls. "Kiss your woman!"

Someone whistles in agreement.

My heart jumps into my throat. I have never kissed Jake. Not once. Not even during our spin-the-bottle phase in junior high. And now we're supposed to kiss here, in

Patty's restaurant? A nervous laugh flutters past my lips. This was not a detail we discussed when we made our game plan on Saturday.

"Yeah, Jake, kiss her," Lily says.

I dare a glimpse, just one. Enough to catch Lily's quirked eyebrow, her expression so dry I could douse it with all the coffee Patty just poured and it wouldn't make a difference.

Patty nudges me closer. My back bumps against Jake's bundle of two-by-fours. I look over my shoulder, up into Jake's face, which registers the same panic I'm feeling. He hesitates for a moment, then dips his head and does what everyone urges him to do. He kisses me. Jake is kissing me. Oh my goodness. He smells really, really good. And he's kissing me.

Before I can register anything else, the kiss ends. The onlookers cheer. And I force myself to breathe. In all my schoolgirl fantasies — wherein Jake realized that he was madly in love with me — I never imagined our first kiss would be in front of his great-uncle Al.

Jake clears his throat. "I, um . . . have to get back."

I nod like an overeager bobblehead doll and bite my lip, tasting cinnamon — Big

Red. Only I'm not chewing Big Red gum. I taste it because Jake chews Big Red and his lips were just on mine.

He looks at me one last time before turning around and walking out the door.

Our captive audience returns to what they were doing before Patty caused a scene, like nothing crazy had just transpired in the house of pancakes. I slide into an empty booth, attempting to feign casualness. Setting her mug on the table, Lily sits across from me, tucks a strand of her chin-length strawberry-blonde hair behind her ear, and crosses her arms.

I want to push her eyebrows down her forehead. Instead, I give her some halfhearted jazz hands. "Surprise."

"There is no way you and Jake are engaged."

"Why not?"

"Because as of Saturday, you weren't even dating. I'm pretty sure you would have told me."

Little did she know, we were already "engaged" by the time I attended the Fall Harvest Festival committee meeting. "You know what they say about whirlwind romances."

She gives me an exasperated look. "You spent an entire week agonizing over paint samples when it came to updating your bathroom."

"So?"

She plops her elbows on the table and curls her long fingers around the mug. "So you expect me to believe that Jake proposed to you on Saturday, out of nowhere, and you said yes?"

Patty approaches, humming "Here Comes the Bride." She sets a mug in front of me, fills it up, gives my arm an excited squeeze, then waddles away. I wilt beneath Lily's deadpan stare. Who am I kidding? I can't keep this from her. I look around to make sure the coast is clear of eavesdroppers, then lean over the table and tell her the story — starting with the bucket list discovery and ending with the fiasco just now in Patty's House of Pancakes, as well as everything in between. By the time I finish the last word, I feel as though I've shed three layers of body armor.

Ribbons of steam curl up from the dark liquid in our cups, clouding the space between us, but not so much that I can't see Lily gaping.

"Would you please say something?"

She dips her chin. "Have you gone insane?"

The question puts me on the defensive. I

didn't realize until now how much I was counting on her support. "My dad is dying."

"I know, but —"

"This is my chance to give him something before he's gone."

"A fake wedding?"

"The experience of walking his only daughter down the aisle."

"But Emma, it's not real. You're giving him an illusion."

Her words cut. I don't let myself examine the wound. I can't afford to. This is my chance to do something for Dad, and we've already told my parents. Jake phoned last night to say he'd told his father as well, and he was just as happy as my parents are. As we sit here and speak, the news is spreading all over Mayfair. I've set this train in motion, and now I must ride it to its foregone conclusion — my father walking me down that aisle, which is exactly what I want. I can't let Lily's disapproval distract me from that.

I look down at my mug until the steam disappears. Patty makes the best coffee in town, and I can't bring myself to take a sip. "I should get going. The Montgomerys' new puppy is scheduled for vaccinations at nine."

"Emma . . ."

"What?"

"I'm worried about you, okay? We never really talk about your dad or how you're doing. I'm afraid you're using this as an excuse to avoid reality."

"I'm not avoiding anything."

"The last thing you need added to the mix is a broken heart."

My exasperation grows. "A broken heart? Lily, it's Jake. My heart is safe."

She stares at me in that way she does — cutting straight through the nonsense, getting right to the bone.

"This is for my dad."

"Does Jake know that? Because it seems like a pretty drastic favor to offer a person."

"Jake knows what it's like to live with regret. He doesn't want that burden on my shoulders." If only my best friend could feel the same. "That's all this is."

She couldn't look any more skeptical if she tried. "I think it's a disaster waiting to happen."

"No, a disaster would be finding Dad's bucket list after it was too late to do anything." I shake my head and move to stand. "I was hoping for your support, but I guess that's too much to ask."

She reaches across the table to stop me. "I needed you to hear me say it. But now that we're clear, okay."

"Okay?"

Lily shrugs. "We're best friends. If you really think this is something you have to do, then I'm here for you. Disaster and all."

I melt into the booth. "Good, because I need help planning the wedding."

FIVE

After coffee with Lily, I spend the rest of the day with animals, doing well-checks, diagnosing various ailments, prescribing medicine, and administering vaccinations. Edna Pearl, owner of the local dance studio, brings in her parrot, Polly, right before I close, under the pretense of sickly behavior. Really, I think she wants an excuse to pepper me with questions about the engagement announcement. I end up staying fifteen minutes past five, poking and prodding a perfectly healthy parrot to the backdrop of, "*Squawk!* Can't believe it. *Squawk!* Jake and Emma."

As soon as Edna and Polly leave, I head over to my parents', hitch Dad's minitrailer to the back of my Honda, and drive out to Sawyer Farm — passed down from Al Sawyer to his son, Wayne, who now runs it with his son, Steve. They stock the town with Christmas trees in the winter, strawberries and raspberries in the summer, and every imaginable size and shape of gourd and pumpkin in the fall. Since Lily grudgingly agreed to help me with the wedding, the least I can do is help her with the decorations for Mayfair's Fall Harvest Festival, and the best place to get decorations is Sawyer Farm.

As I drive the backcountry roads, the crisp air whips strands of hair from my ponytail. I crank up Miranda Lambert and try to lose myself in the colors — green leaves surrendering to red and orange and gold, their foliage made brighter against a bruised sky. It's best if I don't think — not about Jake or that kiss or the ring on my finger or Lily's disapproval or my pesky doubts or Dad's waning life. Instead, I belt along with Miranda until I turn down the road that winds toward the farm. Gravel crunches beneath my tires as I catch sight of a familiar Chevy parked amid a smattering of pumpkins in front of the Sawyers' big barn. I turn down the music and squint at the plates, but of course it's Jake's truck. The rust is in all the right places.

What's he doing here?

I pull up beside his truck and step outside, twisting the ring around my finger. Pumpkins, gourds, hay bales. Decorations for the town square. That's what I've come for.

The screen door to the farmhouse squeals open and out steps Wayne, then Jake, then Wayne's wife, Sandy, who spots me first. As soon as she does, her storklike legs take her down the porch steps and eat up the short distance between us. She wraps her long arms around me and nearly lifts me off the ground. "I knew you two would get married someday!"

Apparently, they've heard the news.

"If Papa Al hadn't told us, I'm not sure Jake would have made a peep. I've been trying to get him to share the details ever since he brought over my new rocking chair, but you know Jake. Never one to blather."

I glance toward the men.

Wayne gives me a friendly wave, skirts around the new rocking chair — polished walnut, beautifully designed — and steps off the porch. "Congratulations, Emma."

"Thanks."

"Jake tells us the big day isn't too far away."

"October twenty-fifth," I say, silently scolding my erratic heartbeat. It's Jake. I have no reason for the sudden bout of nerves. Except for the whole kissing thing.

Jake steps off the porch, too, and stands

by my side.

"We insisted you have the wedding here at the farm, but Jake said he'd have to speak with you about it first." Sandy looks at me eagerly, as if waiting for me to make the decision here and now. "It'd be a free venue. And with the date approaching so quickly, it might be the only one available."

Wayne wraps his arm around Sandy's waist, highlighting their height difference. While she is tall and lanky, he is short and stocky. On any other couple, the disparity might look awkward, but not on them. "Give the girl time to breathe, Sandy. She just got here."

"I can't help it. I'm just so excited."

Wayne pulls Sandy closer, kisses her cheek, then nods toward a tractor hitched to a hayrack near the barn. "You ready to load up?"

I nod. Next week the farm will open to the public. Not only pumpkins and hayrack rides, but a petting zoo and a corn maze bigger than any other in northern Wisconsin. Sawyer Farm puts our tiny town on the map. "Thanks for giving us first pick. Lily will be thrilled."

"Not a problem. Now, how about I give you two a ride out to the patch before the rain starts up? Jake, you can help your fiancée load up for the festival and discuss the location of your wedding along the way."

"Oh . . . um . . ." I peek at Jake, who wears an inscrutable expression. "You probably have to get back to the hardware store."

"I have time for a hayrack ride."

"Good. Let me just pull the tractor around." Wayne heads off while Sandy begins explaining the many benefits that come with having the wedding at the farm. She doesn't quit until Wayne pulls up on his tractor and Jake and I climb into the hayrack. We settle onto the bench in the back and wave at Sandy while we slowly ride away.

When she's out of earshot, Jake clears his throat. "About that kiss . . ."

I let out a nervous laugh. "Yeah."

"I'm really sorry."

"Me too." We ride over some rough terrain. I set my hands on the bench and curl my fingers beneath the wood so as not to jostle up against Jake. I don't want to set off any more alarms in his head. Between Liam's comment about my childhood crush last night and Jake being forced to kiss me this morning, he no doubt has plenty going off already. Poor Jake is probably worried I'm getting false ideas, reading too much into his offer.

He wipes his hands down his jeans. "We should probably come up with a plan."

"So it doesn't happen again."

He gives me a self-deprecating, sideways smile. "I was thinking more about how we're going to play this out."

"Oh." The hayrack ride brings us closer to a field dotted with rows and rows of orange.

"I mean, the Bunco Babes will probably expect a certain level of . . ."

"Affection?"

His dimples flash. "Only if you can stand it."

And just like that, the tension seeps from my muscles. I loosen my grip on the bench. Jake is such a good sport. "So what exactly do you have in mind?"

He looks down at my hand, then takes it in his. "This seems easy enough."

Swallowing, I stare at our interlaced fingers — his large and tan, mine small and a bit paler. "Not too horrible," I tease.

"Almost natural."

"We'll get there."

He relaxes back against the bench.

I smile. "You didn't know what you were signing up for, did you?"

"I knew."

Smiling, I look around at the rolling hills, dotted with maples and oaks. "So we're getting married at Sawyer Farm?"

"Only if you want."

A pinch of giddiness wiggles in my chest. I can imagine it — the crisp weather, an azure sky, the melody of Canon in D or maybe even "Ave Maria" as the guests stand and I slip my arm around Dad's. "I think it's perfect."

"Good."

We ride the rest of the way in comfortable silence — the kind carved from years of knowing one another. When Wayne pulls to a stop, Jake helps me off the hayrack and we wander up and down the rows of pumpkins — large, small, circular, oval, lumpy, and smooth. It's a wonderfully diverse crop this year.

"Emma?" Jake asks.

I straighten from examining some gourds.

Jake nudges a pumpkin with his shoe. "Why did you break your engagement to Chase?"

The question escapes into the cool air and floats between us. This is a topic we haven't talked about. When it first happened, Jake was living in Milwaukee. He kept in contact with Liam but not me. When he came back to Mayfair a year and a half ago, he was a wounded man, picking up the pieces of his grieving family after Ben's death. My broken engagement didn't seem important. Since then we have always managed to skirt around the issue. Chase and Jake were friends, and I hurt Chase badly when I called things off. I never, ever intended to, but intentions don't mean much when someone's hurting. I got the feeling Jake wanted to stay out of it. Yet now he asks. I stuff my hands into the pockets of my corduroy jacket. "I'd just found out my dad had cancer."

He cocks his head.

"Something like that has a way of making you think, you know? Make a good, hard assessment of your life."

His eyes contain an ocean's worth of understanding, because Jake knows.

"The diagnosis changed him."

"Chase?"

"No, my dad. He started living with so much courage. I realized that when I said yes to Chase, it wasn't because I loved him. It was because I didn't want to lose him." I gather several gourds into my arms, Jake grabs two pumpkins by their stems, and we make our way back to the hayrack to drop off our first load. "It's ironic."

"What is?"

"I called off my wedding because of my dad's cancer. Now I'm having another one because of the same thing."

A hint of pain flickers across Jake's face, only I don't know what it's for. Or who it's for. "Do you wish you never would have called off the first one? I mean, if you hadn't, you wouldn't be in this mess now, pretending to be engaged to me."

I grab some smaller pumpkins nearby and place them beside the two big ones. "No regrets."

Six

"They're what?" I stop in front of To Have and To Hold, the only bridal boutique in the county, so fast that Lily bumps into me from behind.

"Golfing, honey," Mom says again.

"Liam, Dad, and Jake?"

Mom scrunches her forehead as if I am being purposefully obtuse, then bustles Lily and me through the front doors. Dresses of every fabric and design spill off racks. Chiffon, organza, satin, and lace. Ball gowns with exorbitantly long trains, short gowns with no train at all, and everything in between. Along with veils and shoes and jewelry galore. The place is like an overstuffed wedding turkey. I turn around, ready to continue my line of questioning with Mom, but I've already lost her. The sudden onslaught of white has mesmerized her, drawing her in like an insect to the light. This is her happy place.

Me? I can't seem to find one.

We are five days from October, a full week into my engagement, and only four weeks from the wedding day. Two emergencies at the clinic — one of which resulted in euthanizing an eight-year-old Lab — on top of all my regularly scheduled appointments hurled me into a put-out-the-fire mentality. All this week, I've managed to avoid Lily completely and Liam for the most part. Dad has been his usual rocklike self. And Mom has turned into a spaz. According to her, "We have no time!" Which is exactly what I don't want to hear, because on the other side of that aisle is a reality I'm not ready to face.

"Emma, you have to try this on." Mom glides to the nearest display, her hand outstretched like she can't resist touching the poufed skirt.

I take in the layers of bustled organza and wrinkle my nose. I did enough of this two years ago to know what looks good on my body and what doesn't. Bustled organza might work for stick-thin, tall models. For a five-foot-four gal with some muscle on her bones? Not so much. "Mom."

She turns. "What?"

"Why are Dad, Liam, and Jake golfing?" Jake doesn't even like putt-putt.

Mom arches her eyebrow. "Why are you

so fixated on the golf?"

"I just . . . Jake . . . doesn't golf." Never mind that this means Jake will be spending the entire morning with Liam, when both of us have gone out of our way to avoid him. I ran into him once this past week over at Mom and Dad's, and the entire time he grinned at me like I was free entertainment. Now Jake is partaking in the one sport that drags on into an eternity with my smirky-faced brother, who will no doubt use that eternity to razz my poor fiancé.

Mom slides a few dresses along one of the racks. "Your father loves golf, and now that Jake is officially a part of the family, he invited him to go along."

I worry my lip. This is no good.

Mom pulls a mermaid-style dress with one too many sequins off its hanger and holds it up to my body. "What do you think, Lily?"

Lily rubs her chin, beholding all the sparkles, then scrunches her nose and shakes her head. "How's Liam doing?" she asks. "I haven't seen him in a while."

"He's fine." I avoid looking her in the eyes when I answer. I can tell by the tone of her question that she's inquiring about more than Liam's general well-being. She wants to know what he thinks about the engagement.

208

A young woman with bangles on each wrist offers to start us a room. Mom hands over the two dresses that have caught her attention.

"We should all get together tonight," Lily says. "Hang out."

"That's a wonderful idea!" Mom runs her fingers along the train of another dress. "We could make use of the fire pit. We haven't done that in a long time."

I eye my best friend. She's had a thing for my brother ever since we realized cooties were a plot devised by parents to keep boys and girls apart for as long as possible. What I can't figure out is whether her suggestion is an excuse to hang out with Liam or if it's her attempt to find out if Liam knows the truth.

"It could be our reward for a day of hard work." Lily holds up her iPhone. "I've got a whole list of things we need to accomplish today if we're going to pull off a wedding by the twenty-fifth."

"The first backyard fire of the season. Your dad will love it." Mom squeezes my elbow and gives me a reassuring smile. "Now, let's find you a dress."

So that's what I do. Or try, at least. It's hard to muster up the enthusiasm when my mind keeps playing out golf course scenarios, wherein Jake crumbles beneath the weight of Liam's questions and spills the truth to not only him, but also my dad. I imagine the disappointment and hurt on Dad's face. And that uncrossed item on his bucket list. It would taunt me for the rest of my life. To add even more angst to the situation, sporadic flickers of giddiness at the memory of Jake's kiss and our hand-holding at Sawyer Farm bubble to the surface.

I need to get a grip.

Doing my best to attend to the task at hand, I nod or shake my head at the dresses Lily and Mom select, until I grow tired of all the white and head over to the bridesmaid section. I hold up a periwinkle monstrosity with an impossibly short skirt and puffy sleeves. "Hey, Lily! How about this for the maid of honor?"

She steps away from a rack and joins me.

I hang the dress up and pull out another — calf-length and seafoam green. "This would bring out your eyes."

"Are you asking me to be your maid of honor?"

"Isn't that assumed?"

"Wow. I've never been a maid of honor at a fake wedding before."

"Shhh!" I dart a look over my shoulder.

"Don't worry, she can't hear." There's an

undercurrent to Lily's words. I can tell she wants to say something more, but she presses her lips together.

I should be grateful that she's keeping her opinions to herself. After all, I asked Lily for her support. But her silent disapproval rankles. "You should be thrilled about this, you know. I'm giving you an excuse to dance with Liam."

"That is one way to look at things." She peeks at Mom, then dips her chin and leans closer. "Does your brother know?"

I shake my head, then wander toward Mom, eager to escape Lily's questions. She follows. Halfway there I stop. Directly in front of me is the dress I've always envisioned wearing on my wedding day, all the way back when I was a little girl obsessed with Cinderella. It's the dress I scoured every boutique across the upper Midwest for two years ago but could never find. Yet here it is, in this bridal shop not more than twenty minutes from my home. A strapless ball gown with a sweetheart neckline, a chapel train, intricate beadwork, and an accompanying jacket.

"It's beautiful," Lily says.

"It's perfect." I run my fingers along the lace sleeve of the jacket, then check the tag. "And it's my size."

211

Lily and I smile at each other. Fake wedding or not, we can't help ourselves. I take the dress off the rack and hurry toward the changing room. The woman with the bangles assists, zipping and buttoning and adjusting, while Lily and Mom wait impatiently outside, telling us to hurry up already.

When I step out of the changing room, Mom's eyes fill with tears.

I take in my reflection, and that giddy feeling swells. I twirl, relishing the rustling sound the skirt makes, and smooth my hand over my waist.

Mom dabs her eyes with a wadded-up tissue. "I have to buy it for you."

"No way." The words come too quickly, but there's no way I'm letting her spend a dime on this wedding. Even if it weren't fake, even if Jake and I were planning on actually being married, my parents have a mountain of medical bills to climb. "I have money saved up."

"And it's half off," the woman with the bangles adds.

The front doors of To Have and To Hold swing open, letting in a gust of chilly autumn air. Jake strides inside, so out of the blue I don't have time to react. When he spots me in front of the mirror, he stops, his dark hair ruffled from the wind. His attention travels up the length of the dress, then lands on my face, but before I can decode his expression Mom jumps out of her seat and throws herself in front of me like a shield. "Jake, you can't see her!"

"Mom —"

"It's tradition, Emma. He can't see you in your dress. It's bad luck!" She holds up her hands. "Jake, close your eyes!"

Jake covers his eyes with his palms.

"Mom, this is silly." Not to mention confusing. Jake isn't supposed to be here. He's supposed to be out on the golf course with Liam and Dad. I look around my mother. "Jake, you don't have to cover your eyes."

"Yes, he does!" She shoves me toward the changing room.

I go willingly and hurry out of the dress as fast as one can hurry out of a wedding gown. By the time I'm back in my jeans, hoodie, and cross trainers, I've had plenty of time to replay the look on Jake's face — panicked before he saw me, stunned after. I'm not sure which one has me hurrying more. As soon as I step out of the dressing room, Jake takes my elbow. "Can I speak with you for a second?"

"Sure, of course." I glance at Lily, then

follow him outside. "What's wrong?"

"Liam knows."

"What?"

"Your brother. He knows."

"How?"

"You know Liam. He was asking so many questions, and he wouldn't let me get away with half answers. Finally, I had to pull him aside and tell him what was going on."

The warmth drains from my face. "What did he say?"

"He laughed."

"He laughed?"

Jake rubs the back of his neck and nods.

"Is he going to say anything?"

"I don't think so."

"You didn't ask him?"

"We didn't have much time."

A groan slips past my lips. I do not want to talk to Liam about any of this. I especially don't want to hear him express the same doubts Lily did.

"I'm sorry, Emma."

"You have no reason to apologize. I'm the one who's put you in such an awkward position."

"Actually, I asked you, remember?"

I look down at the ground and cross my arms to ward off the chill in the air.

"That was a really pretty dress."

When I look up, Jake stands closer than before. "Thanks."

Mom pokes her head outside. "Hey you two, Lily had the most fabulous idea!"

Jake and I turn our heads toward her at the same time.

"I was telling her how your father and I are taking dance lessons tomorrow night. She thought you two should join us. Practice up for your first dance as a married couple."

Another groan pushes up my throat, but I swallow it down.

"So . . ." Mom beams at us. "What do you say?"

I squint against the sun and start to shake my head, because I am not going to make Jake suffer through dance lessons. But he shifts behind me. "Sounds like fun."

If only his voice didn't drip with uncertainty.

SEVEN

The fire crackles and pops and breathes smoke into the star-strewn sky, the gentlest of breezes carrying it slightly north, where the woods line the edge of my parents' backyard. The smell of burning wood mingles with the crisp air as I pull my stocking cap more snuggly over my ears and lean forward in my chair, closer to the heat. Across the fire, Lily lets out a burst of laughter that echoes into the night. She stands beside Liam, who stabs marshmallow upon marshmallow onto a roasting fork.

Somehow I managed to thwart his attempt to accost me when I arrived fifteen minutes ago. Liam rarely listens to me, but my "Not now" came out so sharp and ominous, he actually backed off. I'm positive the reprieve will not last, but I'll take it for now.

I look up the length of the long backyard. So far, no Jake. Dad pokes the pile of burning wood with a fire iron. Sparks of glowing embers jump from the flames, then slowly extinguish into black. He sets the iron stick aside, slides his hands inside the pockets of his Green Bay Packers fleece jacket, and sits down beside me with a groan. "Your old man's getting old."

The words hit me the wrong way, rupturing a pocket of fear I try to leave alone. Fifty-seven is not old. It is much, much too young. I gaze into the fire, praying that this fake wedding can be something we all laugh about together in ten years. Something crazy Emma did for Dad, who was miraculously healed.

"How's your heart, Emma-girl?" Dad asks.

I look down at my shoes and smile a little. Cancer has zapped his patience for small talk. He has replaced the standard and largely accepted *How are you doing?* with this bad boy. And he will not let anyone get away with *fine.* He will poke and prod until something more substantial than smoke arises. "My heart is hoping God will heal you."

Dad sets his hand on the armrest of his chair and seems to contemplate my answer.

I bite my lip, trying to keep it together, but I don't deal well with unknowns. Not when I was a child and not as an adult either. I attempt to loosen the growing tightness in my throat. I attempt to be strong. But the words swell until I can't hold them back any longer. "You can't die."

"We all die, Emma."

"You know what I mean." I shake my head, unable to fathom a world without my father. "I don't think I can handle it."

"God's not asking you to handle it right now. Right now, I'm here." He pats my knee, as if I need the extra reassurance. "And when the day comes and I'm no longer here, God will equip you with what you need to handle it then."

This is another thing cancer has done — taught my father the art of living in each moment. He doesn't look ahead. He doesn't let himself spiral into a storm of what-ifs. He relies on God's strength for today and trusts him with tomorrow. For me, it's a constant struggle. I let out a puff of breath. "You make it sound so simple."

"Trust *is* simple." He holds up his pointer finger. "Not easy, but simple."

The sound of a car door slamming and more of Lily's laughter cuts our conversation short. I look toward the house and spot Mom, closing the distance between us. She skirts around the fire and offers us a bowl of candy corn — my long-standing favorite.

Dad's too. I take a few pieces and pop one into my mouth.

"I do believe your fiancé just pulled up in his truck," Mom says.

"Speaking of your fiancé . . ." Dad takes a handful for himself.

Something about the serious set of his brow makes me stop chewing. "Yeah?"

"My heart is heavy, Emma."

My muscles tense. Does Dad suspect something? And if he does, would he run with it anyway? Like the surprise party on my twenty-first birthday. I knew about the party, and I'm almost positive my parents knew I knew, but when I walked into the restaurant, I did my best rendition of shocked and neither called my bluff.

"As your father, I feel it's my responsibility to tell you" — he sets his hand over his chest and shakes his head — "that he is truly an awful golfer."

I roll my eyes, trying not to give away my relief. "Har, har."

"But I guess there are worse things." He finishes off the rest of his candy corn as Jake appears around the corner of the house. He strides toward us, something strapped around his chest. Dad pats my knee again and stands, because the lawn chairs are doubled up — three sets of two around the fire pit — and apparently, the chair closest to mine belongs to my fiancé. When Jake approaches, Dad slaps him on the arm. "I was just telling my daughter about your golfing skills."

Jake chuckles, the glow from the fire flickering along his jawline.

"You brought your guitar," I say, sitting up straighter.

He runs his thumb beneath the strap. "Figured some music might be fun."

"Of course it will." Mom gives Jake a hug, then she and Dad sit in the pair of chairs to our left.

"Sorry I'm late." Jake pulls the strap of his guitar case over his head and sits beside me. "I was working in my shed and lost track of time."

I stick my hands beneath my knees. "What were you working on?"

"A gift."

"Care to be less vague, Mr. Nonspecific?" I ask, raising my eyebrow.

He raises one of his eyebrows back at me, leaving it at that, then leans forward and bumps his knee against mine. "Hanging in there, kiddo?"

The nickname and the gesture trigger a major bout of déjà vu. All of a sudden, I am eighteen again, sitting next to this same fire pit and this same boy, only it's the night of my graduation party. I had been warming my hands by the fire, the temperature much lower than it should have been for late May, when Jake sat beside me and bumped his knee against mine. "Doing all right there, kiddo?"

I wasn't going to let him get away with it. "You aren't allowed to call me that."

"No?"

"I am officially a high school graduate. I'm not a kid anymore, Jake."

"So I've noticed." I'm not sure what warmed my skin more — the fire or the words or the long look we shared after them. All day, there had been a palpable chemistry between us. I was sure he could feel it too. There had even been flirting.

He popped a few knuckles, a nervous habit. "So . . . there's something I've been wanting to tell you."

My heart rate picked up speed, growing faster and faster the longer Jake delayed saying whatever he wanted to say. Maybe if I helped him along, encouraged him a little. I leaned forward. "Jake, I —"

"Chase."

The name drew me back. "Chase?"

Jake wiped his hands along the thighs of his jeans and nodded.

I glanced past the fire, where Chase stood chatting with my brother. "What about him?"

"He likes you."

"Oh." My hopes plummeted so hard and fast I could do nothing but blink. Jake wasn't going to profess his feelings for me, because Jake didn't have any feelings for me. He was checking to see how I felt about his friend. I felt like an idiot.

"Nothing to say?" he asked.

Trying my best to hide my disappointment, I smiled too brightly. "I think Chase is really great."

"So you like him too?"

"Let's just say that if Chase asked me out, I wouldn't say no."

Jake leaned back in his seat, his expression hidden by the night. "Okay, then."

I narrowed my eyes at him. "Why didn't Chase just tell me himself?"

"Because he's a chicken."

The fire lets out a pop, pulling me back into the present, away from the memory. But not the lesson I learned from it. Jake has only ever had platonic feelings toward me. I am the queen at misreading him. Still, the feelings I put to death back then are doing their best to resurrect themselves now, and I'm not sure I have the strength to fight them.

"Anybody want one?" Liam holds up his roasting fork, which bows toward the ground with the weight of what appears to be an entire bag of jumbo marshmallows.

We all laugh.

The fire crackles as we enjoy our s'mores, and conversation gives way to reminiscing, and reminiscing gives way to Jake and his guitar. As he strums the chords, I close my eyes and relish this moment, right now. With a fire and music and all the people I love most.

EIGHT

My lofty goal for the evening? Do not look like an idiot in front of Jake. Which may sound simple enough, unless you've seen me dance. I had a few words with Lily over her idea on Saturday. She laughed, until I suggested that the maid of honor and best man should join us. I wish I hadn't, because now the maid of honor sits shotgun in my Honda and the best man sits in the middle of the backseat, grinning as I recite the complete story of my engagement with as much matter-of-factness as possible.

When I finish, Liam lets out a whistle. "Wow."

I grip the steering wheel tighter and turn onto the gravel road leading toward our destination.

"That's a pretty big offer for Jake to make."

"That's what I said," Lily mumbles.

I ignore her. "You know what happened

with Ben. He doesn't want me to feel the same regret that he feels."

Liam doesn't look convinced.

"Please, Liam. I know you probably think this is the dumbest idea in the world, but can you please not say anything to anyone?"

"I never said it was a dumb idea."

Lily whips her head around. "What?"

My grip loosens on the wheel. "Really?"

"It'll be like one last hurrah for Dad. Family will be there. Friends too." He leans forward between my seat and Lily's and props his elbows on our armrests. "Mom and Dad are both thrilled about it."

"But it's not real," Lily says.

"Neither is Santa, but you don't hear kids complaining."

Lily makes a face. "What does that have to do with anything?"

"I'm just saying that, sometimes, reality is overrated."

Sitting up straighter, I make eye contact with Liam in the rearview mirror. "So does that mean you'll behave?"

"Don't I always?"

It'll have to be good enough, because we have arrived. I pull up behind Jake's Chevy and park. Edna Pearl gives dance lessons in her husband's old barn, everything from your basic box step to the Viennese Waltz, all beneath the watchful eye and occasional commentary of her parrot, Polly. Edna and her husband never had any children of their own, but they did inherit her grandfather's bird after he passed twenty years ago.

The waning daylight fades in the west as we climb out of my car. Jake's truck door slams shut. Gravel crunches beneath his feet as he walks over, making our threesome into a familiar foursome. All of us seem to inhale at the same time, creating an awkward pause that has my insides doing some impressive acrobatics.

Liam chuckles, then offers his hand with a bow to Lily. "May I have this dance?"

With a rosy hue blossoming in her cheeks, she slips her hand into his and the two disappear inside the barn, leaving Jake and me alone, at dusk, surrounded by plowed fields and milk cows lowing in the distance.

I fiddle with the hem of my shirt. "Jake, thanks for doing this." It seems that's all I can say to him these days — thank you.

"You know, I'm not too bad of a dancer."

"Liar." I smile up at him. "I've danced with you before, Sawyer." Back in high school gym class, when I was the quiet, artsy sophomore and Jake was the cute, athletic senior. When the dreaded four-square unit came up, he offered to be my partner. Even then, he cared about my feelings. Didn't want me to be partnerless. Or maybe he wasn't willing to make a fool out of himself in front of any of the other girls. He couldn't have known, as we laughed and fumbled, that I lived for those ridiculous four-square lessons.

"Gym class was a long time ago, Tate." There's a teasing twinkle in his eye, one that makes them look extra blue. "A lot's changed since then."

So much, and yet nothing at all. "I'll believe it when I see it."

The familiar melody and crooning of Elvis Presley's "Can't Help Falling in Love" emanates from the barn. The lyrics have my insides resuming their circus act.

"Looks like they're starting without us." Jake holds out his arm, motioning for me to go ahead. As soon as we step inside, I spot Dad waltzing Mom around the floor while Liam engages Lily in a spastic polka, hopping her across the barn in complete disregard of the music's beat. They swoop past Polly, who squawks from her bird stand.

The music stops.

Liam does too. "Hey, I was just getting the hang of it."

Lily looks flushed. I can see the grin itch-ing to take full shape.

"We were doing the box step, dear." Edna lets out a long-suffering sigh, then spots Jake and me standing in the barn door. "The bride and groom are here!"

Dad turns around and smiles at me. There's a glow to his cheeks. "Hey, sweetheart."

"Hi, Dad."

Edna claps her hands, gathering our attention. "You, my lovelies, are late."

"Sorry," Jake says.

I nod toward the parrot, who shuffles along her perch. "How's Polly?"

"As fit as a fiddle. Now, Mr. Sawyer, do you know the basic box step, or would you like me to lead you through it?"

"I think I'm good."

"Okay, then! Let's start again. Remember your carriage, men. And ladies, you follow their lead." Edna flips on the stereo. "Take your women, gentlemen."

Jake presses his warm palm against the small of my back and takes my hand, his grip firm and confident as he moves us in perfect synchronization to Elvis's crooning and Edna's counting above the music.

I narrow my eyes up at him. "Jacob Elliott Sawyer."

His cheeks dimple. "I'm just getting

warmed up."

Elvis turns into Vince Gill who turns into Harry Connick Jr. And just like that, my worry dissolves. It's impossible to look like an idiot with Jake leading me around the dance floor. Edna focuses most of her attention on Dad, because Liam is hopeless and Jake doesn't need instruction. Jake has the box step mastered. We laugh and we tease and we dance until Edna turns off the music and teaches us the basic step for swing dancing. Jake wasn't kidding about getting warmed up. He already knows the basics, and then some, delighting Edna so much that she steals my partner, calling out instructions to Liam and Dad while Jake twirls and flings her around. He keeps catching my eye as he does so, smiling smugly. I smile back, arms crossed, shaking my head, because this is most definitely not the same Jake who stepped on my toes during four-square.

When Edna finally lets him go, he helps me figure out the steps to Sammy Davis Jr.'s "Love Me or Leave Me," and then "Jump, Jive an' Wail" comes on, and we're off. I don't even have to think. Not about my steps, or Dad's cancer, or even what will happen after the wedding.

"Where in the world did you learn how to dance?"

"In college." He twirls me around. "I had to take some sort of fitness elective, and my roommate convinced me dance would be fun."

I let him fling me out and pull me in. "Remind me to thank your roommate someday."

"Will do."

I look over at Dad, flirting with Mom, his rhythm nowhere near as good as Jake's but much better than Liam's, and I decide that my brother is right. Reality is overrated. This wedding has made my parents happy. And honestly? It's made me happy too. Maybe swapping out my present reality for this shinier, happier version — where Jake is my fiancé and Dad is healthy — wouldn't be the worst thing in the world. Like the make-believe games Liam and I used to play when we were little kids. They were only really fun when we fully committed.

The music fades. Jake twirls me around one last time, then dips me toward the floor. And as we smile at one another, trying to catch our breath, I find myself thinking, for the first time in a long time, that God might give us a miracle yet. He can do it. God can heal my father. At some point, I stopped really believing that. But with Jake looking down at me and Mom's and Lily's laughter mingling with Edna's coaching and Polly's squawks, I can imagine that maybe, just maybe, there's a happy ending in this after all.

NINE

I had a dream once where I knew I was dreaming. It was right after Dad was diagnosed with cancer, but in the dream, he wasn't sick. In fact, my dad could fly. Not only that, he could take me with him. Even though I knew I was asleep in my bed, I didn't want to wake up. I wanted to exist in that dream forever — with me and my healthy dad and his invisible wings.

I find myself in that same place now, except this time, I'm not asleep.

Between my duties at the clinic, planning a wedding, and helping with the Fall Harvest Festival, avoiding reality has not been as hard as one might think. People around town congratulate me about my engagement and, somehow, I smile and say thank you with a genuineness that borders on alarming. The only thing threatening my happy delusion right now is time. Sighing, I pull two bottles of Baumeister root beer from my fridge, remove the caps with the souvenir bottle opener Lily gave me last Christmas, and scan the calendar magnetized to my freezer.

Despite the hustle and bustle October has ushered into my life, I've done my best to protect each day, draw it out. Resist the rush. I've set new hours at the clinic, closing every Friday at noon so I can enjoy the afternoons and evenings with my parents and Jake. Last weekend we picked pumpkins at Sawyer Farm and had fun carving them while Mom baked the seeds. We've even gone to a couple of high school football games, rooting on our alma mater with Styrofoam cups of hot chocolate. But a day will only stretch so far. Time keeps marching onward, and somehow, here I am, the Fall Harvest Festival today and the wedding next weekend. Like that dreaded alarm clock, it's only a matter of ticktocks before life wrenches me awake.

As far as the wedding goes, Lily and I have managed to finalize most of the details. The ceremony will take place outside at Sawyer Farm. The reception will immediately follow, with barbecue pork sandwiches and a makeshift dance floor in the large barn. We've wrapped burnt peanuts in bright orange plastic wrap for wedding favors. Sent rustic gold invitations with bold red print to family and friends, most of them Dad's. We met with the florist to put together bouquets of red roses, orange calla lilies, burgundy Oriental lilies, and soft green hydrangeas. And we met with Eloise at her bakery, deciding on a caramel cake with ribbons of dark chocolate and buttercream frosting. If Lily rightly suspects I'm catering more to my father's preferences than my own, she keeps it to herself.

The sound of a pounding hammer filters through my opened kitchen window, and a flash of what my dreamworld future could be fills the contours of my imagination — Jake fixing the front porch, a dark-haired, blue-eyed little boy crouching nearby with a toy hammer clutched in his pudgy fist, a girl with blonde curls playing hopscotch on the sidewalk, and my parents stopping by for a Saturday morning visit, enjoying every moment of grandparenthood. My yellow Lab, Samson, nudges his wet nose against my hand, and the vision pops, leaving an empty, sad space in its wake.

Not wanting to be alone with it, I pick up the two bottles of root beer and head out to the porch, Samson on my heels. The screen door creaks open, then whaps shut behind us. I inhale the autumn air deep into my lungs, relishing its freshness. Fall is never long enough, not in northern Wisconsin. Here, the world is all too eager to rush into the cold days of winter. But this year has been a treat. Along with the perfect temperature for sweatshirts and jeans and stocking caps, the leaves have stayed on the trees longer than usual, turning into vibrant shades of gold, yellow, and red. Fall is a season of waiting. A long, drawn-out pause before the world falls asleep, and I find myself cherishing every moment.

Jake finishes wrenching up a loose floorboard, then slides his hammer into his tool belt. I offer him a root beer and he sits down beside me on the step. Samson licks Jake's arm, receives a scratch behind his ear, then trots off to sniff around the bushes.

"To a better porch," I say, raising my bottle.

He clinks his against mine and we drink in comfortable quiet, savoring the frothy sweetness that is old-fashioned Baumeister root beer — nostalgia in a bottle. Finally, when our drinks are half gone, he nudges me with his shoulder. "What are you thinking about so intently over there, Tate?"

I smile down at the step. It's not the first time he's asked the question, one I'm dying to reciprocate, because I never know what he's thinking. Not when it comes to Jake Sawyer. I misread his cues back then, and I still do now. He'll press his hand against the small of my back or whisper something in my ear, and I never know why. To play the part? Or is there something more to it? "I'm thinking that I'm glad the festival is tonight."

"It's kept you and Lily busy."

"Next year when she asks me to be on the committee, I think I'll say no." Next year is something I don't want to think about.

He takes a sip of his root beer. "We should go."

"To the festival?"

He nods.

"We go every year."

"I mean together."

"Oh — yeah." For some reason, my ears turn warm.

"I'll stop by around seven. We can walk over."

"Sure."

"Good." He tips the bottle up to his lips to finish off what remains of his root beer, showing off those ridiculously cute dimples in the process. "It's a date."

TEN

My doorbell rings at seven o'clock sharp. Samson barks, and my heart flutters. All day I've replayed Jake's words and the way he looked when he said them. *Good. It's a date.* They are easily spoken, innocuous words, yet I can't help but assign them meaning. I check my reflection one last time in my downstairs bathroom mirror, grab two cans of green beans off my kitchen counter, wrap a scarf around my neck, give Samson a good-bye kiss between his eyes, and step outside onto the porch.

"Hi," I say, a little too breathlessly.

"You look nice."

"Thanks. So do you." He wears what he normally wears — flannel shirt showing beneath an unzipped Carhartt and well-worn jeans. Only he's clean-shaven and sans his usual baseball hat. I'm probably reading too much into that too.

Jake holds up a plastic bag that already

237

contains one can of pumpkin pie filling and another of cranberry sauce. I place my green beans inside.

"Shall we?" he asks.

Nodding, I pull my hair out from beneath my scarf and zip my coat all the way up. My breaths escape in puffs of iridescent white before disappearing into the night as we stroll through my front yard, down the street, toward the center of town.

I can't tell if the electricity I feel between us is a real thing or self-fabricated. All I know is that I'm hyperaware of all things Jake — the way he shortens his stride to match mine, the way his slightly-longer-than-usual hair curls up a bit over his ear, the closeness of our knuckles. All of it has me more nervous than I should be. "So how's your dad doing?" I ask.

"Pretty good. His arthritis has been flaring up with the colder weather, but he's never been much of a complainer."

"Like father, like son."

Jake smiles.

As we walk and talk about everything but the wedding, I try not to feel guilty about Lily, who called earlier and asked if I wanted to grab a bite to eat at Patty's before heading to the festival. Every year we've gone together, even when I was with Chase, since he always had to work. I felt awkward telling her that I was going with Jake and tried to make up for it by inviting her to join us, then immediately regretted it because I wasn't sure of Jake's intentions. What if his words — *Good. It's a date.* — weren't innocuous at all? What if Jake really did want this to be a date? It didn't matter, though, because Lily declined. We could find each other there. I'm pretty sure her glum tone had less to do with me and more to do with Liam — who is away on another one of his trips and hasn't returned Lily's phone calls.

"You're kind of quiet," Jake says. "Something on your mind?"

"My brother's just being my brother."

"What does that mean?"

"I'm pretty sure he's giving Lily mixed signals. She's starting to fall for him again, and now he's backing off." Our arms swing in rhythm with our footsteps. I can't tell if he wants to take my hand or not, so I leave it out of my pocket, despite the cold and no gloves.

"N-C-L."

"Huh?"

Jake chuckles. "No Commitment Liam."

"Oh, yeah." That had been his nickname in high school. Unfortunately for Lily, the nickname still applies today.

"For what it's worth, I think your brother has always had a thing for Lily. He just doesn't have any clue what to do about it."

"Well, he better figure it out soon. She won't wait forever."

Jake scratches his jaw, his brow furrowing as the growing hum of activity catches my attention. We've officially reached the town square, where children jump in the bounce house, costume-clad teenagers solicit townsfolk to play carnival games, and the animals in the petting zoo oink and squawk and bleat. Several people meander around the baking booths, sampling various pumpkin-inspired recipes, voting for their favorite. Now is when Jake takes my hand, which makes me think the gesture really is for show.

We find Patty first, halfway hidden by a friendly-faced scarecrow. She works in front of a table stacked high with canned food.

"Evening, Patty," Jake says.

She stops sorting the cans into boxes and beams at our joined hands, the whites of her eyes looking even whiter against the night and her dark skin. "Well, if it isn't our town lovebirds."

She has taken to calling us this so often, it's caught on. I can't go in for my Monday morning coffee without hearing the phrase from Jake's great-uncle Al and his buddy Rupert, at least twice. "Seems like a great turnout this year."

"You're telling me. Lily really outdid herself."

Jake sets the plastic bag with our cans on the table. "Here's some more to add to the pantry. Happy fall harvest."

Patty wishes us the same. We wave good-bye and walk through the display of antique tractors — on loan from a few of Mayfair's local farmers — then head straight for the candied apples, which weigh more than any food item should ever be allowed to weigh. We take sticky bites while checking out the jack-o'-lanterns, which range from impressively elaborate to crudely simple, all submitted by Mayfair residents. Jake finds one with an uncanny resemblance to our old history teacher, Mr. DeVree, who had a giant forehead and the world's largest comb-over. I put a tally mark on the sheet in front of it. At the end of the festival, the person with the most tallies takes home a pumpkin-carving trophy. Phil Nixon has seven proudly displayed on the front counter of his convenience store.

"Mr. DeVree gets your vote, huh?"

"For the sake of nostalgia."

Jake slowly tilts his head at the pumpkin. "I'm not sure it's really supposed to be him though."

"Too late. Penciled tally marks cannot be revoked." I toss the remains of my apple into a nearby garbage can and lick the stickiness from my fingers. When I finish, Jake is staring at me. "What?"

"You have some caramel . . ." He touches his lip.

"Oh." Embarrassed, I try to rub the caramel away. "Did I get it?"

"No." Jake steps closer and touches his lip again. "It's right here."

I try more toward the left.

Jake's mouth pulls up into a half smile.

"It's still there?"

"Here, let me." He gently wipes the corner of my upper lip with the pad of his thumb, our bodies so close they are almost touching, the scent of cedar emanating from his skin.

I look up at him through my eyelashes. As our eyes lock, there's something in his expression — an intensity that has my heartbeat picking up speed. For one crazy second, I'm positive he's going to kiss me. But then his eyelids flutter and he steps away.

"Hey, Lily," Jake says, rubbing the back of

his neck.

I spin around and find Lily standing not too far behind us, a sharpness in her green eyes that leaves me feeling flustered, as if I've been caught breaking the rules. "Hey, when'd you get here?"

"A while ago." Her attention flicks from Jake to me. "Was I interrupting something?"

I laugh — a nervous, too-loud laugh that is followed by a silence so painful I'm dying to fill it. Lily might be keeping her thoughts to herself when it comes to this engagement, but her opinion has been clear from the start, and right now I don't want to deal with it. I stick my hands into my coat pockets. "Did you vote for your favorite pumpkin?"

"Not yet."

"Jake and I haven't tasted any of the recipes. We were going to go try some if you want to come along." As much as I don't want to extend the invitation, this is Lily. I can't leave her behind while I trounce off with Jake.

She shrugs.

As we make our way past the gazebo, where Wayne and his son shuck corn like it's the race of their lives, it's obvious that Lily is making a concerted effort to avoid Jake. I can tell he notices it too by the furrow in his brow. It leaves me feeling stuck in the middle — like the two are fighting and it's up to me to get them to make up. "We're getting our dresses altered tomorrow at two," I remind her. The tailor had kindly agreed to come in on a Sunday afternoon to accommodate my hectic schedule.

"I know."

"Have you been fitted for your tux yet?" I ask Jake.

He glances at Lily, whose rotten mood has tossed an invisible blanket of tension over what was shaping up to be a very enjoyable evening. I try to remind myself that she's upset about Liam, but it doesn't help as much as it should. "I went yesterday. Liam's going this Tuesday when he gets back."

We reach the booths with all the baked goods. I try to enjoy the yummy smell of brown sugar, cinnamon, and pumpkin spice, but the awkwardness between my two best friends is beyond distracting. So much so that I barely taste my bite of Clara O'Malley's famous chocolate pumpkin bread.

"So how does this work?" Lily finally asks. "Am I supposed to throw you a bachelorette party? I'm not sure I understand the etiquette for this type of situation."

I shoot Lily a look.

She ignores me. "Is Liam throwing you a bachelor party?"

Jake's furrow deepens. "I'm not really a bachelor party kind of guy."

I hurry over to the next booth, where Eloise stands beside a glorious-looking pumpkin cake with ivory whipped cream frosting, tiny pieces to sample tucked inside Dixie cups. "This looks delicious, Eloise," I say, handing one to Jake, another to Lily.

"If you like it, it's not too late to change your wedding cake order to pumpkin!" She smiles serenely — the perfect picture of a grandmotherly baker. "So, have you two decided where you're going for your honeymoon?"

I swallow my bite of cake, hating Lily's hot stare on the side of my face. "Oh, we're, uh . . . not taking one."

Eloise's serene smile crumples. "No honeymoon? Oh, but you have to take a honeymoon. It's the most romantic part."

Lily's stare does not relent. It is an annoying, unwelcome reminder that this story I'm living isn't real. That it's only a matter of time before the alarm clock goes off and forces me awake. Resentment stirs in my chest. "We didn't have time to plan one."

"Well, maybe you can take a late one, in

the wintertime." Her face brightens. "You could take your wife skiing," she says to Jake. "A nice lodge with a fireplace so you can enjoy a crackling fire at night. Sounds romantic, don't you think?"

Jake agrees, and we thank Eloise for the taste of cake and move on to a whole table filled with pumpkin pie. I don't have an appetite for any of it.

"You'll want to be careful on those ski lifts," Lily says. "Emma's afraid of heights."

"I know," Jake says.

"So, am I supposed to get you a wedding gift?"

I narrow my eyes at my friend.

"Or am I allowed to skip the pretense?"

"Lily," I say sharply.

"It's an honest question."

Maybe so, but I don't want to hear it. "Look, I know you're upset about Liam."

"This has nothing to do with Liam."

Jake pulls at his collar.

I can't stand his discomfort. I can't even stand my own. My frustration mounts. I don't want to deal with this right now. Not tonight. "I'll be back."

"Where are you going?" Jake asks.

"To get some cider." Without giving either a chance to object or follow, I pivot on my heels and weave through the crowd, reality threatening to descend. I do my best to fight it. What is Lily's deal anyway? It's not like my choices are harming anyone, and it's not like she's never made a questionably moral decision before either. Jake understands. Liam understands. I know my mom will understand. So why can't Lily?

As I cross my arms and continue walking, the *clop, clop, clop* of horse hooves and the sound of my name break through my internal venting. I look up from my shoes and spot my parents sitting in a horse-drawn carriage, illuminated by the street-light, finishing the loop around the square. Mom sits on the edge of the bench and waves in my direction as the driver brings the horse to a stop. I walk up beside them.

"What are you doing here all by yourself?" Mom says. "I thought you were coming with Jake."

"I did. I was just trying to find us some cider." I look over my shoulder, toward the baking booths. "He's back there with Lily."

Her mother radar must be on full alert, because her eyes flicker in that way they do whenever she senses I'm in turmoil. "Why don't you take a ride with your dad and I'll go find us some cider."

"Are you sure?"

"Of course. Enjoy a carriage ride with

your dad. I'll find Jake and Lily and let them know where you are." The driver helps Mom down from the carriage, then helps me up. I sit on the bench, wrap my arm around Dad's, and rest my head on his shoulder, savoring the rise and fall of his breathing. We ride without speaking for a while, taking in the sounds of the festival, the clopping of the horse hooves, the crisp evening air, and the moonlight spilling its light onto the tops of the trees. It's not until we round the second corner that I remove my head from his shoulder and look at him. "You've been looking healthy, Dad."

"I've been feeling healthy."

The statement has my hope growing into something desperate and unwieldy, something that refuses to be contained.

"The meds are doing a great job at managing the headaches and nausea."

"Maybe it's not the meds," I offer.

"Maybe."

But he doesn't believe it. I can tell. "You don't think it's possible? All the people who are praying for you to be healed — our whole church, this town — you don't think God can answer?"

"I know he can, honey." He pats my hand. "I'm just not sure he will."

And just like that, the dream I've been living in pops. As if it were nothing more substantial than a soap bubble.

ELEVEN

It's hard to fall asleep after you wake up from a dream as long as mine. I toss and turn in bed, wondering how a night that started with so much promise could turn out like this. I keep thinking about Jake's confusion as I claimed a headache and he walked me home early. I could tell he wasn't sure what went wrong. At what point did the night derail so horribly?

In the morning, I wake up bright and early with swollen eyes and a foggy brain — a crying jag hangover. I don't want to go to church. I want to stay in bed. But if I'm not there, my parents will want to know why. So I take a shower and get dressed and try to cover up the aftereffects of a horrible night's sleep with makeup, then head to Patty's as soon as she opens the doors at seven, hoping a giant cup of hot coffee will do the trick. Not only do I have to make it through church at ten, but I also have to meet up with Lily at two o'clock to have our dresses altered.

I step inside Patty's to the usual early Sunday morning patrons — Randy Crandall, our town selectman, eating a hardy breakfast with his wife; Mick Horowitz, who bears an uncanny resemblance to his schnauzer; and Kathleen Baudin, the town cat lady, who makes a habit of dropping by the clinic to give me pamphlets on the dangers of declawing, as if vet school didn't educate me properly on the subject. Occasionally, she'll even sneak one under the windshield wipers of my car.

Patty appears from the kitchen and sets a plate of eggs and bacon in front of Mick. I join them both at the counter.

"Well, look who it is all bright-eyed and bushy-tailed," Patty says with a playful wink.

"Not feeling the best this morning." I set my purse on the counter. "Hi, Mick."

"Morning, Emma."

"How's Marty's leg doing?" Marty is his schnauzer. I often get their names mixed up.

He cuts apart his eggs with his fork, steam and yolk oozing from the wound. "His limp's mostly gone."

"That's good." I cover a yawn. "Make sure to bring him in if it comes back."

"Will do."

I look at Patty through bleary eyes. "I need coffee, stat. In the biggest cup you have."

"Decaf?"

I give her my best are-you-crazy face. It's a weird suggestion in the morning. Especially since I never do decaf. Not even when I stop by in the afternoon. "Decaf is not my friend, Patty."

She sets her pudgy arms on the counter and leans toward me. "Don't you think you ought to make it your friend?"

All right, now I'm officially confused. I mirror Patty's posture. "Why would I do that?"

"I'm no doctor, but I always thought caffeine wasn't good for the baby."

It takes me a second to fully comprehend what she's implying. When I do, my eyes go buggy. "The baby?" I glance at Mick, who pretends not to listen, then back at the woman behind the counter. "You think I'm pregnant?"

Patty frowns. "Aren't you?"

"No. Why would you think that?"

"Stacy Green told all the gals at bunco on Thursday." I must look pale, because Patty grabs a nearby coffeepot, sets a tall mug in front of me, and fills it to the rim. "She said it was the reason you were getting married so fast."

What an assumption to make! "And you believed her?"

"It's nothing to be ashamed of. A baby is wonderful news."

"Patty, I'm not marrying Jake because I'm pregnant." Anger coalesces with my shock, waking me up before I have a trace of caffeine in my bloodstream. "I'm marrying Jake because I'm in love with him."

The instant the words are out, I realize two things. They are true. And I am a fool.

I pound on Lily's front door, then pace like a caged lion. I feel feral, like I can't exist in my own skin. My mounting anger — at Stacy Green for the rumor, at Patty for believing it, at myself for the position I've put myself in — has me wishing I could crawl out of it. As unfair as it may be, I need a scapegoat. I stop and knock on her door again.

A lock clicks from the other side and the door opens. Lily appears, still in her flannel pajamas. Her brows knit in confusion then worry as she takes in what can no doubt be my frazzled appearance. "Emma? What is wrong with you?"

"What was your deal last night?"

She gives me her deadpan stare, then

opens the door wider. "Do you want to come in?"

No, I don't want to come in. I want to rewind to last night, make Lily behave, make my father take back his words, make the rumor go away, and continue on in happy oblivion. "Did you have to make those comments you made? What happened to giving me your support?"

"I've supported you for the past month."

"No, you haven't. You've been silently judging me."

"I haven't been judging you, Emma. I've been worried about you." Lily's shoulders sag. "At some point, you're going to have to face the fact that your father is dying, and a fake wedding isn't going to fix it."

I can feel myself slowly deflating, right there on Lily's front porch. Because her words are true. As much as I don't want them to be, they are. My father has terminal cancer. All the pretending in the world won't make it go away. And now, to add insult to injury, I have gone and given my heart to a man who never asked for it. "The town thinks I'm pregnant."

Lily bites her lip. "I may have heard that rumor."

"When?"

"Last night, before I met up with you and

Jake. I heard a couple of the Bunco Babes talking about it."

I shake my head, tears welling up in my eyes. "Lily, my dad is dying."

"I know."

"And I'm in love with Jake." I shrug helplessly, because what else is there to do?

She pulls me inside and wraps me in a hug. "Would it help if I made cinnamon rolls?"

TWELVE

It's only nine o'clock when I pull up behind Jake's Chevy and shift into park, idling in his gravel drive. But it feels as though I've lived an entire lifetime since crawling out of bed this morning. After a long heart-to-heart with Lily over cinnamon rolls and coffee, my voice is nearly hoarse and my eyes require Visine. But I know what I have to do. I can't keep pretending. As well-intentioned as Jake and I might have been, it's time to be honest. If only my heart hadn't fallen so hard in the midst of our make-believe, then maybe what I need to do wouldn't feel so impossibly hard.

My future stretches ahead of me — no Dad, no Jake — a landscape too bleak for contemplation. Twisting the now-familiar ring around my finger, I look out the windshield, taking in the expanse of Jake's property. Pine trees dot the periphery of a well-kept yard. A cabin-style ranch home sits on one side of the drive and a two-story man-shed sits on the other, only it's set farther away from the road. Jake has all the benefits of country living — the privacy, the property, the quiet — and none of the hassle or hard work that comes with a farm. Over the past several weeks, people have asked whether we'd live in my bungalow or Jake's cabin. Even though it was not a decision we really had to make, I'd find myself weighing the pros and cons. Usually, Jake's place would win.

Letting out a long breath, I swing open the car door, step outside, and head toward Jake's house, each step heavier than the one before. When I finally muster up the strength to knock, Jake doesn't answer. I turn around and head toward the shed, hoping he's at the hardware store. The place is closed on Sundays, but that doesn't mean Jake's not there, taking inventory or cleaning before church. If he's not here, that will give me more time. To think about what I will say. To rehearse the right words. To drum up the determination.

But a sound comes from the shed as I walk around the corner and stand in the large doorway. The sun shines at my back, illuminating the space inside — filled with beautiful handmade furniture in various stages of completion. Jake stands with his back to me, already dressed in his Sunday church khakis, sanding the top of a gorgeous oak table.

A bit of sawdust tickles my nose and I sneeze.

Jake spins around and broadens his posture, as if attempting to block the lovely table behind him. "Hey." He sets his palm on the edge of it and pulls at his earlobe, strangely flustered. "What are you doing here?"

I step inside and close the distance between us, my heart thudding so slowly, it could be a funeral dirge. The closer I get, the more Jake expands his shoulders and the more charged the air between us seems to grow. By the time I'm all the way there, I reach past him and touch the table, halfway expecting an electrical zap. "Jake, this is really exquisite."

His posture relaxes. "You like it?"

"Like it?" My fingers linger on the wood surface. "I love it."

"Good. Because it's yours."

I look up. "What?"

He smiles. "Patty kept heckling me about a wedding present. And you're always complaining about that small table in your kitchen." He scratches the nape of his neck, making his baseball hat tip up a little. "So I decided to make you a bigger one."

Jake made me a table — one that could comfortably seat a family of six. Does it mean anything to him? Or is this just another one of his kind gestures?

"Hey, Emma." He dips his head to catch my attention. "Is everything okay?"

The concern on his face undoes me. How could I have let myself get into this mess? Why didn't I just say no to Jake's proposition that day on my porch? Laugh it off like any sane, normal person would do? I know why. Because I had been in denial then — and a little bit in shock too. I shake my head. "I can't do this."

"Can't do what?"

I close my eyes. "The wedding."

Jake says nothing.

I take a deep breath and force my voice to come out steady. "I'm so incredibly grateful that you were willing to do this for me and my dad. But it's not real. And I can't keep pretending that it is." I look up at him, hoping and praying he will argue. Hoping and praying he will tell me it was real for him.

He looks down at me, his face etched with desperation, like he wants nothing more than to reach out and sand away my hurt, patch up the broken bits. A hope I don't want to feel bubbles in my heart. It's a hope I've felt once before, after my high school graduation. "Emma, I'm sorry. I thought . . ." He shakes his head and drags his hand down his face. "I thought this would make you happy."

"It did for a while."

"That's all I want, you know. For you to be happy."

Happy.

Like a flower left too long in the sun without any water, my heart wilts. It's not enough. It's not even close. I slip the ring from my finger, place it in Jake's broad palm, and curl his fingers over the gift. He looks bewildered, dumbfounded. Like this is all happening too fast. I want to tell him that *he* makes me happy. I want to tell him that *us* makes me happy. But my throat is too tight to get the words out and I won't put Jake in that position. I won't jeopardize our friendship. So I squeeze his hand, then turn around and walk away.

I hate that he lets me go.

THIRTEEN

I sit inside my parents' house, waiting for them to come home from their usual post-church date, unmoving except for my hand, which strokes Oscar, who purrs on my lap. The front door doesn't open until almost one o'clock.

Mom laughs as she steps inside, and I wonder if they are in a dream of their own, if she is in denial and if Dad is letting her live there. But then I remember our carriage ride and our time in front of the fire and I think no. There is a big difference between avoiding reality by pretending and enjoying reality for as long as it's possible.

Mom hangs her purse on the hook by the door — the one Dad installed just for her since she has a habit of misplacing it around the house — and stops when she turns and sees me on their sofa. "Emma, what are you doing here in the dark?"

Oscar jumps off my lap, away from his free

massage, and lies down in his favorite spot — where the sunlight usually shines in from the large picture window and warms a patch of carpet. But clouds have rolled in and the sun is nowhere to be seen.

"We never saw you at church," she adds. "We didn't see Jake either."

I try to answer, but I can't seem to find my voice.

Dad slips off his shoes, a bag of goodies from Eloise's bakery in hand. He and Mom exchange a concerned look.

"Emma?"

My voice refuses to cooperate. It's like my body has decided that stillness is good, stillness is tolerable, so it will never move again.

Mom takes the bag from Dad, then comes over to me and pulls me off the couch. "Come on. Whatever is bothering you can't be so bad that we can't discuss it over cookies. We got a few extra, in case you and Jake stopped by."

I ignore Dad's inquiring eyes and follow Mom into the kitchen, where she removes three plates and three glasses from a cupboard. Dad walks in behind us and opens the cupboard over the stove, where we've always kept our medicine. He uncaps a pill bottle and shakes a large white capsule into his palm. Mom fills one of the glasses with milk, hands it over, and Dad swallows the pill. His face has a pallor to it that wasn't there yesterday. Or maybe it was and I just wasn't willing to see it. Either way, it's a subtle reminder that I can't go back to dreamworld, even if I wanted to.

"I have to tell you guys something."

Dad looks at me, and Mom waits to respond while she fills the other two glasses with milk and puts the gallon container back in the refrigerator. "We know it's not true, Emma."

The words pull my chin back. "You know?"

"Of course, sweetheart."

"Then why did you . . . ?" I'm so confused. Why did they let me go on then, if they knew Jake and I weren't really engaged? That isn't like them at all.

"We heard the rumor last night and didn't believe it for one second."

I look from Mom to Dad, trying to make sense of her words.

"You and Jake would have told us if you were pregnant. Your father and I know that. This is a small town, and one of the drawbacks of a small town is that rumors fly. Let people think what they will think. They will figure out the truth soon enough."

"We're not getting married," I blurt.

Mom and Dad stare at me, blinking but silent. I wait for my words to sink in. I wait for them to register.

Instead, Mom rattles her head, as if shaking her thoughts into place. "I don't understand. You and Jake aren't getting married at all because of a rumor?"

"No, it's not because of a rumor." I look down at my shoes, unable to face their disappointment. "I'm sorry. For all of it. I'm sorry for lying. I'm sorry for getting your hopes up. But most of all, Dad, I'm sorry that I can't give you that last item on your bucket list."

"My bucket list?"

"I saw it. When you were in Door County. I didn't mean to. I wasn't snooping. I was putting mail on your desk and your journal fell and your bucket list fell with it . . ." I fidget with the zipper of my jacket. "I wish you could walk me down the aisle. More than anything. But I can't keep pretending."

Mom sinks into the closest chair, as if my confession has buckled her knees. "You mean you and Jake were never really engaged?"

Shame sets my cheeks on fire. Now that my feet are firmly planted in reality, it all seems so foolish. What were Jake and I going to do — wait it out until my dad was gone and then come out with the truth? "I don't know what I was thinking. It was the only thing you couldn't cross off your list. So I went home and Jake was there, like Jake always is and . . . I don't know. I'd been feeling so helpless and it was something I could do."

Dad walks across the kitchen and stands next to Mom at the table. "Emma."

A braver woman would look up, but right now, I am not brave. I'm the exact opposite of brave.

"I wrote that list two years ago, when you were engaged to Chase."

I bite my lip. Mom has forgotten all about the stack of plates, the glasses of milk on the counter, the cookies in the bag. I think I might have permanently stolen her appetite.

"Sit down," Dad says as he drops into a chair next to Mom.

I obey without question.

Dad lets out a long sigh. "Please look at me."

I pull my attention away from my jacket zipper and force myself to give my father the attention he deserves.

"Do I want to give you away? Yes. It is something I have imagined from the moment you wrapped those tiny fingers around mine. But Emma, walking you down the aisle was never about me. It was about you."

My eyes blur out of focus. I blink furiously, determinedly.

"For your joy." Dad reaches across the table and sets his hand over mine. "Giving you away would only be special if the man I was giving you away to was prepared to love and cherish you the way I've always loved and cherished you."

My chin trembles. "I wish that guy could be Jake."

Mom and Dad don't look shocked. I think they've always known. I think that's why they believed us when we made the announcement. They never questioned my side of the equation.

"Maybe it will be," Dad says.

I shake my head. "I gave him the opportunity and he didn't take it." I picture Jake, unmoving as I handed him back his grandmother's ring. "He didn't even reach."

"Sometimes we men are slow to figure things out." Dad smiles. "Give him some time. He might come around."

As much as I would love for Dad to be right, I can't help but think that if Jake hasn't figured it out by now, he's never going to figure it out.

FOURTEEN

Raindrops spit from a bloated sky and splatter against my windshield. The sunny morning has given way to a dreary afternoon, appropriate weather for cancellations. I do not hem and haw or drag my heels or dip my toe into the water. I don't even let Lily help me. I created the mess. The least I can do is clean it up. So as soon as I leave my parents' house, I dive in, trying not to imagine the news spreading across Mayfair faster than kennel cough. I have already called and canceled the barbecue, the flowers, the alterations — leaving voice mail messages wherever live people were taking the Sabbath off. All I have left is the cake. Jake can take care of the venue, since it's his aunt and uncle's place.

My heart hurts, but I refuse to indulge in any wallowing. I'm not going to spend whatever time remains with my dad pining after Jake. I pull up to the curb and park my car as thunder rumbles in the distance, the black horizon hinting at the wrath to come. I climb out of my car, hurry across the street through the cold drizzle, and step inside the warmth of Eloise's bakery. I am glad she opens her shop on Sunday afternoons.

She smiles behind the counter, her face wrinkled with age and laugh lines. "Emma! What can I get for you this afternoon — some muffins?"

"Four of your chocolate cupcakes." Because it's my vet technician's birthday tomorrow and I'd like to take him a treat for all the extra hours he's been working. "And I need to cancel the wedding cake."

Her eyes widen. "Cancel the cake? But you have to have cake at the wedding."

"There isn't going to be a wedding." The tone of my voice does not invite further questions. I can answer them later, when my emotions aren't so raw.

Eloise's face falls. "Oh, well, I'm sure sorry to hear about that."

"Me too."

She processes my payment and hands me a container of cupcakes as the pitter-patter of raindrops turns into a downpour that pounds against the roof of the bakery. I turn around and look out the window. Normally,

I'd wait inside and enjoy a muffin and some hot tea until the downpour passes, but I can feel Eloise studying the back of my head. Staying would only invite questions. I'd rather get wet. Clutching the cupcakes under one arm, I pull up the hood of my jacket, toss a wave over my shoulder, and make a mad dash outside, over the curb, out into the street.

"Emma!"

I stop in the middle of the road. Turn slowly. And my breath catches. Because it's Jake. Standing several paces away, his hat and the shoulders of his jacket soaked through, his chest heaving as though he sprinted all the way from his house.

"Jake?" I shield my eyes. "What are you doing?"

"I'm a liar," he shouts over at me.

"What?" I squint through the rain, positive the din from the storm warped Jake's words.

He steps closer, joining me in the middle of the street, and the storm around us is nothing compared to the one raging in his eyes. "Earlier today I lied. When I told you that your happiness is all I care about." Rain wets his lips. "It should be, but it's not."

I shake my head, unwilling to believe. Unwilling to hope.

269

"I left because of you."

"What?"

"All those years ago. The reason I left town is because I couldn't watch you get married to Chase. What I should have told you this morning, what I should have told you that day I offered to marry you on the porch, what I should have told you that night after you graduated high school" — he wipes his hand down his face — "is that I love you."

I can't breathe. I can't even move.

"I feel like I've loved you forever, but I've never been able to say it. The timing was never right. You were my best friend's kid sister. I was going to college and then you were with Chase and then Ben died and your dad was diagnosed with cancer. And I never could tell if you felt the same way. But no regrets, remember?" Before I fully process what he's saying, Jake gets down on his knee, in the middle of the street, in the middle of the rain, and takes out a small velvet box from the pocket of his coat.

My hand moves to my chest.

He opens the box and inside is the same ring I've worn every day since we sat in Jake's idling truck outside my parents' home. Only he's offering it to me now, not to make our story more believable but

270

because this is real. Jake is down on one knee in the middle of the street in the pouring rain, and there's only one reason I know of for a man to get on one knee . . .

"Marry me."

Emotion climbs up my throat. I cup my hand over my mouth to trap the sob inside.

"I don't want a wedding, Emma. I want a marriage. To you. Because nothing — and I mean *nothing* — would make me happier than spending the rest of my life trying to make you happy." Jake looks up at me through the rain, waiting as his breath escapes in clouds of white.

Unable to remove my hand from my mouth, unable to show Jake the smile forming beneath my palm, I nod, my heart swelling with so much joy I think it might explode.

"Yes?"

I nod again, faster, and remove my hand. "Yes!"

And just like that, Jake has me in his arms. He twirls me in a circle, then kisses me — a rain-soaked, wonderful kiss with my feet off the ground, a kiss a thousand times better and more passionate than our first kiss in Patty's. And then we are both laughing, like we can't believe this moment. Like we can't believe ourselves.

"Do you really mean yes — not because of your dad's bucket list, but because this is what you want?"

"Jake, this is what I've wanted since the second grade."

He sets me down and presses his wet forehead against mine. "I am an idiot."

"Hey, that's my fiancé you're talking about. My real-life, not-fake fiancé." I stand up on my tiptoes and press my lips against his. It's a wonderful, giddy, heart-pattering feeling kissing Jake. I'm not sure I'll ever get over the wonder of it. "Now, if you don't mind, I'd really like that ring back."

Jake doesn't hesitate. As soon as it's back on my finger, he turns my hand up and kisses my palm. "Don't take it off again, okay?"

I shake my head. "Never."

FIFTEEN

Lily fixes my veil in the kitchen of the Sawyers' farmhouse, her eyes alight with all the excitement and happiness a maid of honor should feel for the bride. "Are you ready?"

I breathe in the beauty of this moment and the messy path that led to it. Our lives are such a muddled pot of heartache and blessing, loss and triumph, sorrow and joy. I nod and wring my hands, a lump already in my throat. "I think so."

Lily opens the door and we step out onto the porch, into the late October air. My father turns around, so handsome in his tuxedo, and a breath of forever passes between us. One I will carry with me for the rest of my life. I dab my knuckle beneath my lashes, a vain attempt to save my makeup.

I don't know how much time we have. His tumor is growing every day and his headaches are worsening. We could have two whole months — sixty lifetimes, each encompassed within a single day. Or he could be gone in two weeks. I don't know how this story will end. But I do know that I can enjoy right now. My father has taught me this. Today, he is here. So I will praise God for today, and trust in his provision for tomorrow.

He cups my cheek with his palm. "You, my daughter, are too stunning for words."

A tear gathers and spills.

Dad catches it on his thumb, then holds out his arm, and the three of us walk through the yard, beneath a canopy of trees that have not yet lost all their color, toward the rows of white chairs filled with family and friends, and the soothing melody of Lily's sister playing "Clair de Lune" on her violin. We stop in front of a pair of trees that hide us from view of our guests. Lily gives me a hug, hands me my bouquet of flowers, then joins Liam ahead. He winks at me with a proud smile on his face. Lily takes his arm and they make their way down the aisle. There is a brief pause of anticipation as the violin stops, then starts up again with Canon in D. Everyone stands. The sunlight dapples through the leaves.

I look up at my dad — the man who has

loved and cherished and protected me from the moment I entered this world. "Are you ready?"

"Emma, I've been ready for twenty-seven years."

Wrapping my arm tighter around his, I let my father lead me down the aisle. Toward Jake, my groom. The man who will love and cherish and protect me for as long as we both shall live.

ACKNOWLEDGMENTS

I'm a wordy person, so when Becky Philpott contacted me about writing a novella for their Year of Weddings series, I was honored but also a little frightened. Novels I could do. Novellas? Not so sure.

I had no idea that I would have so much fun writing this story! I fell in love with Jake and Emma and the small, quirky town of Mayfair, Wisconsin. I hope readers fall in love too!

A few shout-outs are most definitely in order . . .

A hearty thanks to all the people who have made this novella better than I could ever manage on my own — Becky Philpott, Jean Bloom, and Karli Cajka. It was a pleasure working with you!

Thank you to the entire team at Zondervan for inviting me to take part in such a fun project, Elizabeth Hudson for your passion and enthusiasm, and an especially loud shout-out to my fellow "bridesmaids." It's been an honor and a joy celebrating these novellas together!

Thank you to Marie Bates for giving me a sneak peek inside the life of a veterinarian, and to Joel Malm for helping me figure out the perfect occupation for adventure-seeking Liam. Any inaccuracies in the portrayal are all mine!

Carrie Pendergrass for sharing your husband's words to you at a time I really needed to hear them. They became the words Emma's dad shared with Emma in the horse carriage ride when she really needed to hear them. I pray they encourage readers as much as they did me!

Thanks, of course, to my agent, Rachelle Gardner, for all you do to get my work out there.

To my amazingly supportive husband and my wonderful family for all you do so that I can write.

To a lavishly good God for allowing me to do something that brings me such joy and for providing the words when I'm feeling wrung dry.

And to my fabulous readers — the ones who take that joy and multiply it exponentially with your support, your presence, and your encouragement. It's an honor to write stories for you, and I will continue as the Lord allows!

DISCUSSION QUESTIONS

1. In the beginning of the story, Emma finds her dad's bucket list. What are some things you would write on your own bucket list?
2. Jake knows what it's like to live with regret. Do you have any regrets in your life? Have you ever done something out of your comfort zone in order to avoid having regrets?
3. Emma saw her and Jake's "engagement" as a morally gray area. Do you agree? If you were in Emma's position, would you have done what she did? Of all the characters in *An October Bride,* who's reaction to the fake engagement did you relate to the most?
4. Halfway through the novel, Emma decides to enter completely into the fantasy world she is currently living in. Have you ever lived in denial about something in your life? What happened to finally make you face reality?

5. Emma has a lot of special relationships in this novel — her relationship with Jake, her relationship with Lily, and her relationship with her dad and her mom. Which relationship did you enjoy the most? What are some relationships you have in your own life?

6. There are a lot of quirky secondary characters in this story. Which one was your favorite?

ABOUT THE AUTHOR

Katie Ganshert graduated from the University of Wisconsin in Madison with a degree in education and worked as a fifth-grade teacher for several years before staying home to write full-time. She was born and raised in the Midwest, where she lives with her husband, their young son, and their goofy black Lab, Bubba. When she's not busy writing or playing or reading or snuggling, she is obsessing over the paperwork and the waiting that comes with adoption. Visit her website at katieganshert.com.

■ ■ ■ ■ ■

A NOVEMBER BRIDE

BETH K. VOGT

■ ■ ■ ■ ■

To Those Still Waiting for
Happily Ever After
". . . happy are those who trust in you."
Psalm 84:12b (NLT)

ONE

This was Sadie's star moment. The reason she collected recipes and watched cooking shows. Why she made color-coded, computerized grocery lists cross-referenced by availability and quality of items, store locations, and layouts. Spent hours shopping for fresh produce and meats and poultry — and sales, always sales.

At last, it was time for the presentation of the prepared dish.

She turned from the professional-grade oven, heat wafting against her back, dampening the cloth of her white chef jacket. *Was it still clean?* With a flourish and a well-practiced smile, she held the steaming dish aloft in her gloved hands. Inhaled the aroma of chicken in the bubbling sauce of Italian dressing, and topped with lightly browned, grated Parmesan cheese. At the last second, she remembered to nudge the oven door closed with her shoulder.

Hold the smile. Always hold the smile.

"Oh, this smells delectable."

Ugh. Maybe not the best word. Too late now.

Sadie set the deep red stoneware dish on the waiting trivet, turning it just so, knowing a trusty cameraman would capture just the right angle. "Boneless chicken breasts. Grated cheese. Italian dressing. And, for those of you who are gluten-free, I used a coating of crushed cornflakes instead of bread crumbs."

She stood tall, despite the tightness in the small of her back, recounting the other dishes she'd made that day.

And smile.

"There you have it. A week's worth of dinners: chicken Parmesan, chicken piccata, salmon Sedona cakes served with English muffins, crown rack of lamb, and braised beef short ribs." She resisted the urge to push the bangs back from her face. The focus was on the meals she'd prepared, not her. "On the next segment of *Your Personal Chef,* I'll share another week's worth of dinners, including —"

When notes from the Peer Gynt Suite No. 1 sounded from her smartphone on the desk in the corner of the kitchen, Sadie closed her eyes, her mouth twisting. "A call? Really? We were almost finished."

Silence — and then her phone sounded again.

"It's a good thing this show is a figment of my imagination, or I'd have blown some network's budget a gazillion times with all my retakes." Sadie tugged off one padded oven mitt with her teeth and tossed it on the counter. Pulled off the other one and laid it next to its partner.

If anyone ever knew she talked to herself — and an invisible audience and production crew — while she cooked for her clients, they'd take away her culinary school diploma and parboil it.

Her phone rang again.

"I'm coming. And you, whoever you are, just ruined my cooking show." Sadie slipped off her navy blue clogs and pulled off her tie-dye bandana. She'd wash her hands and redo her hair before returning to the kitchen.

Wait. She'd set her phone out, hoping to hear from Matt so they could firm up plans for their date tonight. Sure enough, Matt's photo showed on the display.

SADIE — NEED TO CANCEL.

Again?

DO YOU HAVE TO WORK LATE?

Sadie tapped her sock-covered toes against the tile floor as she waited for Matt's reply.

So they wouldn't be seeing that new action movie getting all the great write-ups. She could always toss together dinner and take it to him. Pasta was simple. And a Caprese salad . . .

Matt's next message interrupted her musing.

DON'T KNOW HOW ELSE TO SAY THIS. IT'S BEEN FUN. BUT I'M DATING SOMEONE ELSE. MET HER AT WORK.

Sadie's fingers froze on the keypad. *What?* Her mind scrolled through the past few weeks. *How many times had Matt backed out of their dates? He hadn't been working late. Who knew what he'd been doing?*

She didn't want to know. She wasn't naïve — she just didn't want details.

With deliberate precision she erased Matt's last message, ignoring the new ones appearing on her screen. With each *ping* she hit the red delete button. She didn't want to read his excuse. His apology — if he even offered one.

Delete.

Delete.

With her phone silent, Sadie blinked away the sting at the back of her eyes, rubbing her finger against her left eye. When would she break the nervous habit that had begun in grade school? Some habits you never outgrow . . . and some things you learn to ignore or cover up with a fake smile. A glance at the clock showed she didn't have time to indulge in a cry that would redden her nose and turn her face a blotchy mess. The Hartnett children would arrive home from school in a couple of hours — with their too-inquisitive nanny — and she needed to have the chicken Parmesan stored in the fridge and the kitchen immaculate. After that, well, after that, she needed to head home. By herself. Speed-walk to her front door because, with the fall weather lingering in the warmer degrees, kids were bound to be playing in the park across the street from her house.

Why hadn't the Realtor told her before she bought the house that the city planned to put in a playground? Sadie could only hope her neighbors didn't notice her daily ignore-the-park routine. She could handle kids one, maybe two, at a time. But assembled all together on a playground? Of course, the Realtor would have no way of knowing about her memories of elementary school and how some days, just the sight of kids gathered around a swing set or slide reduced Sadie to a grade-schooler again.

Once safe inside, she'd make herself dinner. Ensure the kitchen was spotless. And do her Monday routine. After all, Matt dumping her was no reason to break her now predictable evening. It was beginning to feel as if being dumped by text was a certainty too.

Okay, now she was being pitiful. And she would not let Matt and his dump-by-text reduce her to a pathetic woman.

With silent footsteps, Sadie retreated to the bathroom just off the kitchen, avoiding her reflection in the hammered-copper framed mirror. She finger-brushed her short hair and covered it with the bandana. Then she ran cold water over her hands and pressed her fingers against her eyes, praying away the burn behind her eyelids. *Not now.* Then she washed her hands, breathing in the scent of pine soap that lingered in the room.

The breakfast meals were labeled and stored: scrambled egg and sausage burritos, pancakes, and an assortment of muffins. The week's dinners were put away, too, except for tonight's spinach salad, which was in the fridge waiting to be served with the chicken Parmesan.

By three o'clock, the last of the dirty dishes were washed and dried, put in their proper places, and she'd left the alphabetical list of meals on the counter, as Mrs.

Hartnett preferred. She already had her own copy of the list in her file so she could keep track of what recipes she used that week, and not repeat a meal too soon.

As she slipped out of her chef's jacket, marred with bits of evidence from today's cooking, and put on her navy blue polo shirt, the front door swung open.

"Chef Sadie! Are you still here?" Jill, the Hartnetts' ten-year-old daughter, half-ran from the foyer into the kitchen, her auburn pigtails flying.

"Yes, Jilly, I'm still here." Sadie stepped from the bathroom, stuffed her bandana in her soft-sided satchel, and knelt down as the girl raced for a hug.

"Did you make us dinner?"

"Of course — a whole week's worth. And breakfast too."

"Did you make us anything else?"

Jill's younger brother, Carter, all freckles and missing front teeth, came over and wiggled his way into the hug. "Didja, Chef Sadie?"

"Now, why would I do that?"

"Because you like us — and because you always do."

Sadie stole another double hug, the cool of the Colorado outside still clinging to their faces. "Who told you I liked you?"

"You did!"

"Well then, yes, I left a surprise for you in the cookie jar." She rose to her feet as the children released her and ran to discover their treat.

"They were so excited to come home and see what you'd made for them." The nanny, Miss Marci, hung the children's backpacks in the airlock between the kitchen and the garage.

"And I looked forward to seeing them. I made a double batch of snickerdoodles, and I set aside a few for you."

"The Hartnetts got lucky the day they hired you."

"I love cooking for them. Why work in a restaurant kitchen where I'd rarely meet the people who ate my food? Have a good night, Marci."

Settled in the safety of her Volvo sedan, Sadie leaned back against the seat, her hands gripping the steering wheel, eyes closed. Why didn't she keep a spare set of her glasses with her for when her eyes got tired?

She'd been dumped via text. *Again.* Was the pounding in her brain caused by a long day on her feet — or by Matt's *not* working late? She opened her eyes, stared straight ahead, the whispered words slipping past her lips part promise, part prayer. "God, I don't care if I ever date another man — ever, ever, again. And I don't know which aggravates me more: being asked out by text or being dumped by text. Don't men know how to have a real, face-to-face conversation anymore?"

When Erik closed his eyes, he could imagine he was back in college, facing off against the pitcher of an opposing team.

The second he opened his eyes, he was back in the batting cage. He swung the metal bat back and forth at waist level before positioning it up over his left shoulder. Inhaled the air laden with sweat and the aroma of the prepackaged pizzas they served at the snack bars. Tightened his gloved hands around the handle of the bat, left hand on top of right. Stilled his breathing, shutting out the sounds around him — the mechanical whir and release of pitching machines, the shuffling of the other batters' feet, and the tapping of the bats on the rubber mats.

Concentrate, Davis. Clear the bases.

He'd set the pitching speed for seventy miles per hour. He'd start easy and then ramp up the machine's speed, just like his college coach had taught him. Those years were far back in his mental rearview mirror, but some habits were hard to break — and swinging a bat was still the best way for him to work off tension.

The *tink* of metal against padded rawhide echoed in the partitioned-off cage surrounded by walls of chain link as the first baseball collided with his bat. Before the first fifteen minutes were up, he'd be sweaty and loose. And maybe, just maybe, he wouldn't be trying to figure out what time it was, wondering if there was a voice mail on his cell phone.

Another swing — but this time he only tipped the ball.

He was either going to get the project or he wasn't. Thanks to a recommendation from a friend who was crazy for outdoor obstacle races and now helped organize Raging Inferno Races, the group had seen Erik's portfolio. His references. All he could do now was wait.

His next hit was an easy out.

Maybe he should remind himself of all the reasons he left his "real job" as an in-house copywriter at an advertising agency to become a full-time freelance writer and editor — swing! — but he'd tossed down fifty bucks to stand in a batting cage to avoid thinking. To avoid his phone.

Was he paying his bills? Yes. Was he picking up new clients every month? Yes. Then what was the big deal about this project?

Who was he kidding? The chance to manage the advertising campaign for a national obstacle-challenge race would put a strong foundation beneath him. The exposure, not to mention the additional steady pay, along with the chance to grow as the organization expanded their races to more cities every year, meant both stability and professional credibility.

So much for not thinking. Still, he didn't go near his phone, tucked in the outer pocket of his backpack, until he'd worked out in the batting cage for half an hour. His long-sleeved T-shirt formed to his chest, damp with sweat, and he wiped at his forehead and beard with the back of his arm.

I trust you with this, God. Really I do. But you know what I'm hoping for: a phone call and a yes.

Less than three minutes — and one brief voice mail and follow-up phone call later — he had his answer. Erik allowed himself a "Yes!" and a fist pump between his sedan and an SUV, stopping at the sound of a kid's laughter. He then stunned the teen boy into silence by handing him twenty bucks. "Have fun at the batting cages."

"Are you kidding me, mister?"

"Nope. Today's a great day for me — and you too."

"Thanks!"

And now, Erik knew of another way he wanted to celebrate. He voice-dialed the necessary number.

"This is Sadie McAllister, your personal chef."

"I'd like to arrange a special dinner for two, please." Erik grinned at his reflection in the SUV's side window even as he tried to sound like a potential client.

"I'm sorry, I don't do private — Erik! Are you pranking me?"

"This is a serious request. I have something worth celebrating."

It took Sadie ten seconds to figure it out. "You got that race account, didn't you?"

"Yes, ma'am, I did!" Tucking his phone between his ear and shoulder, Erik slid into his Subaru, leaving the door open so the cool of the late fall afternoon would pull the stuffiness from the car. "Still need to sign the contract, but I'll do that once they fax it to me tomorrow."

"Then I'm most definitely going to cook you dinner. How about I grill steaks Saturday night?"

Sadie was the only one who grilled steak the way he liked. "Are you sure Matt will give you up for a Saturday? If you already have plans he could join us . . . I could bring Lydia . . ."

"Funny thing about Matt." It was impossible not to detect the forced cheerfulness in Sadie's voice. "We're not seeing each other anymore."

"But weren't you going out tonight?"

"I really don't want to talk about it." It sounded as if Sadie turned on a hand mixer. "If you want to celebrate with Lydia Saturday — or even bring her —"

"No. No, Saturday's for celebrating with my best friend."

"I'll have a sixteen-ounce New York strip — grilled just the way you like it, topped with caramelized onions. Baked potato. Fresh baked focaccia bread. And for dessert —"

"Surprise me."

"Six o'clock?"

"See you then, Sadie J."

"It's a date. And, Erik?"

"Yeah?"

"I'm proud of you."

Erik tossed the phone on the dash, leaning back in the driver's seat. So, this was what success felt like. Part independence, part self-satisfaction, mixed all together with the challenge of accomplishing the tasks ahead of him. Heady stuff.

He could do this. Stand on his own two feet. Build a stable life for himself — and feel like he was worth celebrating. Prove to his father he was somebody — even if his dad wasn't around to see it.

TWO

Sadie preferred to cook alone. But today her employer, the usually-at-work-by-now Felicia Cooper, trailed her from refrigerator to stove to sink to countertop and back again, snitching tastes of every dish Sadie had prepared for Felicia and her husband.

She no longer wondered why the Coopers employed a personal chef for just the two of them. The couple could spend their accountant-dentist double income however they wanted — she enjoyed cooking for two adults just as much as she enjoyed cooking for the Hartnetts.

"I'm not really working from home today, you know."

Sadie rearranged the slices of green and red peppers sautéing in the skillet with thin circles of onion, inhaling the distinctive aroma. *"Hmm."*

"We've been seeing an infertility specialist."

Okay. Sadie hadn't expected her employer to divulge something quite that intimate. Mrs. Cooper was stretching the definition of a personal chef. Sadie lowered the heat and added the strips of seasoned skirt steak. Was she supposed to respond? And say what? *I'm sorry? Congratulations?*

"The doctor harvested my eggs a month ago. Tomorrow she's going to implant the embryos." Felicia paced the kitchen, nibbling on a sliver of green pepper. "Who knows? We could have triplets! How could I go to work today and crunch numbers with the possibility of triplets in my future?"

"Understandable."

"We've been trying to have a baby for four years." Felicia completed another rapid circuit around the island, causing Sadie to sidestep her on the way to the sink. "I had no idea putting off having a baby until I was thirty-nine was going to complicate my life so much. You're married, right?"

Sadie stilled. Why, oh why, hadn't Mrs. Cooper just gone to work today? "No. Still single."

"But you're not even in your thirties yet." The woman took another slice of pepper from the pile Sadie had set aside for her. "Pete and I didn't even get married until I was thirty-two. And then we wanted to have 'our' time, you know? Now I wish we'd had children right away. Maybe we'd have avoided all this infertility angst."

The mostly one-sided conversation finally ended when Mrs. Cooper gathered up her leather purse and her car keys and decided to go to Starbucks, declaring, "I'll be off caffeine for months if I get pregnant."

Sadie exhaled, taking in the tasks still needing to be completed. How was she supposed to prepare the couple's meals when her attempts to concentrate on the recipes were interrupted by Mrs. Cooper? Of course, now all she had to deal with were echoes of her employer's voice.

Was infertility in her future — if she even managed to fall in love and get married before old age arrived? Would she be forced to listen to the ticking of her biological clock while waiting for some man to find her and propose? He was probably lost and wouldn't even bother to text and ask for directions to her home.

She wanted kids. She'd be a good mom. Available. One who made three nutritious and delicious home-cooked meals each day. Who showed up for their kids' school performances and parent-teacher conferences.

She could always adopt as a single mom.

That was an option. Look at all the celebrities who did that nowadays.

Was solo motherhood her dream?

No.

Maybe she needed to face reality. Maybe she needed to stop dreaming . . . stop waiting for Mr. Right to text her and say, "I'm here! Want to get married and have a couple of kids?"

Maybe it was time to go after what she wanted . . . or find another dream.

With "Take My Breath Away" playing in the background, Erik settled into one corner of Sadie's charcoal-gray sectional couch. Only a true best friend would humor his love for eighties music. Stretching his arms over his head, he tried to find some room for dessert . . . somewhere. "That was, as always, a perfect steak."

"How hard is it to walk a prime cut of beef past my stove? You won't even let me warm it up to rare." Sadie set a plate loaded with a slice of three-layer coconut cake next to two frothy mugs of Irish coffee on the one-of-a-kind shadowbox coffee table. The design showcased an eclectic assortment of antique items: an eggbeater, a tin star-shaped cookie cutter, a silver-handled carving set — even a couple of faded recipe cards. "Such a waste of my indoor gas grill."

"Best decision you ever made — installing a grill in your kitchen. Most women want the party bathroom with the supersize sunken bathtub." Erik picked up a fork and dug into the cake. He ate a quarter of the slice, eyes closed as he savored the blend of moist cake and shredded coconut sprinkled over the thick creamy icing. "Now this . . . we could have skipped dinner and gone straight to dessert."

"You're worth celebrating." Sadie had curled into the opposite corner of the couch and pushed up the sleeves of her white cardigan.

"Thanks to your cooking, I'll be doubling my time on the tread-desk tomorrow."

"You and that crazy tread-desk." She cradled a mug of coffee in her hands, tucking her feet underneath her. "I still don't understand how you work on your computer and run on your treadmill at the same time."

"I don't. I work and *walk* at the same time. It's multitasking at its best." Erik raised his mug of coffee, knowing the fragrance of cream and Irish whisky only hinted at the delicious taste. "Cheers. So, how are you doing about Matt?"

"It's not as if this hasn't happened before. My wedding ceremony will probably be done by text."

"That would be original." Erik paused with his fork over the half eaten slice of cake. "Don't worry about it, Sadie. He wasn't the one."

"Easy for you to say — you won't be an old woman birthing babies once you decide to get married — if you ever do." Sadie brushed her bangs to the side of her forehead. "Look at me, Erik. I'm thirty. And as single as a girl can get."

"So what? I'm thirty — and am I worried about it?"

"It's not the same thing. You're a guy — and a commitment-phobe at that."

"I beg your pardon?"

"Oh, come on. You date a woman, what? Three, maybe four months? And then you're done. Your relationships have an expiration date on them that sets off some sort of internal alarm. *Warning, warning. This relationship is about to be terminated . . .*" Sadie hid a giggle by taking another sip of her coffee. "I do give you credit for remaining friends with all your exes."

"I've never met a woman that I wanted to commit matrimony with." Erik wasn't being completely honest with Sadie, but she didn't need to know that. "And thirty is not old."

"Thirty isn't old for you because, while

you do have that commitment alert, you do not have a biological clock."

"Excuse me?" Erik brushed a few crumbs from his close-cropped beard.

Sadie tossed him a napkin. "You heard me: biological clock. I admit it. I want to get married. I want to have kids. And the older I get, the harder that gets."

"Who have you been talking to?" Maybe he needed to move to a chair — let Sadie stretch out like this was an analyst's couch. "Some woman who wants to get pregnant, right?"

"Yes, if you must know. One of my employers is having infertility treatments."

"A lot of older couples deal with that."

"She's in her late thirties."

"And you're thirty, Sadie. Three-oh. Relax." Erik didn't see a single muscle slacken in his uptight friend. "And what about you and me?"

"What about you and me . . . what?"

"You said I only date a woman three or four months. You and I didn't date for three or four months."

Sadie waved off his comment. "We never dated, Erik."

She was doing it again. So what if he rarely mentioned their barely-begun-before-it-ended summer romance — they had been a couple. Sort of. "Yes, we did. The summer before I left for college. We held hands when we went hiking and at Elitch Gardens. And don't you remember I kissed you on the roller coaster?"

"Kiss? What kiss?" Sadie broke eye contact, setting down her coffee and then shifting back into the corner of the couch.

"Well, I remember kissing you — even if it was twelve years ago." Erik moved down the couch and leaned toward her, not surprised that she smelled of the kitchen: garlic and onions sautéed in butter — some of his favorite things. "But given that I was an inexperienced eighteen-year-old back then, kissing you now might be more memorable for both of us. Want to give it a try?"

Sadie placed a hand against his chest, her fingers splayed against the red-and-black striped flannel shirt, preventing him from moving any closer. "Don't be ridiculous. Friends don't kiss each other."

He winked at her, covering her hand with his. If he kept it light, maybe she wouldn't notice how fast his heart was beating. "Why not? You're single. I'm single — just hit three months with Lydia, which means, according to you, she's as good as gone. How about it?"

Erik scanned Sadie's face. She never once blinked her brown eyes, the way she outlined them with a soft shade of forest green accentuating their almond shape. She caught the corner of her bottom lip between her teeth. He hadn't kissed Sadie since he was eighteen. If she said yes to his seemingly flippant, "How about it?" he would make sure she didn't forget this kiss. And he wouldn't stop at one, either.

"No, thank you. I want a man who's looking for a long-term relationship — as in *I do.*" She gave him a slow once-over, almost as if she was seeing his deepest secrets. "Will you marry me?"

Her words were a cold splash of water. She'd made it clear that she had no romantic feelings toward him. Erik sat back, crossing his arms over his chest. "I offered to kiss you, not marry you, Sadie."

"According to you, we've already kissed." Sadie maintained a teasing tone. "Let's move our relationship to the next level and get married. They always say you should marry your best friend."

"Who are these all-wise, all-knowing *they,* anyway?" Erik needed to find a way to regain control of the conversation. "We're not characters in a *When Harry Met Sally* remake who have to sabotage a friendship by getting married."

"You're absolutely right." Sadie eased away from Erik, sliding off the couch to collect the empty coffee mugs. He wished he could figure out a way to continue the banter and pull her back close to him. "And we don't have to confuse our friendship by kissing. Now that we've got that all sorted out, I'll pack up the leftover cake for you to take home."

After Erik left, Sadie took control of her Bose music system, switching the eighties music Erik preferred back to the rich, full notes of Pavane Op. 50. The soft echo of his chuckle returned as she ran her hand across the back of the couch, where he'd tossed his jean jacket — knowing she couldn't leave it lying around for more than a minute. She rearranged the trio of brass candlesticks — shortest to tallest — and restacked the antique classic books on the mantel that Erik had disordered. He'd started the tradition back when she rented her first apartment after she'd started the Broadmoor culinary apprenticeship program. Every visit, he'd rearrange something — switching pictures on the wall or even the condiments on the shelves in her fridge — and then see how long it took her to find what he'd disordered.

Violins played in the background as Sadie hit speed dial on her smartphone. Then she started a final wipe down of her kitchen counters, the faint aroma of sautéed onions mixing with the astringent scent of kitchen cleanser. "The candlesticks and books on the mantel."

"Man! What was that? Thirty seconds?"

"Yep. Try harder next time."

"Thanks for celebrating with me. Sorry you didn't kiss me?"

Sadie forced a laugh past the burn in her throat. "Not in the least. Sorry you didn't accept my marriage proposal?"

"Not in the least. Goodnight, Sadie Jupiter."

"Wrong again."

"I'll guess your middle name one of these days."

"Uh-huh. You haven't yet, and there are only so many words that begin with the letter *J*. Goodnight."

"I'll call you."

"Sure you will — when you get hungry for a home-cooked meal."

His laughter couldn't quite tug a smile onto her lips as she disconnected the call.

Don't you remember our kiss?

Somehow he'd believed her when she'd

said no. When she'd said his kiss wasn't memorable.

After knowing her for seventeen years, Erik couldn't tell when she was lying.

She'd replayed that awkward moment when they were caught somewhere between friendship and the possibility of falling in love over and over in her mind for weeks after it happened.

They were best friends who talked and went bowling together. Best friends who talked and watched movies together. Best friends who talked and hiked together.

And then one day as they walked Cottonwood Creek Trail, Erik had slung his arm oh so casually across her shoulders and then let his arm slide down around her waist. Being snugged up against his lean body, the scent of the Colorado summer — sunshine and fresh air all mixed up with wildflowers and just-mowed grass — radiating off of him, caused all of Sadie's senses to go on high alert. The warmth in his cobalt blue eyes sparked a response inside her — a sense of security she'd lacked for years. When he slipped his hand around hers, intertwining their fingers, and asked, "Okay?" she'd smiled and whispered, "Okay."

It wasn't until a week later, during a day

trip to Elitch Gardens, that he kissed her.

"Having fun?"

"Sure."

Erik tugged at her hands fisted around the roller coaster's lock bar. "You're scared."

She stared straight ahead, the early evening breeze cool against her neck from her newly cut-short hair. "I always feel like the cars are going to careen off the track."

Erik wrapped an arm around her waist, pulling her into the curve of his arm, his lips close to her ear. "Come here. I'll hold onto you."

She loosened her grip, realizing sweat slicked the bar. But her eyes watched their slow ascent up the side of the first hill of the roller coaster, her breathing keeping pace with the rattle of the cars.

"Sadie." Erik's whisper pulled her attention away from the hill, even as his fingers traced her jaw and tugged her face toward him.

"I'm —"

He pressed his lips against hers, silencing her protest. What should she do? Erik was her best friend . . . but things between them were changing — had changed. Sadie let go of the safety bar and dared to close her eyes, to slip her hand up to his shoulder just as the cars crested the hill.

One second Erik was kissing her, the pressure of his mouth an unexpected enticement.

The next, he threw his hands in the air, laughing and whooping, his yells blending with everyone else's in the cars behind them as the roller coaster descended in a rush of speed and wind and noise past the other side of the hill and around a curve.

"Isn't this great?"

The swerve of the car jostled them together again.

"Great."

"Not scared anymore?"

"No. No, I'm not scared anymore."

And that was enough of that.

Sadie folded the damp dishrag and laid it across the edge of her double sink. Left the light over the sink on low. Straightened the couch cushions. Turned off the tableside lamps.

Twelve years. Too long ago to still be affected by an adolescent kiss that hadn't meant anything to Erik. She'd managed to restore their relationship to friends-only status with little resistance from him — and friends they remained.

And one trustworthy friend was worth more than becoming one of Erik's too-many-to-count girlfriends. Oh, she could probably count them if she tried. Name them all too. And it didn't bother her that

her name wasn't on the list.
  Not at all.

THREE

She'd expected to find the Hartnetts' kitchen empty. Solitude was part of her usual routine that began at nine o'clock sharp and included donning a freshly laundered chef's coat and savoring one cup of black coffee with one spoonful of sugar and a swirl of milk that she preheated in the microwave.

But today, the last Monday of September, her routine stalled before it even started. Why was Mrs. Hartnett sitting in the breakfast nook, the morning's newspaper spread out in front of her, a glass of orange juice in her hand?

"Mrs. Hartnett?"

Had she misread the calendar? Was today a holiday?

"Good morning, Sadie. Didn't mean to surprise you. I'm going in late because I wanted to talk with you."

Sadie swallowed back the sour taste that

rose in her throat. Had she made a mistake with the previous week's meals?

"*Everything's fine.* The kids loved what you made last week. They even requested the Parmesan chicken again soon." Mrs. Hartnett folded the newspaper. "Pour yourself some coffee and come sit down. I won't keep you too long. I know you have a schedule."

Seated across from Mrs. Hartnett, Sadie set her mug of coffee — black for the moment — in front of her, positioning her hands beneath the table, clenching and unclenching them. Older than her by ten years or more, Mrs. Hartnett wore her hair in a sophisticated page-boy cut that she'd let go gray. The muted silver color set off her blue eyes in a striking manner.

"So, would you like to talk about meals? Suggest something?"

"I'd like to talk about your job." She held up her hand, a smile stretched across her coral-colored lips. "Don't worry. I'm not firing you. Remember, I said nothing is wrong. But I am getting promoted, which involves a transfer to Oregon. And I'd like to know if you'd go with us — as our family's private chef."

Sadie choked on her first sip of coffee, and not because of the unsweetened bitterness. "I . . . beg your pardon?"

"I know it would be a huge change, asking you to move. But you do such a wonderful job cooking for our family. And I'll be working longer hours, at least at first. Ron will be telecommuting, as well as traveling back here each month. We don't want him worrying about meals."

"Where in Oregon?" She had to ask something, just to have time to unravel her thoughts. *Move? Cook for one family?*

"Portland."

"When do you leave?"

"I'm expected there after the first of the year."

"That soon?"

"They'd like to have me sooner, but I told them I didn't want to disrupt the children's school and holidays."

Sadie risked taking another small sip of her coffee. "I don't know what to say."

"Say you'll consider it." Mrs. Hartnett slid a brown folder across the table. "Here's some information about Portland. And Ron did some research about salaries for private chefs, as well as cost of living."

"Okay."

"We could do this one of two ways: look for a house with a separate living space for you or you could find your own apartment.

And of course, we would pay for your moving expenses. We're ready to negotiate a good salary. Why don't we plan on talking in a week or ten days?" She waited for Sadie to nod. "Oh, and I forgot to mention that I have a good friend in Portland who is connected with a cooking school there. She's interested in talking with you about possible teaching opportunities."

Sadie nodded again, uncertain what to say.

Mrs. Hartnett rose to her feet. "Now, it's time for me to get to work. They're announcing my promotion today and I don't want to miss the champagne toast."

Only after her employer left did Sadie remember she was still wearing her coat. She hung it in the foyer closet and slipped into her chef's jacket. Then she went to the bathroom, switching on the light, checking her makeup and hair while she washed her hands. Mrs. Hartnett's maid had switched out the pine-scented hand soap for something scented with lemon. Sadie's so-carefully lined eyes stared back at her.

"Don't look at me. I don't know what you should do."

This is what Phillip had in mind when he called to see if I wanted to hang out?

Erik adjusted his pace to match his best

friend's, which was slowed down by a stroller the size of a mini-Mack truck and the multicolor, flowered diaper bag slung on his shoulder. If he'd known they'd be babysitting, he would have stayed at home, walked on his tread-desk, and brainstormed ideas for the race account.

"You sure you don't want to push?" Phillip angled the stroller toward Erik as they walked through the neighborhood, slowing his steps even further, as if expecting him to switch places.

"No, thanks. You're the dad. You steer that thing."

Phillip didn't even bother holding back his laughter. "There's a baby in here, buddy — not a bomb."

"I'd rather handle a load of dynamite." Erik shoved his hands in the pockets of his Windbreaker, ducking under a tree branch covered in brilliant yellow leaves. "You push and talk. I'll walk and talk."

"I didn't realize we'd be babysitting." Phillip stopped the stroller long enough to stow the diaper bag underneath and then eased it off the sidewalk into the street. "That's better. I hate dodging mailboxes and trash cans. And I apologize. Ashley mentioned her hair appointment after I'd called you."

"No problem." Erik rounded a parked SUV and came alongside Phillip. "I read somewhere that walking is considered a form of exercise too."

"I could try a jog."

"Isn't the goal to keep Annalisa asleep?"

"You'll enjoy our time together more if she does."

"Keep walking."

This was one of the last days of Indian summer. Soon cool weather would lay claim to the days. Silence fell between them. That was one of the things Erik appreciated about Phillip. He was a pastor, comfortable in a church pulpit, but didn't feel the need to talk all the time — about God or anything else.

Even so, Phillip spoke first. "So, how are you doing being self-employed? Feeling settled?"

Erik stared ahead at the gradual incline of the neighborhood street. "You ask me that every time we get together. It's only been eight months. Can't you wait until I hit my first anniversary?"

"Is it going as well as you hoped?"

"That wasn't even eight *seconds.*" Erik scratched his beard. "I enjoy being my own boss. I'm paying the bills — no need to wait tables or be a telemarketer. And I just got hired by the Raging Inferno Race Company — the one that does those insane obstacle races. Javelin throws. Mud crawls. Rope climbs. It's my best gig yet."

"Congratulations. So, no regrets, then?"

"No regrets — yet. I don't miss my old job. And I have time to work on my Great American Novel — although it's more like the world's worst first draft."

"Anytime you want me to read it . . ."

"I know, I know. You're game. I'll remember."

Erik's phone played the first notes of "It's Still Rock and Roll to Me," and he pulled it from his pocket. "One sec. Let me just make certain this isn't a work call." He scanned the text. Pocketed his phone again. "Huh."

"Huh what?"

"That was Sadie."

"Is everything okay?"

"Yeah. Sure. She usually doesn't text during a workday. But she said she didn't want to wait to tell me some news — and we'd talk later."

Phillip stopped. "What's the news — don't keep me waiting."

"Her employer got a promotion — and is moving to Oregon. They want Sadie to move with them as their private chef."

"Wow, that's an amazing opportunity."

"Yeah. Wow."

"Anything else?"

"She's thinking about it." The phrase had looked wrong on Erik's cell, now it sounded wrong. Why was Sadie even thinking about the job offer?

Sadie had lived in Colorado all her life. She'd bought her first house two years ago and fixed it up room by room. Her friends were here.

"Erik?"

He was rubbing his hand across his jaw when Phillip's voice pulled him back to the moment. "What?"

"What are you thinking about?"

"I don't think Sadie will take that job."

"You don't think she'll take that job — or you don't *want* her to take that job?"

"What kind of question is that?"

"Answer the question. Do you want Sadie to take the job?"

"It doesn't matter what I want." Erik shrugged. "I don't tell her what to do. Sadie and I are just friends."

"So you've said ever since I've known you. But let me ask you this. Are you being honest with yourself?" Phillip's voice remained level, but it felt as if his words carried the weight of a lawyer cross-examining a witness. "I've watched you date other women.

325

You like them for a couple of months, and then you're done. The only woman you've ever been loyal to is Sadie."

"Excuse me?"

"Could it be that you're in love with her?"

"You're a pastor, Phillip, not a relationship guru."

"I do couples counseling, you know."

"Sadie and I are not a couple." Erik kicked a rock so that it skittered across the street. "The one time I ever tried to change our relationship to something romantic, she backed away so fast I was left holding thin air."

"Oh-ho! And when was this?"

"Go ahead, laugh. It doesn't matter anyway — it happened so long ago she doesn't even remember that I kissed her."

"But you do?"

"It doesn't matter."

"Erik." Phillip settled one hand on Erik's shoulder. "We aren't in high school anymore. And I'm asking you a question, man to man. Are you in love with Sadie?"

"I never thought she'd move away. I never thought I wouldn't see her every week. Sadie's my best friend."

"The more important question, my friend? Is that all you want her to be?"

Four

Erik pressed the Stop button on the treadmill's control panel, his steps slowing. He'd spent several hours working on the race project, as well as a few other deadlines. Then he'd set aside his laptop and worked up a decent sweat while he ran, praying the entire time. The last ten minutes, his intercessions fell into a rhythm matching the pounding of his feet on the treadmill.

Help me do this, God.

I want to do this.

I can do this. I can be the kind of man Sadie deserves.

He grabbed the bottle of water from his dresser and gulped down half of it. And now he was going to do it. But first he'd shower and pray a little more.

"Hey, Sadie, this is Erik."

"I know who this is, Erik. If you remember, I was there when you went

327

through puberty and your voice changed."

Erik pressed his fist against the bedroom wall. *Really?* He'd put in a full morning brainstorming ideas for his new account. He'd spent an hour running on the treadmill. He was hungry. Tired. And now he was calling to ask Sadie out — because Phillip had put him up to it — and she had to knock him all the way back to puberty?

"You still there?"

"Yes." Erik hummed a few bars of "Born in the U.S.A." Some people counted to ten when they felt as if they were losing their grip on their patience. He hummed. And this was no time to get testy. He would treat Sadie like, well, like a woman. Not like his best friend.

"Are you humming?"

"What? No." Erik stepped up on the treadmill again. Hit Start — keeping the pace low and slow.

"You sure? Because you only do that when you're trying not to lose your temper."

If this conversation didn't improve soon, he was going to sing the entire song at the top of his lungs.

"Sadie, would you go out with me?"

Silence — and then she laughed. Not her off-tune giggle that always made him smile, but a laugh that probably had her doubled over. When she spoke again, her words were punctuated with gasps for air. "Erik . . . first you asked me if I wanted to kiss you . . . and I said no. You . . . you turned down . . . my marriage proposal . . . Why are you asking me out?"

Of course she was going to make this difficult. *Keep walking, Davis. Charm her.*

"Hey, you refused to kiss me. And that wasn't a real proposal."

Charming. Now they sounded like two grade schoolers.

"You didn't really want me to kiss you. What was that line you used? *'I've become a much better kisser. Want to try again?'* " Sadie's imitation of him was not even close. "Is that how you set a romantic mood for every woman you date?"

Was he supposed to take Sadie's verbal slicing and dicing without even flinching? If he continued his pursuit of a date, she'd leave him in little pieces, just like the ingredients for the Cobb salad she'd served him last month. Was he a man or an avocado?

"Okay, so I don't want to marry you and you don't want to kiss me." Erik stiffened his spine and asked again. "But you didn't answer my question: Will you go out on a date with me?"

"Come on, Erik, I need to —"

"You need to answer my question. When a man asks you out, you need to tell him yes or no."

"You're asking me out?"

"Yes."

"Why?"

Couldn't the woman just say yes and let it be? "Because I want to go out with you."

"As friends?"

"As a man and a woman. On a date."

"But you and I — together — we're not a man and a woman. We're best friends."

Erik fought back the urge to start humming again. "Now that's absurd."

"You know what I mean."

Why had he ever thought asking Sadie out was a good idea? Oh, yeah, because Phillip had gotten into his head and convinced him he might be in love with Sadie. Right now, he wasn't even sure he liked her.

But he wasn't quitting — not yet, anyway. "Sadie, will you go out with me, please?"

"No."

No? "What do you mean, no?"

"You asked. I answered. No, I will not go out with you. I don't believe in mercy dates or practical joke dates or whatever this is. If you ever want another late-night meal — any meal at all — cooked by me, end this conversation now. Good-bye, Erik."

The last Thursday of the month — and Sadie was about to be surrounded by a horde of men and their sons. Again.

"I wouldn't be here if you hadn't agreed to help me with this class." Sadie stood side by side with her friend Mel, setting up cooking stations around the counters in the church kitchen. "When the men's ministry director asked if I wanted to teach a series of cooking classes to dads and sons, I should have said no. *N-O.* How hard is it to say that two-letter word?"

"You go through this every month, Sadie." Mel wore an apron emblazoned with the logo of her upscale catering company, Trifles. "Relax. We'll have fun."

"You're only saying that because you think Keegan Fletcher is hot."

"I do not."

"Then I'll help him and his son tonight."

"Oh no you won't."

"My point exactly."

Sadie glanced at the clock. In fifteen minutes, twenty-two dads and sons would fill the church's kitchen, ready for a third cooking lesson.

"This will be a unique way for the dads to bond with their sons, Sadie."

331

An echo of the director's voice persuading her to teach the class broke through her concentration. Weeks ago he'd stood there, shaking her hand and nodding up and down like a bobblehead doll, and Sadie found herself bobbling a yes back.

"I'm a personal chef. When you and I graduated from the Broadmoor's culinary apprenticeship, I never imagined teaching a bunch of guys how to cook."

"The classes have been an absolute hit, Sadie. Didn't you tell me they already asked you to teach it again?"

"Well, the one thing I know is that men like bacon. And they wanted the dads and sons to bond during the classes, so it was easy to come up with Bonding with Bacon."

"You've already done the hard work and made a lesson plan. You can just use it again." Mel pulled her black hair into a short ponytail. "Week one: the basics of knife sharpening and an appetizer of Man Candy."

"Those guys couldn't get enough of maple syrup caramelized over thick cut bacon. And since I sharpened the knives myself, no one ended up in the emergency room." Sadie set out several large containers of gel sanitizer. "They weren't too happy the next week when I mentioned we were making a wedge salad with bacon — until I showed them all the extra bacon I'd brought along so they would have enough to snack on."

"That was a bit of brilliance — bacon and more bacon." At the sound of the doors swinging open and boyish laughter intermingling with the rumble of men's voices, Mel snapped her fingers. "And now it's time to handle the motley crew . . . I mean class, one more month."

Sadie positioned herself at the front of the kitchen, knowing Mel would finish the prep. "All right, guys, remember to put on your aprons and don't forget to wash your hands with soap and water and then use the sanitizer. Then choose a work station."

Toby, an eleven-year-old with Down syndrome, ran over and engulfed her in a hug. "Hey, Miss Sadie."

"Hey, Toby."

"What are we making tonight?"

"I hope you're hungry. Tonight we're making 50-50 burgers and sweet potato fries."

Toby tightened his arms around her again, his grin lopsided, his brown eyes shining behind his glasses. "My favorite."

Sadie exchanged smiles with Toby's father, a tall, lean man, whose hair was the same sandy color as his son's. Everything they'd made was Toby's favorite. "Great. Don't forget to wash your hands."

There was no such thing as making too much food when it came to this class. Leftovers were rare. Tonight her plan was to demonstrate the proper technique for cutting julienne fries and forming a hamburger patty. Then she'd cook the sweet potato fries while Mel assisted the dads and sons in prepping and cooking their hamburgers.

Justin Boyle, one of the several single dads in the class, interrupted her as she piled scrubbed sweet potatoes on the counter. "I was wondering if you could recommend a good basic cookbook? These classes have inspired me to be a bit more creative. Branch out beyond chicken nuggets and hot dogs."

"Glad to hear that." Sadie laid her knives on the counter. "I'd be glad to give you some suggestions."

"Great." Justin cleared his throat. "Maybe . . . maybe we could meet for coffee at The Tattered Cover and browse the cookbook section?"

Sadie bit her lip, warmth heating her face. "Maybe we could."

They were interrupted by Toby returning to ask what he could do next to help.

Justin backed up. "I'll call you."

"Sure."

Now all she had to do was teach the group how to julienne potatoes and how to form hamburger patties — and not wonder whether she'd just been asked out on a bona fide date.

"Tonight we are making 50-50 burgers. We'll be using half ground beef and half ground bacon." After rubbing a squirt of sanitizer into her hands, Sadie grabbed a handful of the mixture from the glass bowl in front of her. "You'll each make your own hamburger, and get to eat it tonight. But first, I'm going to teach you the best technique for forming a burger. Shape your patty, and then press a crater in one side of it" — she and Mel showed the class how to do this, moving around the room to each dad-and-son pairing — "making sure the crater is about the size of a silver dollar. This allows space inside the burger for the juices to expand, but they won't run outside the patty."

Bert, one of the dads who came with his thirteen-year-old son, raised his hand. "Does the crater go up or down when we grill the burger?"

"It doesn't matter."

"How do we know when the burger is done?"

"Good question, Bert. Normally when we

discuss cooking meat, we talk about rare, medium, and well-done. But not with a 50-50 burger. You don't want to eat raw bacon. So these burgers are served either medium-well or well — I recommend well." Sadie held up a meat thermometer. "You can use a thermometer like this one to check the temperature. Or another way to test if a burger is done is to see if the juices run clear and the patty is firm to the touch in the center."

Before starting to cook the burgers, she talked the group through the prep for the sweet potato fries with Manchego cheese and rosemary.

"While Chef Mel helps you cook your burgers, I'll work on the sweet potato fries. Here's what I want you to remember: the thinner the cut, the crispier the fries. So, a shoestring cut will be crispier than a julienne. I'm going to use a deep fryer tonight — a two-step process — but baking them and then tossing them in the cheese and rosemary is another, healthier option. And yes, I have handouts with all the recipes and information for you to add to your notebooks."

For two hours the hum of voices, intermingled with laughter, filled the church kitchen. The salty aroma of bacon and beef and the sizzle of fries scented with rosemary and the nutty aroma of Manchego cheese laced the air.

As much as she insisted she didn't want to teach the class, Sadie relished seeing the satisfaction on the dads' faces as they tasted their burgers. How they congratulated their sons for following the recipe even as they joked about who made the better burger. As they cleaned up the kitchen, she encouraged them to try out their newfound skills on families and friends.

"Don't forget, class: 'Cooking is at once child's play and adult joy. And cooking done with care is an act of love.' "

With Mel nearby, she even managed a nonchalant, "Looking forward to it," when Justin said, "I'll call about going to look at cookbooks" as he left for the night.

"So, how are things going with you and Matt?" Mel removed her stained apron, leaning back against the kitchen counter, not bothering to hide the huge yawn that almost swallowed her words.

Her friend's question caused Sadie to do a second wipe down of the counters with a healthy dose of cleaner. Generally speaking, the more a cleaner stung her eyes, the more Sadie liked it. How had she not mentioned the drive-by breakup by text? Oh, that's right. They'd spent the evening in a room loaded with testosterone and calories — and Mel had spent a lot of that time checking up on Keegan Fletcher and his son.

"Things aren't 'going' with Matt. He dumped me — by text."

"What?" Mel straightened, hands on her hips. "Sadie — how do you find these guys?"

"Are you blaming me for that man's lack of social skills?"

"No, of course not." Mel folded her apron and set it by her animal-print, suede purse. "But didn't the last guy you dated dump you by text too?"

"Yes. And the guy before him." Sadie held up the white dishrag, waving it like a surrender flag. "Don't ask anymore. I give up."

"I'm sorry, Sadie."

"No — I'm *Sorry Sadie*."

Once again, she bordered on pathetic.

"I did have a guy ask me out this week, but I turned him down." Well, two guys if she counted Justin's invitation as a real date.

"Who? Why'd you turn him down?"

"It was Erik — and that's why I turned him down."

"*Erik*-Erik? Why would he ask you out? You two have been friends since middle school! You're like brother and sister."

"Well, it's probably because I proposed to him."

"What?"

Mel's bug-eyed expression caused Sadie to bust out laughing, which eased the tightness in her chest. "But that was only because he asked if I wanted to kiss him."

Mel grabbed her by the shoulders, giving her a slight shake. "Explain yourself right now. This is Erik, right? The one you asked to the Sadie Hawkins Dance — and he turned you down."

"Yes, that Erik."

"Why is he suggesting you kiss each other — and why are you proposing?"

Sadie shrugged her shoulders, and Mel released her. "It was just a crazy conversation. I had hassled Erik about being afraid of commitment. And then somehow he said he was a much better kisser than the last time we kissed —"

"Whoa. When did you two kiss?"

"Years ago. When we were eighteen. One kiss. It was a mistake. Since then, we've been friends — and nothing but friends."

"You, uh, didn't want to find out if he *was* a much better kisser?"

"Stop!"

"All right, so how did you end up proposing to a man you won't even kiss?"

"It was a joke — that's all."

"So, besides Erik offering to kiss you, and you proposing to him — it's been a normal week?"

Why was Mel asking so many questions? Sadie was done with men — dating them and talking about them. "Well, like I said, Erik did ask me out on a date."

"And this is a *normal* week?"

"I turned him down."

"Oh — on a non-normal week, you'd accept?"

"No."

"Why not?"

Sadie slipped into her jacket, thankful for its warmth since the weather had turned cool overnight. "Mel — that is a ridiculous question."

"Are you dating anyone?"

"Not at the moment." Sadie didn't mention Justin because, really, cookbook shopping wasn't a date. Was it?

"Is Erik dating anyone?"

"No — he said he just hit the three-month mark with Lydia, so he's unattached. But, once again, he's managed to remain friends. They both admitted there was no real romance between them — and that was that."

"If you say so."

"Oh, I know Erik's dating modus operandi. To his credit, he always ends up friends with all of the women."

"No hard feelings? No stalker ex-girlfriends?"

"None."

"So, if both of you are unattached, why don't you go out with him?"

Sadie shoved her hands into her pockets. "Mel, are you listening to me? Erik and I are friends — best friends. And that's the way I like it."

"So, you're happy working and watching the cooking channel?"

"It's been one week since I was dumped — and I find a lot of good recipes that way. Just last week —"

"You're scared to say yes."

"Why would I be scared?"

"You tell me. What are you afraid of?"

Nothing. And everything. Not that she'd tell Mel that. She didn't want to go on an emotional roller-coaster ride again with Erik.

"I heard a quote once. 'Life begins at the end of your comfort zone.' You like to be comfortable. Play it safe."

"What's wrong with that?"

"What do you think explorers would have discovered if they played it safe? Or what would inventors have created?" Mel stood in the middle of the kitchen, refusing to budge. "Didn't you listen to anything our instructors taught us in school? The importance of trying new things? I double-dog dare you to go on a date — one date — with Erik."

"This isn't grade school."

"No, it's not. So stop acting like a scared little girl, afraid someone's going to hurt you. Call Erik up and tell him your calendar cleared up and you're available."

Fine. Two could play the grade-school game.

"You just dared me to get outside of my comfort zone. What will you do?"

Mel stood with her hand on her hip, the glint in her eye causing Sadie to wish she hadn't asked the question.

"It's more like what will *I* do for *you.*"

"What's that supposed to mean?"

"Remember how I was invited to be on the morning news last month and how I shared a breakfast recipe? The station manager called me last week and asked if I could recommend another chef to do a guest spot."

Mel stared at her, a wicked smile on her lips. Sadie waited. And waited.

Nothing.

"You're not going to use Erik as the bait

for a chance to do the cooking segment."

Silence.

"You're not that kind of friend, Mel."

"I'm not?"

"Mel!"

"Here's how this goes down: You call Erik and tell him you had a change of heart. That you'd love to go out with him. And then I'll call the station manager and give him your name and phone number." Mel stuck out her hand. "Deal?"

Sadie was not going to be cornered into a date with Erik. She grabbed her small leather purse, marched past Mel, switching off the kitchen lights. Without a word, Mel slipped on her coat and shouldered her purse, passing Sadie. As she headed for the parking lot, Sadie scrambled after her, the heels of her clogs tapping against the asphalt.

"Fine. I'll do it."

"You're a smart woman, Sadie. Of course, you did graduate top of the class." Mel motioned to her. "Go ahead, call Erik."

The cold night air nipped at her nose and fingers. "Now?"

"Yes. *Now.* I'm not going to listen to the entire conversation, but I want to see you dial the number and make sure he answers. Then I'll leave you two alone while you make plans for your date." Mel shook her head and *tsked* when Sadie muttered something under her breath. "Ah, ah, ah. No threats. I'm your liaison to TV land, remember?"

FIVE

Erik hunkered down in his Subaru outside Sadie's house in the older section of northern Denver. The arrival of October saw the small grouping of aspen trees in her front yard turning golden. Once past the white-picket fence Sadie scraped down and painted each spring, a brick pathway led to the front door, painted a rich forest green and adorned with a gold scripted *M*. Laughter floated over from the park across the street as children conquered the monkey bars and followed one another up and down the circular slide.

This was a *date*.

Not a sort-of date. Not a fill-in-at-the-last-minute-because-the-person-I-asked-couldn't-make-it date.

A *D-A-T-E*.

All he had to do was knock on the door and greet Sadie when she answered. Act natural. He'd been to her house hundreds of times.

But never for a date — not since the summer after high school when his particular-to-a-fault best friend had made it clear that she had no interest in a romance with him.

Erik stared at the front door, feeling as if he were standing two body-lengths off second base, trying to make the decision between stealing third or running back to second.

Sadie may not remember those few weeks during the summer before he left for college. When they'd held hands. And shared one too-brief kiss. But he did. Sadie's non-reaction to his kiss made it obvious she preferred friendship with him rather than his inept attempts at romance.

He was thirty now. An adult. This date had more riding on it than the immature longings of an eighteen-year-old. He knew what he was doing. Why he was here. What he wanted.

Who he wanted.

Make your move, Davis.

The day hinted at the beginnings of another idyllic display of Indian summer. Leaves crunched under his feet and the sun warmed his shoulders. Maybe he should have planned something outdoors.

The chimes of the doorbell sounded

through the house, and only a few seconds later, Sadie swung open the door. No bright-colored bandana hid her deep-brown hair. Her makeup — the barest hint of blush, a touch of eye shadow and eyeliner — impeccable. The jeans and pale-green blouse accented her figure, proving that she didn't use her profession as an excuse to overindulge.

"Ready to go?" She eased the door shut behind her as she joined him on the small porch.

"Hello to you too." Erik stayed put, close enough to catch a hint of her perfume that smelled of vanilla. Did she just grab the expensive Mexican vanilla she liked to cook with and dab it behind her ears? "Is this how you greet all your dates? Don't you want to invite me inside, show me your home?"

"You were here ten days ago. You know what my house looks like. You helped me move, remember?"

"Go back inside."

"What? That's ridiculous."

"Back inside." He turned her to face the door. "Let's try this again and act like we haven't known each other since we were thirteen."

"Is this a pretend date — or a real one?"

"It's real, Miss McAllister, I assure you. You're acting like we're going to hang out together."

"We are —"

"Please." Erik held up his hand and closed his eyes. "I invited you out on a date. You accepted. We do this my way."

"Do you enforce absurd rules like this with all your dates?"

Erik refused to answer, hoping the heat blazing in her eyes wouldn't singe the other side of the door.

Then he sang the chorus of "Born in the U.S.A." to cool down. Sang it again because he figured Sadie needed a chance to cool down too.

Squaring his shoulders, Erik knocked on the door again. And waited. Rang the doorbell. And waited.

Finally, Sadie opened the door — wearing her blue Japanese kimono robe, belted tight around her waist.

"Oh, Erik — you're early. Come on in. I'm sorry I'm not quite ready." She ran up the stairs leading to her loft, pausing halfway and leaning over the railing. "If you're thirsty, there are some sodas or tea in the fridge. Or water. Back in a few."

He should follow her and march her back downstairs and out to his car. But was she wearing anything underneath that silky robe? No reason to call her bluff and end up embarrassing them both.

Nope. This was when he would disorder something in Sadie J.'s space.

What section of the open concept living room that flowed right into the dining room would he disrupt today?

Sadie's sacred kitchen.

To the casual observer, the kitchen looked as spotless as a staged home's, ready for an onslaught of potential buyers. The stainless steel counters were bare of appliances. The clear glass cabinets displayed artistically arranged white dishes.

Sadie kept her treasured collection of cookbooks — dozens of them — in a side cabinet that was more of a nook beside the refrigerator. One by one, he turned them upside down. Did he dare rearrange them too? At the sound of Sadie's footsteps on the stairs, Erik grabbed two cans of soda from the fridge, and met her at the foot of the stairs.

"What are you doing?"

He offered her a can. "Soda?"

"No, thank you." Sadie tilted her head. "You know I don't drink diet. What are you up to?"

"Nothing. Wasn't thinking. Do you want

something else?"

"No. I'm fine."

She'd changed into a denim skirt, tall black boots, and a purple sweater. "If you're ready, let's go."

"You don't want a tour of my house?"

"No, I'm good. After you, Sadie."

"Are you going to watch the otters all day long?" Erik's close whisper caused a shiver up Sadie's neck.

Sadie leaned toward the plexiglass tank, following the motions of the long, lithe animals frolicking in the water. *Watch the otters.* Ignore how Erik's low tone created a warmth in her body that made her want to lean *toward* him, not away. "I love otters. Usually when I try to see them at the zoo, they're sleeping. Or the exhibit is closed for renovation."

"You come here often?"

Was that a hint of disappointment in Erik's voice?

"No — I can't think of the last time I came to the aquarium — or the zoo. Probably during some elementary-school field trip." Sadie crouched down to watch the underwater otter ballet, the heat from Erik's closeness evaporating. She'd probably been on some class trip her mother had assured her would be fun. And then Sadie had hung back from her classmates, staying near the teacher — where it was safe. "Do you know otters hold hands when they sleep?"

"They do?"

"Yes — so they don't float away from one another. Isn't that adorable?"

Several younger children pressed forward to watch the animals, pushing and shoving one another to get the best spot, causing Sadie to ease to the right side of the tank. She never took her eyes off the trio of otters sliding through the water, swimming around the blue bucket filled with a chunk of fish-laden ice.

Five minutes later, she turned to share a laugh with Erik. Where was he? She slipped through the crowd, rounding the corner of the exhibit to find him talking with a college-aged girl overseeing the display of faux barrels overflowing with stuffed otters.

"The real ones are much more fun to watch," Sadie said, walking up behind him.

"Yes, but you can't take one home with you." Erik held up a medium-sized brown-and-white, stuffed otter, using it to plant a kiss on the tip of her nose.

Sadie stepped back. "That tickles."

"Then let's hope he behaves when you take him home."

"This is for me?"

"Of course. You can't come to the aquarium and not get a souvenir." Erik pocketed his receipt and thanked the cashier. "Don't forget to name him."

"Erik."

"What?"

"That's his name — Erik."

"You have to be more creative than that. Something like Nanuk or Oscar or Swimmy."

"Swimmy?"

"It's better than Erik."

"You said I get to name him — and I did." She tucked the plush memento into the top of her black cross-body purse. "Thank you."

"You're welcome. But that furry thing looks nothing like me."

"You're right — whiskers but no beard."

"You've never liked my beard, have you?"

Sadie scanned Erik's face: his deep-set blue eyes, hawkish nose, and firm jaw. "I admit I wasn't too happy a few years ago when you announced you were growing it."

"Why not?"

"I wasn't crazy about the whole lumberjack look." Sadie reached up and touched the dark blond hair covering his jaw. "But your beard is nice. You keep it trimmed — not all wild and crazy like Karl

352

Marx or . . . or one of those Duck Dynasty guys."

Erik's boom of laughter caused the people around them to stop and stare. "That's quite a jump in history — Karl Marx to Duck Dynasty."

"You know what I mean." She dropped her hand, tucking it into the pocket of her skirt. "It'll be a long time before I give you a compliment again."

And it would be even longer before she touched Erik Davis's face again. His beard was soft. And his full lips had curved into a much-too-alluring smile. Where had the thought of letting her fingers trail up to the hair along his temple, which he also kept trimmed close, come from? Followed quickly by a desire to kiss him.

"You want to go see the mermaids?"

What? Sadie shook her head, clearing her thoughts. *The mermaid show.* "No, I don't think so."

Erik linked his arm through hers. "You never dreamed about being a beautiful underwater sea creature?"

"No."

She'd dreamed about being beautiful for years — all the while enduring the teasing of classmates. A taunt whispered across her mind. *Pirate.* But if you were the only kid in class wearing an eye patch, what else would your classmates call you? Disappearing into the ocean had never been part of the dream. Becoming invisible, yes.

"Sadie?"

Sadie pulled her hand away from her left eye. "What?"

"Do you have a headache?"

"No. No. I'm fine. Lead on to the next exhibit."

It'd been worth crawling underneath the exhibit to the viewing half domes to make Sadie laugh again. Of course, the space was built to accommodate children, not grown men. Through the haze of blue water, distorted multicolored fish darted by against the backdrop of the faint outlines of the people standing around the tank. Where was Sadie? How long did he need to stay under here to get her talking to him again? And why had she suddenly gone silent?

As he backed out into the open space again and rose to his feet, he bumped into someone. "Sorry about that."

"No problem — Erik?"

Dusting his hands off, Erik turned and faced Charlie Ferguson from church.

"Hey, Charlie. You here with the family?"

"Yep. Angie's talking with Sadie."

"Perfect day for the aquarium, isn't it?" The two joined Sadie and Angie and the Fergusons' three children. "Did you all watch the mermaid show?"

"We sure did." Angie looked from Erik to Sadie and back again. "So, what brings you two to the aquarium?"

Erik draped his arm around Sadie's shoulder, unable to ignore the way she stilled. "We're on a date."

Now Sadie went ramrod stiff. "We're not dating . . ."

"Yes, yes we are. Dating, I mean." Erik kept the smile on his face despite Sadie's swift kick to his ankle. *Ouch.* "I asked Sadie out and she accepted. So this is a date."

"Wow, that was fast." Angie's eyes widened. "Last I heard, you were dating Lydia."

"Um, yeah. I was. But now I'm not." *Great.* He sounded like a jerk. "I'm out with Sadie. Today."

"That's wonderful." Angie waved as Charlie tugged her toward the next display of fish. "Well, we'll see you at church."

When the family turned away, Sadie aimed another kick at his ankle.

"Come on, Sadie! Are you trying to cripple me?"

"What are you doing, telling them that

we're dating?"

"This is a date."

"This is a between-you-and-me date. You don't have to announce it to the whole church."

"I didn't announce it —"

Sadie stomped away, forcing Erik to double-time it to keep up with her. "Angie's going to put us on the prayer chain!"

"What? The prayer chain is for prayer requests."

Sadie bowed her head, hands clasped together, her voice a muted whisper. "We need to pray for Sadie and Erik. Yes, they're dating! I saw them at the Denver Aquarium! It was so cute! We need for God's will to be done in their relationship. We need to pray that they stay pure and not give in to temptation . . ."

"Now you're being absurd."

"You have obviously never volunteered for the prayer chain."

"Yeah, and if that's what really happens, I don't plan to either." Erik risked taking her hand and pulling her toward the exit, keeping space between them in case she decided to kick him again. "Are you hungry? I thought we could have lunch at the Cheesecake Factory."

"Bribing me with cheesecake isn't going

to make me forgive you."

"It's worked in the past, Sadie JuJube. Cheesecake is my go-to plan when I need you to like me again."

"Humph." Sadie allowed him to lead her toward the exit. "It's a good thing I like cheesecake. And you're wrong again."

"I'll figure out your middle name one day."

"So you think, my friend. Seventeen years and counting."

"I'm no quitter. You should know that about me by now."

Six

Sadie ran her hand down the front of her chef's coat, pressing a palm against the queasiness in her stomach. She never had flying-out-of-formation butterflies when she stood before an "audience" in the Hartnetts' kitchen — or the Coopers'. Yes, this morning's audience was live — but they were also invisible. She'd just pretend they were as imaginary as the ones who were presented with her weekly meals.

Even though the local morning show was on a commercial break, she refused to mess with her bright red bandana. No need to risk getting it misaligned — or pulling it off altogether. *Relax.* The set was almost like home: truncated counter, a range and sink, her already-prepared pistachio encrusted pork loin sitting off to one side, all the ingredients separated out into clear glass bowls surrounding a prepped, uncooked pork loin.

"Mel said the two of you went to culinary school together?" Derrick Franklin, the male counterpart of the morning team, continued a steady stream of questions during the commercial break.

"Yes. At the Broadmoor."

"Are you working at a restaurant now?"

"No, I'm a private chef for several families in the metro area."

"Interesting." He faced the TV camera as the lights came up. "Time for our segment. Cynthia does the intro and then we're on. Just relax and pretend we're talking in your kitchen."

As she stared into the bright glow of the lights, Sadie tried to swallow, the smile on her face causing her lips to tremble. Why hadn't she asked for a bottle of water?

We're just talking in the kitchen. Pretending to cook. It couldn't be simpler. In less than five minutes, you're out of here.

Sadie stood in the Coopers' kitchen, the cup of coffee gone cold in her hand. She'd stored the groceries in the fridge. Changed into her chef's coat. Set out her menu and her knives. And here she stood, already half an hour behind schedule.

Imaginary lights, camera, action!

Today she couldn't even conjure up a

smile for an imaginary audience.

Of course, being an utter failure on live TV — knowing *real people* had witnessed her on-air mortification — well, that was enough to make her want to abandon cooking all together.

The debacle had happened two days ago, and thinking about it still caused her to groan out loud. She'd flustered — if not completely frustrated — Derrick Franklin. Once the segment was over, he'd walked off the set with nothing more than a curt, "Thank you for your time." And she was almost certain the cameraman had covered up a laugh with a lousy imitation cough.

When the station manager asked her to bring in a fun recipe, she'd selected a favorite, one she'd prepared dozens of times. She'd chatted with the host during the commercial break. Sure, she'd felt a little nervous, but didn't everyone?

And the minute they went live . . . she couldn't remember how to boil water. Franklin had to almost drag every word out of her, filling in the awful silences with statements like "And before we came on the air, didn't you mention something about trimming the fat off the pork loin?" Franklin's eyes pleaded with Sadie to relax. Be normal. Be anything other than a freaked-out chef.

She'd hacked on the piece of meat while mumbling about needing to remember to remove the "silver skin" too. But did she explain that was a tendon membrane? *No.* And if the camera zoomed in while she prepared the stone-ground mustard, honey, and red wine sauce, then everyone in the Denver area saw her hands shaking like she needed a stiff drink.

The ring of her cell phone shattered the memory. Erik. He'd called her twice a day since her death-by-morning-show disaster. She retrieved the ingredients for chicken cacciatore from the fridge, piling them on the counter. "I'm fine, Erik."

"Are you convincing me — or yourself?"

"Very funny."

"Sadie, you weren't that bad."

"You've never lied to me before. Don't start now."

"You're making this worse than it was."

"I was there, Erik." Sadie turned on the water and began rinsing the fresh vegetables in the sink. "I didn't even remember my own recipe for pistachio encrusted pork loin."

"Always a favorite of mine."

"I couldn't say pistachio. *Pistachio.*"

"You did now."

"I sounded as unintelligible as Tom, the

Muppets' Swedish Chef."

"You did not — wait a minute. The Swedish Chef's name was *Tom*?"

"I saw it on YouTube once — it was some sort of ad lib by Danny Kaye during a skit." Sadie slumped against the counter. "It doesn't matter. I flopped."

"Stop beating up my best friend, will you? You looked adorable."

"No one who is scared to death looks adorable."

"I did not call to argue with you."

"Fine." Sadie pressed her damp forefinger and middle finger to her left eye. *Headache coming on.* "You don't usually call me during work hours anyway."

"True — you don't answer your phone."

"I'm off-schedule." And not likely to catch up if she kept chatting with Erik. "What do you need?"

"I wanted to see if you'd go out with me again."

Another date? Was Erik just trying to make her feel better?

"Why?"

"The proper response is yes or no — and I sincerely hope you say yes, Sadie Jasmine."

"A Disney princess name?"

"Jasmine happens to be a flower, too, you know."

"Whichever — you're still wrong."

"Fine. I'll keep guessing."

"You always do."

"Back to my question: Will you go out with me again? Please?"

She silenced the *why* demanding to be asked again. The first date had been fun. Just for a moment a dangerous emotion had flared, but she'd extinguished that quickly enough. And she did need to keep herself busy.

"Sure. I'll go out with you again. What are we doing?"

"That's a surprise. Just be comfortable — and ready for a good time."

"Anything else?"

"Yes. Call Mel. She's worried about you."

Sadie slumped against the edge of the sink. "Mel called you?"

"Only ten times. Call her."

"I will. I'm just so embarrassed — and I let her down."

"Mel's your friend — she's on your side, Sadie. She told me she wishes she'd gone with you so she could've helped."

Something between a whimper and giggle escaped Sadie's lips. "Oh, that would have entertained the TV audience."

"Well, at least you laughed."

"Barely."

"It's a start. Now get to work. I know how you hate to be off-schedule. See you Saturday."

How odd that Erik was asking her out when their friendship started all because she had asked him to the Sadie Hawkins Dance.

She could do this.

The middle-school hallways were filled with the sounds of students talking as they opened their lockers and slammed them shut. The overhead clock in the hallway ticked down the last five minutes before homeroom started. Guys and girls yelled hellos, laughter clogged the air, and occasionally someone yelled "Hi, Sadie" and broke her concentration.

The rules for the Sadie Hawkins Day Dance were clear: A girl could ask a guy to the dance on November 13. And it wasn't as if she hadn't talked to Erik Davis. They were lab partners in science. Sometimes he even called her when he missed school and needed to find out about the day's assignment.

So why was she sweating through her Just Do It Nike T-shirt?

Sadie positioned herself next to Erik's locker. He often arrived in a rush, racing the homeroom bell, shoving his backpack into the locker, slamming the door shut with a metallic clang.

All she needed was one minute. Less, even.

And there he was, blond hair disheveled, his gray T-shirt wrinkled.

She chewed on her bottom lip. "Hey, Erik."

"Sadie." He manipulated the lock and swung open his locker. Shifted his backpack from his shoulder and shoved it inside. Grabbed a few books.

She gulped a breath, forced a grin. "So . . . I was wondering if you wanted to go to the Sadie Hawkins Dance with me next Friday. It'd be fun."

Now came the yes, and they could go their separate ways and she could breathe again.

"Um . . . the Sadie Hawkins Dance?"

Did Erik's voice crack? Poor guy.

"Yeah, you know. They've been announcing it over the intercom every morning."

"Yeah. That." Erik jumped as the bell rang for homeroom. "I don't think so, Sadie. Thanks anyway. Gotta go — we're gonna be late."

She watched him lope off down the hallway, never once looking back.

He said no.

No.

Her cheeks burned and her lungs ached when she tried to draw a breath. Instead of going to homeroom, she marched to the girls' bathroom, avoiding her reflection in the mirror over the sinks. She locked herself in a stall, leaning back against the cold metal door.

It didn't matter. It was a stupid dance. And Erik was a stupid boy.

Sadie squeezed her eyes shut, knuckling away the lone tear that managed to escape and trail down her face.

She'd go to the dance by herself. Lots of girls did.

And nobody knew she'd asked Erik Davis — and that he'd said no. She could only hope he wouldn't tell his buddies and laugh at her.

Well, if he did, she'd make sure he flunked science — even if it meant she had to flunk it too.

As she began setting up to cook, the clatter of pots and pans jarred her back to the present. She could laugh at that memory now, knowing how she and Erik both ended up at the dance by themselves. How they'd hung back by the refreshments, watching their classmates dance. And how they'd talked. About their teachers. And how Erik liked to play baseball. And Sadie liked to bake. And then they started inventing crazy secret lives for the chaperones. By the end of the evening, the entire middle-school faculty was a front for a secret agency that battled crime.

And she and Erik weren't just lab partners anymore . . . they had become friends.

SEVEN

"You're supposed to let me lead." Erik repositioned Sadie so she stood facing him again. His big toe was probably swelling from the way she'd tromped on it.

"I'll let you lead once you know what you're doing." Sadie watched her feet, trying to keep up with the rhythm of some song about Joshua and the battle of Jericho. Who knew you could swing dance to a song retelling a Bible story?

"We're both *beginners*. Stop leading and follow me."

Other couples moved across the wooden floor in the small room on the upper floor of the Mercury Café in Denver, swinging and swirling around them. They laughed and smiled whether they were getting the dance moves right or not.

Strings of tiny white lights covered the ceiling. Halfway through the free hour-long lesson, she and Erik still looked as if they were involved in some sort of stand-up arm wrestling contest. Why couldn't they catch on to the instructors' directions?

"Breathe, Sadie. Of course, if you pass out on me, it'd be easier to take charge."

"Ha-ha. You're hysterical."

"And you're still not relaxed."

Sadie risked looking at Erik. "I *am* relaxed."

"This" — Erik contorted his face into something between a frown and a grimace — "does not communicate relaxed."

"I'm concentrating." She closed her eyes. Listened to the music for a moment to recapture the beat. Opened her eyes as Erik tried to maneuver her through another swing-dance step.

"Don't concentrate so hard. Have fun."

Sadie clenched her teeth. "How can I have fun when I don't know what I'm doing?"

Erik swung her in yet another awkward circle, pulling her up against him. "Sadie, most of the people here don't know what they're doing."

She nodded to a young couple who executed a perfect underarm twirl. "They do."

"They're cheaters. Very good, experienced cheaters who could teach the class — but still cheaters." He swayed back and forth, his hand warm against her back. "You know why I wanted to do this tonight?"

"To publicly humiliate both of *us*?"

"No." In one smooth motion he slid his arms around her waist and pulled her up against him, positioning her arms around his shoulders. "Because if I had to do it over again, I would have said yes when you asked me to the Sadie Hawkins Dance when we were thirteen. I'm catching up on past regrets."

Sadie stared straight ahead, which meant the only thing she could see was Erik's gray shirt pocket. Where had that statement come from? They swayed back and forth like two middle schoolers, their feet shuffling on the floor, while other couples stayed up to swing-dance speed. Erik hummed along with the music and Sadie inhaled the faint scent of fabric softener that clung to his clothes.

"We're dancing too slow."

"I'm content." Erik rested his chin on top of her head and continued to hum for a few seconds. "I'm holding you. You're letting me lead. And you haven't stepped on my foot in a couple of minutes. It's turning out to be a good evening, don't you think?"

When Erik moved his head to look down at her, Sadie made the mistake of looking up, her cheek brushing against the soft cotton fabric of his shirt. In the muted light of the room, Sadie tried to decipher the way Erik's eyes warmed . . . He was close enough to kiss, if she wanted to do something that crazy.

On a swift intake of breath, Sadie realized she wanted to kiss him. She did. If his arms tightened around her, or if he tipped his head the slightest bit closer — she'd close her eyes and say yes to this longing.

And then the song ended. The dancers slowed. Moved away. And Erik released her.

The moment faded with the last notes of the music.

By the time the class ended, Erik had coaxed her into trying the basic steps again — and they'd managed to master them. Well, almost. But she'd laughed at her missteps, not tensed up. And Erik ended the final dance with a silly flourish, dipping her and dropping the lightest of kisses on her cheek.

Silly man.

On the ride home, Sadie tucked herself into the passenger's seat, her hands folded in her lap, as she watched the blur of houses along Broadway pass by outside the car window. She and Erik had never danced together before. It was . . . unfamiliar . . . to

370

be that close to him for an hour. To feel the pressure of his hands guiding her, to be so near that his beard brushed against her face, to feel his arm wrapped around her waist, to listen to him hum . . . and to wonder if he could feel her heart beating like she could feel his.

"Tired?"

"Hmm." She shook her head, dispelling her thoughts. "In a good way."

"I'm glad. We'll try it again sometime."

"Sure."

They would? When — and why? And would it be a date — or would they be back to "best friends only" status again?

Outside her house, Erik stepped up onto the small front porch while she searched in her purse for her key and slipped it into the lock.

"You want to come in? I could make some coffee."

"I don't think so."

A small pang — something indefinable — tripped her heart. "Oh. I understand. On deadline?"

"No." Erik stood in the shadows. "That's not it at all. It's because of this."

Before she realized his intent, Erik leaned forward, closing the distance between them, and kissed her.

He didn't touch her, save for the firm pressure of his lips against hers.

Erik pulled away the barest of inches. "Sadie?"

"Yes?"

"I'm going to kiss you again."

He didn't wait for her to say *no* or *yes* or *please*. He cradled her face with his hands, which were cool from the fall night air, his thumbs caressing her skin and sending shivers down her neck. His kiss coaxed a response from her, his lips soft against hers, the taste of his mouth enticing in its newness. Sadie leaned into Erik, savoring the touch of his hands against her skin, the warmth of his mouth. When he ended the kiss, Sadie's hand clutched the front of his coat, as if anchoring herself to him.

"And that, my dear Sadie" — Erik rested his forehead against hers, his breath warming her lips in an echo of their kiss — "is why I'm not coming in."

Enough said.

He pulled her close again and, for one moment, Sadie held her breath, but instead of kissing her again, Erik unlocked the front door, thanks to the key that was waiting in the lock.

"I really enjoyed myself tonight." Sadie half-closed the door.

Erik's eyes glinted in the porch light. "I did too. And the dancing was fun too."

The sound of Erik's laughter slid into the house as she closed the door. Sadie leaned against the door, embracing the memory of his kiss.

EIGHT

What was Erik doing standing outside Whole Foods Market in the middle of the day, wearing his dark gray coat with the red plaid scarf she'd given him last Christmas, and holding two insulated cups, one of which he raised and tipped oh-so-slightly in her direction?

Sadie forced herself to maintain a slow pace. There would be no running across this parking lot, not with a light dusting of snow slicking the surface. She wasn't going to do a face plant in front of him, thank you very much.

"For me?"

"Yes — you're the one who muddies a good cup of coffee with milk and sugar. And I asked the barista to heat your cream before adding it to the coffee." As he handed her the unexpected treat, he leaned in and brushed a kiss across her lips as if it was the most natural thing in the world.

Sadie spoke once she caught her breath. "What are you doing here?"

"Well, you mentioned you had to shop for the Coopers when we talked earlier. I thought I'd tag along. Push your cart."

Sweet — but Erik was going to be a huge distraction. Sadie needed to focus on her list, not the man next to her, who'd snagged a black metal cart from the corral by the front door.

"Where to? Fruits and veggies? Seafood? Desserts? Frozen foods?"

"I don't know if this is a good idea. I have a system I like to follow . . ."

"Of course you do. Just consider me your shadow. I'll tag along — all that I'm in charge of is pushing the cart and refilling your coffee. I won't say another word."

Erik controlled himself while she scanned her list: tri-tip roast, chicken Florentine, smoked garlic stuffed prime rib, handmade wild mushroom truffle pesto ravioli, and duck confit. The produce section proved his downfall.

"You know I can juggle, right?" Erik sorted through a pile of oranges, selecting three, and began tossing them in the air, increasing his speed.

"Yes, I know you can juggle."

"Toss me another one."

"I'm shopping." Sadie was on the hunt for fresh herbs: thyme, sage, parsley, rosemary, and tarragon. "If you keep talking to me, I'm going to forget something."

"Come on — toss me another one."

A small group of children gathered around him. Sadie tossed him another orange. Let him entertain kiddos. She had work to do.

Erik found her in the market's expansive cheese area.

"Hey. Sorry about that."

"It's okay." Sadie added Pecorino cheese to her cart. "I'm just on a tight schedule today."

"Don't you usually shop and then go home and do prep?"

"Yes. But I'm meeting Justin Boyle at The Tattered Cover later."

"Oh?"

"He's one of the single dads in the cooking class I teach at the church. You know him — he makes custom fishing rods. He wants to start cooking regular meals for his son — get away from fast food and chicken nuggets. So he asked me to meet him at five and help him find a good beginner's cookbook."

"Why don't you just give him one of your cookbooks?" Erik stuffed his hands in his jeans pockets. "You've got enough."

"I have a collection — not a lending library." Sadie added a brick of Fontina cheese to the supplies. "Oh, no turning my books upside down. Not nice."

"Took you long enough to notice. What was that — two weeks?"

"I noticed two days later — I've just been busy."

"So you and Justin are going on a date, huh?"

"I don't think it's a date —" Was it? "I'm just giving him some extra help outside of class."

"Is his son coming too?"

"I don't think so."

"Then it's a date."

"I'm helping him . . ."

Erik didn't seem convinced.

"Fine. Be that way."

Erik pushed the cart. No joking. No juggling. After helping her carry her bags to the car, he gave her a swift wave.

"Talk to you soon. Have fun tonight."

"Thanks. I will."

No kiss.

Why was Sadie going on a date with that guy?

Didn't their two dates and one kiss — well, two kisses, which kept replaying in his mind — signify anything to her?

He was a teenager again and back up on that roller coaster, afraid Sadie was going to toss him over the side.

Not this time.

He was thirty, not eighteen. This time, he wasn't going to wonder what happened. He wasn't giving Sadie up without a fight. But he only had a few hours to plan his offensive maneuver.

So this was the life of a private investigator — lurking in between store shelves, watching the door, hoping some store clerk wouldn't show up and accuse you of shoplifting?

Erik held his ground in the greeting card section of the bookstore, his attention on The Tattered Cover's front doors. He even had a few cards in his hands, which he may or may not get to use, depending on how tonight went.

"Isn't that her?"

At Lydia's whispered question, he looked up from the card adorned with a retro black-and-white photo of a man and woman embracing under the words: For My Love: C'mere you!

Sadie at nine o'clock.

Took her long enough to get here. Of

course, she was the one who was punctual. He had been early.

"Yep, that's her."

What was she doing, looking that cute in a navy blue jacket, white scarf arranged at the collar, and a pair of black skinny jeans tucked in black boots?

And there was Justin, greeting her with a friendly hug. Motioning to the Starbucks coffee bar. Sadie shook her head. Looked as if it was book browsing first, coffee later.

Fine. He could put his plan into action all the sooner.

Erik set the cards back in the rack. "You ready for this? Okay, remember the plan: We interrupt Sadie and Justin. You distract Justin — to the point he takes you to coffee, not Sadie."

Erik straightened his shoulders. Yeah, as far as Sadie was concerned, he was a goner. He just wasn't sure Sadie would ever speak to him again after tonight's lovesick shenanigans.

Lydia offered him a smirk — a sympathetic smirk, but a smirk nonetheless. "You must love her an awful lot to sabotage her date, Erik."

The word *love* slammed into his gut. To admit it to himself was one thing. To hear an ex-girlfriend say it — out loud — was

379

something else altogether.

"I do, Lydia."

"Which is why you and I didn't work out. Why did you even date me when you were in love with Sadie?"

"I just realized it. It took me seventeen years to figure it out."

"Talk about slow."

"Yeah — but I'm catching up fast. Let's go."

Sadie's and Justin's laughter floated over from one of the aisles in the cookbook section.

"Sadie, what a surprise!" Erik could only hope his voice sounded nonchalant.

"Erik?" The pages of the open book rippled through Sadie's fingers.

He stepped forward, gripping Justin's outstretched hand. "I'm Erik Davis." He'd thought this next sentence out all afternoon. If he went the "I'm Sadie's boyfriend" route, he put seventeen years on the line — and all his hopes for a future. "I'm Sadie's best friend."

"Nice to meet you, Erik. I've seen you at church."

"And this is Lydia, a friend of mine."

"Sadie — Erik's told me so much about you." Lydia enacted her part perfectly, offering Justin a warm smile and managing to position herself between the two men. "Hello, Justin."

"Lydia."

Erik ran his hand down the spines of the closest books. "So, how's the cookbook browsing going?"

"We just started." Sadie's posture was rigid, her tone glacial.

"You like to cook, Justin?" Lydia might not be able to thaw out Sadie, but Justin couldn't take his eyes off the tall brunette.

"I'm taking the father-son cooking class Sadie's been teaching at our church. Ever since my wife died almost two years ago, my son and I have survived on frozen food and takeout."

"I'm so sorry for your loss." Lydia angled her body toward the widower. "I have a wonderful recipe for beef stroganoff. Of course, I'm not in Sadie's league. I spend more time fly-fishing than cooking."

"Fly-fishing?"

"Yes. My father taught me. Do you fly-fish?"

"I make custom rods."

Lydia's look of surprised admiration was Oscar worthy. "No, really?"

"Yes."

"That's amazing. I'd love to see them sometime."

"Sure."

Erik knew his cue. "Aren't some of your rods featured in a book?"

"Yeah, yeah they are." Justin barely glanced at Erik. "How did you know that?"

"Sadie must have mentioned it to me."

"There's no time like the present." Lydia was a pro. He would make sure he loaded her Starbucks card with an extra twenty-five dollars. "Maybe the book's here."

"Oh, I don't know . . ."

It figured Justin Boyle would play it humble.

"It wouldn't hurt to look." Lydia tucked her arm through Justin's. "Shall we?"

Justin hesitated. "You don't mind, Sadie?"

"No, no, I don't mind at all. I'll keep looking through the shelves."

"Anyone interested in coffee?" Erik pulled out his wallet. "I can go order for us."

Everyone declined, and soon he and Sadie were left standing between the shelves.

Sadie slammed the cookbook shut. "Erik Davis, you ought to be ashamed of yourself."

"I don't know what you're talking about."

"You knew I was going to be here with Justin."

"So suspicious, Sadie J."

"Do you deny that you arranged to be

here with Lydia at the same time?"

"Is this when I take the fifth?" Erik held his hands up, hoping Sadie backed down soon.

"This is when you go home."

"But then you'll be left here all alone."

"Only until Justin comes back."

"But if, um, my suspicions are correct, he's not going to be coming back anytime soon."

She advanced on him, one slow step at a time. "Did you sic Lydia on that poor man?"

"Are you kidding me? Did you see Lydia? Did you see Justin looking at Lydia? And they both like fly-fishing — they're perfect for each other."

"What? Now you're a matchmaker?"

"Justin's happy. Lydia's happy. I'm happy." He took the book from her hands. "What about you? Are you happy?"

"Me? I'm discovering that my best friend is a conniving stalker."

"All's fair in love, sweetheart. All's fair."

NINE

It was barely seven in the morning on a Saturday. Sadie wasn't asleep, but she wasn't up and at 'em, either. She'd go grocery shopping later, after coordinating her planned menu with the sales at the local grocery stores, but for now she needed quiet. And answers. Still in bed, her blankets smoothed over her legs, her pillows arranged behind her back, she balanced her Bible against her knees.

So, Sadie, what do you think about Oregon? Have you made a decision?

Mrs. Hartnett's question, left via voice mail on Thursday, had haunted her the last few days. Stay or go? Should she or shouldn't she?

Sadie had flipped through her Bible for the last forty-five minutes, finding her "anchor" verses — passages that had helped her in the past. Comforted her when she was hurt. Guided her when she had other decisions to make. Today she'd stopped at Psalm 143:8, "Let me hear Your lovingkindness in the morning; For I trust in You; Teach me the way in which I should walk; For to You I lift up my soul."

She pressed her hand against the page, as if she could soak in the truth. She needed a direct message from God. She loved her job, loved the Hartnett kids. What they were offering her was the chance to pursue some new adventures, as well as the chance to be closer to her parents. And what was holding her here except her beloved routine? Of course, no one in Oregon would know her as the girl who freaked out on the local morning news show — not that the incident bothered her anymore. Much.

And then there was Erik . . . but what exactly was going on between them, anyway? Why the sudden romantic turn in their friendship? And what would happen in a few months when his internal warning system blared?

At the sound of an elephant trumpeting through her bedroom, Sadie's hand slid off the page, ripping it partway from the binding.

An elephant? She silenced her phone before answering it.

"Hello?"

"Hey, Sadie Jehoshaphat!"

"Now you're messing with my ringtones and guessing some obscure Bible name? Honestly, Erik, if you're calling to say you're sorry for the other night, you now have two reasons to apologize."

"I'm calling to ask if you'll go out with me."

"I'm not even certain I'm talking to you."

"Well, talk to me long enough to say, 'Yes, Erik, I'll go out with you.' "

Sadie choked on her giggle.

"You can't be that mad at me if you're laughing."

Sadie ran her fingers through her unwashed hair. "Erik . . ."

"Yes, I'll go out with you."

It was useless to resist the man — and did she even want to? "Yes, I'll go out with you."

"Perfect. I'll pick you up at eight o'clock."

"Tonight?"

"No, this morning. See you then."

When he hung up, Sadie stared at the screen. *This morning?*

Where were they going? What should she wear — and how was she supposed to be ready in an hour?

When Erik showed up, Sadie had showered and changed into a pair of comfortable jeans — ones that she normally wore around the house. She accessorized them with a yellow sweater, opting to wear her hair loose. She applied her makeup but finally gave in and slipped on her glasses, an admission to a lurking headache. In all the years they'd known each other, Erik might have seen her wear her glasses a dozen times.

When she opened the door after Erik's knock, the first words out of his mouth were, "Forgive me?"

He bowed his head, looking at her through lowered lashes, his bottom lip poking out like a pouty three-year-old's.

No way was she responding to that. "Overdoing it a bit, aren't you?"

"And I thought I had it down pretty well."

"I know you too well."

"I disagree." He lifted her hand and pressed a warm kiss against it. "You know me perfectly."

Sadie fought the desire to step into Erik's arms and give him a real good-morning kiss. She wasn't sure what had gotten into her best friend, but she liked it — a lot.

"So where are we going?"

"To breakfast."

"Perfect. I'm starving." Sadie linked her arm through his, enjoying the feel of his fingers intertwined between hers. "And where are we going for breakfast?"

"Have you ever gone to the Brown Palace's brunch?"

"No — but isn't that served on Sundays?"

"Yes, but I didn't know that when I planned this date. And the Broadmoor's brunch is —"

"On Sunday too."

"And it's also where you did your culinary training, so why would you want to go eat there?"

"Well, there is that."

Erik ushered her into his car. "I did find a very elite place to eat."

"Really? Where?"

"My apartment. I thought I'd make you breakfast."

"What?"

"Don't worry. We're being chaperoned."

"You're kidding me."

"No. If we're going to be careful about being alone in your house now that we're dating, we need to uphold the same standards at my apartment."

She had to wait to continue the conversation until Erik was settled in the driver's seat. "You did not ask someone to come to your house and chaperone us. We're adults, not teenagers."

"Agreed." Erik offered her a quick smile.

"The question is: Which is the worse temptation?"

Good question. This grown-up Erik was much more tempting than the eighteen-year-old version. "Erik, who is at your house?"

"Nobody yet — but there will be."

Once they arrived, Sadie gripped her seat belt. "I am not getting out of this car until you tell me who else is going to be joining us for breakfast."

He covered her hand with his. "You know me better than anyone, right?"

"Ye-es."

"Well, then come to my apartment, knowing that I am perfectly trustworthy. Nothing is going to happen — except breakfast."

"It never occurred to me that anything else might happen."

"Of course not. And I'll try not to be hurt that the thought of kissing me again hasn't kept you awake."

"I didn't say that."

"Really? That's nice to know."

"Let's go have breakfast, please."

Erik needed to remember that this morning was about breakfast — waffles, bacon, orange juice — and nothing else. But he'd need to work hard to concentrate on cooking and not on whether Sadie would let him kiss her again before the end of the day. Or the bigger question: Was Sadie having anything besides "best friend" feelings for him?

No matter what, he had a plan in place to ensure the only thing they indulged in at his apartment was breakfast.

Once Sadie was settled at the table — cleared of the pile of mail and magazines — he opened his laptop and activated Skype.

"We're Skyping with someone?"

"Phillip and Ashley. I don't think Annalisa is joining us."

"Excuse me?"

"Hold on a second." Erik activated the video chat. "Hey, Phillip."

"Morning, Erik." Phillip's hair looked damp, as if he'd just showered. "Sadie there?"

"Yes." He positioned the laptop so Phillip could see Sadie. Phillip waved, prompting Sadie to wave back.

Phillip cleared his throat and put on his best I-mean-business face. "Okay, so here are the ground rules for you two: Keep the laptop powered up and open while you're having breakfast. Keep Skype open at all times. And you stay where we can see you. Pretty simple. Other than that, enjoy yourselves."

"Where's Ashley?"

"She's getting Annalisa dressed. She'll be joining the Skype session too — Ashley, not the baby. I'll be sitting over here working on my sermon about self-control."

"Subtle. Very subtle." Erik tossed his friend a salute. "Well, I'm going to get started."

"Do you want any help?" Sadie half-rose from her seat.

"No, thank you. I'm the chef today. But I do have some orange juice if you'd like — freshly squeezed."

"You're kidding me." Sadie retrieved two small glasses from the table and joined him in the kitchen.

"Well, that's what it said on the label. And it has pulp in it too."

"Hey, you two!" Phillip's voice came from the laptop screen. "Can't see you."

Erik pulled a container of juice from the fridge. "Will you carry the laptop in here, please?"

"Sure."

When she returned, Erik was setting up a Belgian-waffle maker.

"Waffles?"

"Yep — homemade, if you ignore the mix. And do you prefer sausage or bacon?"

"Bacon."

"Ah, a woman after my own heart. I have both — but why zap sausage in the microwave if we both want bacon?"

He was showing Sadie the extent of his cooking skills. But once it was all made — and served on real plates, not paper — she'd be impressed.

She sipped from the glass of juice, angling her hip against the counter. "Is there anything you want me to do?"

"Just stand there and look pretty. I've got this."

Sadie shook her head, as if dismissing his comment.

"What?"

"Nothing. Forget about it. Focus on your waffles."

"Are you disagreeing with the 'I've got this part' — or the 'look pretty' part?"

Sadie waved away his question. "Don't mind me. Show me your skills, chef."

"Hey." Erik took her hand, pulling her close, and using his other hand to tilt her chin up so she had to make eye contact with him. "I don't care if you know I'm a lousy cook — you've probably already figured that out. But you have to know you're beautiful to me."

He pressed his forehead to hers, when she

looked away. "Sadie?"

"It's okay, Erik. I don't want to talk about it." She motioned toward the laptop on the counter. "We're not alone."

"He can't hear us. Besides, he's deep into Greek verbs by now." Erik lowered his voice. "Do you remember asking me to the Sadie Hawkins Dance?"

She sniffed and offered him the hint of a smile. "Of course I do. You said no and practically ran to homeroom."

"You want to know why I said no?"

"I know why — you didn't want to go with me."

"Nope." Erik traced the curve of her face with the back of his hand. Her skin was so soft. "I couldn't believe a cute girl like you was asking a nobody like me to the dance."

"What?"

He pressed a kiss to her temple. Today the scent of vanilla lingered in her hair. "I thought it was a joke — like maybe your girlfriends were watching, laughing."

"After all I went through in grade school — wearing an eye patch and being teased? Being called a pirate by those mean girls?"

"Well, I didn't know that then, did I?"

"No, I guess you didn't."

"All I knew was this cute girl with long brown hair asked me out to a dance . . .

and I was too scared to say yes." Erik slipped his arms around Sadie's waist, easing her closer. "If you asked me today, I'd say yes. And the whole time we were dancing, I'd be wondering if . . ."

"You'd be wondering if . . . ?"

"If you'd let me kiss you goodnight."

"I don't believe in kissing on the first date."

"But this is our third date."

"We were discussing the Sadie Hawkins Dance that never was."

"Were we?" He pressed a kiss to one corner of Sadie's mouth.

"Yes."

"If you say so." He swept his lips across hers and pressed a kiss on the opposite corner of her mouth, noticing how she stopped breathing. How her lips trembled beneath his.

Kissing Sadie was becoming a take-his-breath-away habit. Something he'd like to do every day of his life. The way she'd leaned into him, wrapping her arms around his waist and then slipping them up around his back and pulling him closer, made him think that maybe, just maybe, she enjoyed kissing him too. The way she exhaled his name on a sigh as he sought the warm curve of her throat, and then ran her fingers through his hair and gently tugged him back to her and whispered, "Kiss me again."

She didn't have to ask him twice.

They weren't eighteen-year-olds on a roller coaster, but Erik felt as if he were falling . . . falling deeper in love with the woman in his arms. And he wasn't letting her go this time.

"Hey! Hey! I'm still here!" A sharp, staccato rapping pulled Erik away from Sadie.

He opened his eyes as she buried her face in his shoulder. "Who is that?"

"Um, we forgot about Phillip." Sadie's voice was muffled. "On your computer."

He cradled the back of her head with his hand. "I guess we did." An acrid plume of smoke billowed from the waffle maker on the counter. "And we forgot the waffles, which are now burned."

"Oh, Erik. I'm so sorry." She stepped out of his embrace. "Let me clean up this mess and fix breakfast."

"Absolutely not. I'm fixing you breakfast — but you have to stop being a beautiful distraction. Go. Sit over there and talk with Phillip and Ashley. I'll clean up this . . . charcoal . . . and start again."

TEN

Sadie ran her finger along the edge of the folder where it lay on her desk, then tapped it with her fingers.

Decisions, decisions.

Did she take the job in Oregon or didn't she?

When she got home from work, she received an unexpected phone call from the Hartnetts' friend in Oregon, who spent a good thirty minutes discussing the culinary school and the possible ways she could use Sadie's skills. The information compiled by the Hartnetts — magazine articles about Portland, a spreadsheet detailing salaries for private chefs nationwide with a suggested salary — was fanned out across her dining room table. And of course, her parents, who lived in Northern California, loved the idea of their only child being closer.

Why not say yes? Embrace a new dream for her life?

But what about her life here? What was happening between her and Erik?

Could it become something real? Permanent?

And how was she supposed to know?

Pray.

Wait.

It was November and the Hartnetts needed an answer — soon. Because if she wasn't going to move with them, then they needed time to find another private chef. Someone else . . . preparing meals for Jilly and Carter. The thought refused to settle. She'd been cooking for the family for three years. She knew their likes. Their dislikes. That Jilly liked chocolate cake with chocolate icing for her birthday. That Carter liked baked macaroni and cheese, heavy on the cheese. That Mr. Hartnett preferred lamb and Mrs. Hartnett loved fresh salmon. She'd invested not just time and culinary expertise into the family, she'd invested her heart.

Yes, she and Erik were best friends exploring a romance . . . but she'd never seen Erik commit to a woman. Never in the seventeen years she'd known him. And even if she cut him slack for high school — because, really, what guy knows what he wants in high school? — that still meant he'd never committed to anyone in thirteen years.

Why would Sadie be any different?

So, Erik, is this relationship going anywhere, um, permanent?

No. Absolutely not. She'd already proposed to him once. And his answer to her silly proposal made it clear he wasn't looking for " 'Til death do us part."

Did Sadie even realize how many times he had to stop himself from saying, "I love you"?

Was she ready to take their relationship past the point of no return? They'd always been "just friends," but he wasn't content living on that side of loving Sadie any longer. He wanted the *all* of loving her.

He knew her better than anyone, but now, as they walked through her neighborhood after he'd surprised her by showing up with hot chocolate from the coffee shop two blocks from her house, he couldn't figure out what she was thinking, much less how she felt about him.

"You okay?"

"Me? Sure. I'm fine." Sadie's gaze stayed focused on the horizon. "I've just got some things on my mind."

He let his heart lead his actions, put his arm around her waist, and pulled her close.

This is what he wanted. Sadie by his side. Sadie in his life. Always.

Her shoulders shifted against him as she sighed. "Remember I told you the Hartnetts are moving to Oregon — and that they want me to move with them as their personal chef?"

"I remember."

"I need to give them an answer this week."

"And?" Erik stared straight ahead, the sidewalk stretching out in front of them, covered with fallen leaves.

"And . . . I need to give them an answer."

"So what are you thinking?"

"I love the Hartnetts."

She loved the Hartnetts. What did she feel for him? Where did he stand compared to a family of four that she cooked for once a week?

"I've invested three years of my life in that family. I know them — their likes, their dislikes. I hate the thought of them leaving."

And what about leaving me, Sadie? Erik gritted his teeth, holding back the question.

"I mean, I've lived in Colorado all my life . . . and I love it here . . . but Oregon sounds beautiful too. It sounds like fun to move . . . to experience something new."

Erik shifted, putting a bit of distance

between them.

"And I'd be closer to my parents. They're excited about that possibility. So . . . there are reasons to stay and reasons to go." Halting beneath a leafless tree, she looked up at him. "What do you think?"

What did he think? He *knew* Sadie — had known her since she was thirteen. Watched her pursue with passion her dream of cooking . . . paying her way when her parents said no, insisting she needed to go to college, not settle for cooking school. He was crazy in love with her — his best friend. But they were best friends first. And best friends did not stand in the way of each other's dreams.

What if he asked her to stay . . . and she resented him? And then left a few months later anyway? He knew exactly how that felt — watching someone you love leave you, no matter how many times you asked them to stay.

And what could he offer her, really, besides the promising beginnings of his decision to be his own boss? He'd done his life solo for so many years. He had no experience with how relationships — family — worked. What if he told her that he loved her — and then failed her?

The word "Stay" stalled in his throat,

stuck behind, "I love you."

"I think . . . I think you should go, if that's what you want to do. You'd do a great job. And when the head of the culinary school meets you face-to-face, she'll realize what an asset you'll be and try and steal you away from the Hartnetts."

"You think so?"

"I know so. You're going places, Sadie J."

"Yeah. I guess I am." She moved away from him, her steps foreshadowing the future. "I guess I am."

"What do you mean Erik told you to leave?"

"Oh, Mel." Sadie sat at her friend's dining room table, staring down a bowlful of her signature minestrone soup. "I asked him what he thought I should do about the Hartnetts' job offer — and he said I should go."

"That's it?" Mel held a grater in one hand and a block of Parmesan cheese in the other.

"Yes."

"He thought you should go — and nothing else?"

"Yes. He thought I should go . . . if that's what I wanted to do." Sadie stared at the steam rising off the bowl of soup. "Or something like that."

401

"Aha!" Mel began grating cheese with a frenzy.

"Aha *what*?"

"He doesn't want you to go. I knew it."

"Mel, he never said he didn't want me to go. And we are not discussing this anymore." Sadie stirred the mixture of pasta, vegetables, and broth with her spoon. "I'm getting a headache."

Mel settled into the seat across from her. "You're going to listen to me, headache or no headache."

"Lower your voice. And the last time I listened to you, I agreed to go out with my best friend — and I ended up freaking out on TV."

"And that little fiasco is behind you. You survived, with a little emotional wear and tear, but dreams intact." Mel watched her from across the table. "Sadie, do you love Erik?"

"I'm not answering that question —"

The slam of Mel's spoon rattled the table. "Answer. The. Question."

"Yes. Yes. I love Erik. I do. But it doesn't matter. I'm not going to put my heart on the line and have him walk away from me in three or four months."

"He's stayed with you longer than any other woman."

"As my friend, Mel. *F-r-i-e-n-d.*"

"That's what you tell each other — but we all stopped believing you a long time ago."

"What?"

"I've known you were in love with Erik for years. I thought you'd figure it out — not that I'd have to tell you over a bowl of soup and a loaf of homemade bread."

"If he loves me, Mel, why is he telling me to leave?"

"Have you ever thought that he's just as scared of falling in love as you are?"

"Erik?"

"Yes, Erik." Mel threw her hands up in the air. "Women like to talk about how they've been hurt by guys. Guess what? Guys get hurt too — by their families. By women. Maybe Erik's afraid you don't want him. Asking him out to the Sadie Hawkins Dance when you were thirteen doesn't say you love him now, you know."

"But what if —"

"What if you two end up madly in love with one another — and get married? Then I get to cater your wedding, got it?"

ELEVEN

"So how's it going with Sadie?"

Erik ignored Phillip's question. He could see the batting cages. Hear the metallic *tink* of bats colliding with the baseballs. The rattle of the chain-link fences when the balls collided with them.

Phillip raised his voice. "I asked you a question. You going to answer me?"

Erik faced Phillip, who stood in the middle of the parking lot. Were they really going to have this conversation here?

"Things aren't going with Sadie."

"Are you kidding me? After what I saw on Skype the other weekend? Did you all have a fight?"

"No."

"Then what happened?"

"Sadie's taking the job in Oregon."

"What job?"

"One of the families she cooks for — they're moving to Oregon and they asked her to go with them — as their private chef."

"And she picked them over you? I find that hard to believe."

"There was no picking."

"You asked her to stay, right? Told her that you love her?"

Erik turned around and started walking toward the batting cages again.

"You're an idiot, Davis."

Erik did an about-face. "Hey! Is that something a pastor should say?"

"I'm talking to you guy-to-guy. You love this woman — why are you letting her leave?"

"I don't have any right to ask Sadie to stay here if she wants to go to Oregon."

"Now you're going all noble on me?" When Phillip settled onto one of the park benches, Erik followed, slumping against the back of the seat. "You're dressing up fear in some sort of misguided attempt at being heroic."

"What does that mean?"

"What are you afraid of?"

"Nothing."

"What are you afraid of?"

"Nothing . . . that hasn't already happened. My father abandoned the family when I was twelve years old. He's wandered in and out whenever he felt like it. I

405

remember begging him not to leave — but nothing I said made any difference. Sadie's been my best friend. Do you know when we were in high school that she used to make extra sandwiches, pretend she couldn't eat all of them, and offer one to me? I knew what she was doing. She'd seen my pitiful lunches . . . but she wasn't feeling sorry for me. She was being my friend. Soon she started adding cookies. And brownies. Even at fourteen that girl could love on you with food."

"You guys loved each other all the way back then, huh?"

"We were *friends*. I know what it's like to ask someone to stay — and then watch them leave. I'm not doing it again — not even for Sadie. If she wants to go, well, then she can go. I'm happy for her."

"And how do you feel?"

"It doesn't matter. I'll get over it."

"Just like you got over your dad leaving?"

"I'm fine."

"Have you forgiven him?"

"Do you think that man's ever asked for forgiveness?" Erik tried to swallow the bitter taste that seemed lodged in his throat. "As far as he's concerned, he's never done anything wrong. He didn't want to be married anymore, so he left. If my mom wants to be there when he comes around, well, that's her choice."

"Can I share a different view of forgiveness?"

"Do I have a choice?"

Phillip was silent.

"Sure. Go ahead," Erik said.

"I see forgiveness as both horizontal and vertical." Phillip formed his hands so that they looked like a cross, one up and down, one side to side. "So you and your dad? That's the horizontal aspect of forgiveness. If you went to him and said, 'Dad, I forgive you,' he would look at you like you were crazy, right?"

"Yep. He'd probably say, 'What are you talking about? I didn't do anything to hurt you. My choice was between me and your mother.' "

"So, for now, unless your father changes, unless your father acknowledges that he hurt you by abandoning you, there's nothing you can do about this aspect of forgiveness. *Nothing.*" Phillip waited until Erik looked at him. "You can't say 'I forgive you' because your father doesn't realize any injury has been done."

"Okay. What's your point?"

"But this" — his friend pressed the hand pointing upward against his other hand —

"this you are responsible for. The vertical aspect of forgiveness is between you and God. It happens at the foot of the cross. This is where you have to get on your knees before God and work things out with him. Are you willing to forgive your father? Are you willing to admit that maybe, just maybe, you don't want to forgive him? And then tell God that ugly truth? Because he knows it anyway."

"And then what? God's going to remind me of all those verses about how I'm supposed to forgive. Yeah. I know that. So then I feel guilty because *I can't do it.*"

"No. It's not about condemnation, Erik. It's about staying at the foot of the cross. Telling God you can't do it . . . you can't forgive your dad."

Erik buried his face in his hands. He did not want to do this here, hemmed in by batting cages and a parking lot filled with cars. He didn't want to do this at all. Phillip just let him sit as he inhaled, long and slow. He spoke without looking at his friend. "I hate what my father did. It's even affected how I see God. I'm fine with Jesus, you know? The Son. And the Holy Spirit. But God the Father? No, thank you."

"Then talk to Jesus. Or the Spirit. Ask him to help you . . . one minute, one hour, one day at a time. Ask him to fill you up to overflowing with his forgiveness for your father. You can't forgive your father — yet. But he already has."

Erik stared off into the distance. "I thought we were talking about me and Sadie."

"We were."

"How did we get here?"

"You need to tackle one lie before you can tackle another."

"What's that supposed to mean, oh wise one?"

"Your father abandoned you — even when you asked him not to leave. You're not that child anymore. And Sadie is not abandoning you. You haven't even told her that you love her. You haven't asked her to stay."

"So . . . you're saying it's time for me to grow up."

"It's time for you to tell your best friend you don't want to be friends anymore."

"But what if I tell her I love her and she still leaves me?"

"Then you ask God how you love someone and let them go."

TWELVE

Sadie had burned a bridge.

The bridge leading to Oregon was nothing more than a pile of ashes. Come January, the Hartnetts would be gone and she'd still be in Colorado. Adjusting to the culinary likes and dislikes of a new family. And maybe, just maybe, still dating Erik.

But by then they'd be hitting four months. Erik's commitment meter would be set off — unless God calmed Erik's heart. Unless Erik began to realize he loved her as more than a friend.

Or God changed her heart — and taught her to be content with their friendship again.

"God, I'm staying. Not because Erik asked me to. Not because he loves me — or because you promised me that he would love me." Sadie settled into the seat and closed her eyes, praying her heartbeat would slow. "I'm staying because I know you haven't told me to leave. And if all Erik and

410

I ever are is friends . . . help me be satisfied with that. It's been enough until now."

The breeze ruffled Erik's hair, the late afternoon sun casting him in shadow.

"Interesting to find you here." He lowered himself onto the swing next to Sadie, his feet anchored into the crater of sand worn down after only a year of children playing at this park. He pushed off, matching the motion of his swing to hers.

"True. I've never been a fan of playgrounds." Sadie leaned back, her arms bent at the elbows, watching the horizon sway up and down with the motion of her swing. "Of course, when you spend your time hiding at the top of the slide, hoping the other kids don't find you and call you a bad pirate and force you to walk the plank . . . well, it loses its appeal at an early age."

"I wish I'd known you back then." His voice fought against the pull of the wind.

"What would you have done, Erik?" Sadie kept her face turned to the sky so that Erik didn't see the grimace that twisted her mouth. "Kids can be mean. And having an eye patch for a good part of elementary school and a pair of glasses made me an easy target. *Pirate.*"

411

"I would have defended you. Maybe beat up a couple of bullies."

They swung side by side. Funny, how with almost no effort at all, they fell into an easy rhythm with one another. As he slowed down, his shoes scuffing the earth, Sadie slowed too. Erik gripped the chain links that suspended the swing and pivoted to face her.

"Why'd you ask me to the Sadie Hawkins Dance, Sadie J?"

Really? He wants to know that now?

"You were the new kid in school. You didn't know anybody . . . and sometimes, sometimes you looked lonely." Sadie let her body relax. "And the truth is, even though we were lab partners in science class, you didn't know me — the girl who used to wear an eye patch and get teased. So you were safe."

Erik watched her. "Safe, huh?"

"And cute, in a thirteen-year-old-boy kind of way."

He grabbed the chains of her swing and pulled her closer. "You still think I'm cute?"

"Puh-leeze, Erik."

"Come on. This is an important question. We men have fragile egos."

"I think you're cuter without a beard."

"Oh, thank you very much." Erik held

412

their swings still, anchored together. "Sadie, if I asked you to the dance today, would you say yes?"

"If you asked me . . . to the dance? That's a ridiculous question, Erik. It's not even realistic."

"What if I asked you something else? Would you say yes?"

"Depends on what you asked me."

Erik knew the rules.

When you propose to a woman, you're supposed to be somewhere romantic, not in the middle of a playground. You're supposed to get down on one knee, and deliver a well-practiced speech. Not meander around and ask the woman "Will you say yes" before you even ask her to marry you.

He was getting this wrong in so many ways.

Erik gripped the metal links tighter. "Sadie, would you be my best friend . . . and my wife, for now and always?"

And then, before she could answer, he pulled her close and kissed her.

He didn't know if Sadie would say yes or not . . . but she hadn't pushed him off the swing and run away.

Not even close.

Her hands covered his as she leaned

413

forward into his kiss. If this wasn't a yes, it was the sweetest torture of a no.

Sadie moved back so that mere inches separated them, the hint of vanilla lingering in the air. "Did you just ask me to marry you?"

"Was that a yes?"

He brushed her bangs back from her forehead, cradling her face between his hands. "Yes. I asked you to marry me." He pressed a kiss to her lips as they curved into a smile. "Please tell me you said yes."

"I'm saying yes now. You didn't give me a chance to say anything before. You just kissed me."

"Sorry about that." Erik ran his thumb along the back of her hand. "No, I'm not. There's going to be a lot more of that from here on out."

He stood, pulling her into his arms, moving them away from the swing set. "Looks like you need to tell the Hartnetts you're not going to Oregon."

"No need for that."

"There most certainly is. I have no interest in one of those commuter marriages."

"I already turned down the job." Sadie pressed her hand against his chest. "I couldn't leave Colorado — even if we were just friends. This is home. And God was going to teach me how to be content with our relationship, whatever it was."

"Are you content?"

"I am." Sadie gasped, moving away just as he bent to kiss her again. "Oh my gosh. We've got to plan a wedding!" She tugged at his arm, pulling him toward her house. "I need to start making lists. We have to decide on a cake. A photographer. The wedding party. Guests. When do you want to get married? I always thought a summer wedding would be nice —"

Erik dug his heels into the ground. "Stop."

"What?"

"Sadie, I waited twelve years between our first kiss and the next time I kissed you. I'm not willing to wait even a month to marry you."

"But it takes time to plan a wedding —"

"You're going to make yourself crazy, you know. And you're going to make me crazy too. You, Miss Plan Everything Down to the Last Detail, are going to take all the fun and joy out of this wedding."

"You're right." Sadie linked her arms around his neck.

"I am?"

"Yes. You are. What do you suggest?"

"Leave it all to me."

"Leave it . . . *all* to you?"

"Yes."

"The cake?"

"Yes."

"The photographer?"

"Yes."

"The wedding party?"

"Yes."

"The location?"

"Yes."

"The date?"

"You already know the date."

"I do?"

"Yes, you do. It's the only day we could get married."

"Erik —"

"You keep trying to figure it out . . . and I promise, I won't let you miss our wedding."

"Very funny."

"Oh, I couldn't be more serious, Sadie J. You and I are going to get married very, very soon."

THIRTEEN

It was her wedding day — not that the assembled guests realized that yet.

Sadie paced her loft, waiting for Erik to sneak upstairs and announce, "It's time." Downstairs, thirty-three people — including her parents and Erik's mom — mingled in her living and dining rooms, indulging in a bogus engagement party catered by Mel's business.

Sadie refused to sit down — where? On her bed? — and wrinkle the lace gown she'd found during a whirlwind shopping weekend with Mel and Ashley. Those two women knew how to throw a girl in a dressing room and toss dresses at her until Sadie feared she'd get lost under a pile of ivory and white satin and sashes.

But when she'd slipped on *this* gown, with its fitted silhouette and sheer lace three-quarter sleeves, Sadie had almost not recognized herself when she'd faced her reflection in the mirror.

"Stop."

"Is everything okay?" The heavy black curtain muffled Ashley's voice.

"Just . . . wait."

Sadie reenacted the moment, holding her breath and positioning herself in front of the full-length mirror. Would she catch a glimpse of what she'd seen that morning?

Beautiful.

Warmth flowed through her veins, suffusing her body. How had this happened? Was she beautiful because Erik chose her? Because Erik loved her?

Yes . . . and no. There was more to it than that.

She was being true to herself. She'd chosen her life. Chosen the man she'd love forever and happily ever after.

Footsteps thudded up the wooden stairs and a moment later, Erik's head and shoulders appeared above the railing — *a clean-shaven* Erik.

"Are you ready?"

"Absolutely! Did my parents see you come up here?"

"I don't think so. I told them I was checking on things in the kitchen." His embrace was a sweet moment of sanctuary. "You look gorgeous."

She ran her hand across the soft skin of his jaw. "I still can't believe you shaved off your beard for me."

"You did say you preferred me without it."

"But that didn't mean you had to shave it off."

"I intend to keep my wife happy."

Sadie adjusted his tie, the blue a perfect match to his eyes. "You know we're breaking a major tradition, letting you see me before the ceremony."

"We're breaking so many traditions, what does one more matter? I planned the wedding, not you. We've known each other seventeen years, had three official dates, and are getting married seventeen days after I proposed." Erik paused, cupping his chin in his hand. "Huh. Seventeen years. Seventeen days. Hadn't realized that before."

"It's a numerical coincidence. A good sign."

"I agree. We're also throwing ourselves a surprise wedding on Sadie Hawkins Day, no less." He reached out his hand and tugged her to him. "And if you recall, I saw you earlier when we did the 'reveal' photo. You were gorgeous then too."

"Thank you. For . . . all of this."

"You know, you never told me your full

name. I guess I'm going to finally find out, huh?"

She matched his whisper. "It's Sadie J. Just 'J.' My parents couldn't agree on my middle name, so they let the initial stand."

"That's it?"

"Yes. Disappointed?"

He leaned forward and brushed a kiss across her lips. "How could I be disappointed? I'm marrying my best friend."

Ashley interrupted their romantic moment. "Phillip sent me after the missing groom. He's about to make the announcement and then marry you two, which means he needs Erik in the living room and you in the kitchen. Come on! It's time to surprise everyone."

A few minutes later, her father entered the kitchen. "Your friend Ashley told me that you . . ." His voice trailed off.

Sadie touched the creamy ivory material surrounding the flowers in her bouquet. "Would you mind giving me away?"

"Here?" Her father's eyebrows rose over his tortoiseshell glasses. "Now?"

"Well, not here, in the kitchen. I'd like you to walk me out to the living room —" Sadie paused. Yes, Phillip was informing the guests that the informal party to announce their engagement was actually their wedding too. Gasps echoed all the way through the living room, dining room, and into the kitchen. "— now."

Her father bent and kissed her cheek. "You're putting a little twist on tradition, you know. My grandmother was married in her parents' living room — only they didn't have a single photo of the event."

"I'd forgotten about that." Sadie squeezed her father's arm.

"You'll certainly have some stories to tell your children."

"And probably some explaining to do to our guests."

"Oh, I wouldn't worry about that — I think everyone is enjoying being part of the surprise."

Mel switched on Colbie Caillat's "Realize," the song Erik had selected for the processional, and then stepped back.

"I'll slip into the living room after you." She handed Sadie her phone. "But you have a message."

"I'm not answering my phone now."

"Um, I think you're going to want to read this text message."

Who on earth was texting her now?

SADIE J, I LOVE YOU. WILL YOU MARRY ME?

"One second, Dad." She handed Mel her

bouquet and half-turned as her fingers tapped the keyboard.

I ALREADY SAID YES . . . AND IN JUST A MINUTE I'LL SAY I DO.

HURRY UP, WILL YOU?

STOP TEXTING ME AND I WILL.

She tossed the phone to Mel. "Mute this thing, please. I won't be needing it for a while."

"Yes, ma'am."

"Thanks for such a lovely 'engagement party.' " She winked as she retrieved her bouquet. "Now, if you'll excuse me, there's a man in my living room who wants to marry me — and I don't want to keep him waiting. After all, it's been seventeen years. I think we've both waited quite long enough."

ACKNOWLEDGMENTS

"Give thanks to the Lord for he is good . . ." Psalm 107:1a NIV

The Lord has been so good to me. He's allowed me to live my dream of being a writer — and expanded that dream in unexpected ways. As I wrote Sadie and Erik's story, I was encouraged and supported by many other people:

Rachel Hauck: Thank you for suggesting that I be part of the A Year of Weddings writing team. Your belief in me inspires me. Thank you, too, for helping me brainstorm *A November Bride*. You're brilliant — have I mentioned that?

My family: With every acknowledgment I write, I realize again that I can never truly express the importance of my husband's and my children's support. They make the difference between writing and not writing for me. They understand writing is my dream-coming-true — and they cheer me on and pray for me as I pursue the doors God opens for me.

The Zondervan Team:
· Becky Philpott (editor)
· Karli Cajka (associate editor)
· Natalie Hanemann (freelance editor)

Thank you for your professionalism every step of the way as we produced *A November Bride.* It has been a delight working with all of you.

Rachelle Gardner: Thank you for always having my back. You answer my questions — even more, you *anticipate* my questions. Your representation is invaluable — and your friendship is a blessing.

Nate Huntley: I created a heroine who is a personal chef. The only problem is, I don't spend that much time in the kitchen. Thank you for bringing all your culinary expertise to the rescue and answering all of my cooking questions, starting with "So, what should Sadie cook in this chapter?"

Melissa Christian (a.k.a. Mel): Thank you for helping me understand the Broadmoor Culinary Apprenticeship Program. I respect you and what you do more than you know!

The My Book Therapy Core Team: Led by the inspiring Susan May Warren, My

Book Therapy's "battle cry" is "Get Published. Stay Published." I would add to that: *Find lasting friendships that will encourage you along the writing road.* With each book I write, I am reminded how much I have learned from My Book Therapy, and how thankful I am to be part of this talented team that includes:

- Rachel Hauck
- Reba Hoffman
- Lisa Jordan
- Michelle Lim
- Melissa Tagg
- Alena Tauriainen
- David Warren

DISCUSSION QUESTIONS

1. Sadie and Erik became friends in middle school and remained best friends for years before falling in love. What's your experience with a friendship turning into a romance?

2. Erik planned three fun dates to woo Sadie: a trip to the Denver Aquarium, a night out learning to swing dance at the Mercury Café, and breakfast cooked at his apartment (with online chaperones). What other fun dates would you have planned for Sadie and Erik?

3. Sadie's self-image was affected by a childhood experience: being diagnosed with a lazy eye and having to wear an eye patch and glasses for a number of years during elementary school. She was also teased (bullied) by other classmates. Have you or someone you know ever been bullied by other kids? How did this affect you (or them)?

4. Have you ever gone to a Sadie Hawkins Dance? What was your experience like?

5. Before Erik could move ahead and love Sadie, he had to forgive his father for abandoning the family. Phillip introduced him to a different perspective of forgiveness: horizontal and vertical forgiveness. What did you think of this view of forgiveness to help Erik let go of his hurt? Do you have a favorite scripture passage about forgiveness?

6. Sadie experienced a horrible bout of stage fright during the morning cooking show. If you'd been there with her, how would you have helped her relax?

7. Sadie and Erik surprised their friends and family with an engagement party that was actually their wedding ceremony. What's the most fun thing that's ever happened to you at a wedding?

ABOUT THE AUTHOR

Beth K. Vogt believes God's best is often behind the doors marked "Never." She's the wife of a former Air Force family physician who said she'd never marry a doctor — or anyone in the military. She's a mom of four who said she'd never have kids. She's a former nonfiction writer and editor who said she'd never write fiction. Beth's novels include *Wish You Were Here, Catch a Falling Star,* and *Somebody Like You.*

Visit her website at www.bethvogt.com
Twitter: @bethvogt
Facebook: AuthorBethKVogt

The employees of Thorndike Press hope you have enjoyed this Large Print book. All our Thorndike, Wheeler, and Kennebec Large Print titles are designed for easy reading, and all our books are made to last. Other Thorndike Press Large Print books are available at your library, through selected bookstores, or directly from us.

For information about titles, please call:
(800) 223-1244

or visit our Web site at:
http://gale.cengage.com/thorndike

To share your comments, please write:
Publisher
Thorndike Press
10 Water St., Suite 310
Waterville, ME 04901